CURI
KILLED THE CAT

Joan Cockin

GALILEO PUBLISHERS, CAMBRIDGE

First printed, September 1949

This new edition printed 2023

Galileo Publishers
16 Woodlands Road
Great Shelford, Cambridge CB22 5LW UK

www.galileopublishing.co.uk

Distributed in the USA by:
SCB Distributors
15608 S. New Century Drive
Gardena, CA 90248-2129, USA

and in Australia by:
Peribo Pty Limited
58 Beaumont Road, Mount Kuring-Gai
NSW 2080, Australia

ISBN 978-1-915530-141
epub: 978-1-915530-295
Kindle: 978-1-915530-288

Printed in the EU

CONTENTS

CHAPTER I

THERE was no visible agitation as the Director-General's car drew up at the door. The DG did not like excitement to be manifest in one of his departments. Quiet efficiency was the accent, so, while the group of half a dozen messengers and porters who had been enjoying their tea and the warmth of a great fire in the hall found business unobtrusively elsewhere, old Martins, the head porter, ran solemnly down the stone steps and opened the door of the car before the chauffeur could get there. Encouraged by this achievement, he ventured a more elaborate welcome than usual.

"Good afternoon, sir. Nice weather for a drive, sir."

The great man in the back seat was stuffing into his dispatch-case the papers which, regardless of spring sunshine and Cotswold scenery, had occupied him during the long drive from London, and it was a few seconds before he got out of the car.

"Afternoon," he grunted, and ran up the steps with a lightness unusual in such a massive figure.

In the hall he paused for a moment. Once he had found an assembly of porters enjoying themselves here on Government time, and he was always alert for another infringement of regulations. But the hall was silent today except for the lively crackle of the log fire. He went up the main staircase two steps at a time, as silent and purposeful in his movement as the sleek limousine in which he had arrived. Turning sharply on to the landing, another man coming towards the staircase knocked into him in the shadow and staggered back against the wall with an exclamation.

"Damn you!" he swore. "Can't you use a horn?" and bent over to pick up his stick, which had been sent flying in the collision. Straightening himself to wither the offender he stopped abruptly.

1

"Oh! I—I'm sorry, sir. I didn't know. . ."

"In future kindly look where you are going. We should prefer not to lose you, Stone."

The DG passed on, rather pleased at having administered rebuke and encouragement with such an impartial hand. He quite consciously enjoyed these manifestations of respect for his office. It was proper that men should treat him with a courtesy they did not show their equals. Ordinarily he would have given only the cold rebuke. But Stone was deserving, perhaps, of special treatment—his brilliant Army record for one month in the Middle East, his wound resulting in a permanent limp, his five years in a German prison camp, made him specially deserving of sympathy. Anyway, thought the DG, dismissing thoughts of sentiment, he was an excellent worker.

His own room at the end of the corridor was warm with a coal fire and bright with spring sunshine. The DG was not sensitive to beauty, but he liked this room. Its dignity had qualities of grace and charm lacking in the ponderous Ministry of Works design of his London office. It was a gentleman's room, he thought, while his London place could never be mistaken for anything but a Civil Servant's office.

Miss White was placing some files upon his desk as he came in. She had long ago arranged with the hall porter that when the DG arrived he should give her an emergency ring on the telephone. This gave her time to throw her cigarette in the fire, hide her magazine and compose a devout and efficient expression. As he entered she looked up with a smile that managed to be both submissively welcoming and busily preoccupied.

"Good afternoon, sir. You're earlier than usual today. What a lovely day for a drive!"

"Good afternoon, Miss White. Yes, I had my lunch in the car, and that saved time. Anything important here?"

He sat down at the desk and started thumbing through the files and correspondence, with a glance at the names involved.

A brief look was usually enough for him to estimate the importance of a letter.

Miss White deftly drew out a minute with a priority tab pinned to it.

"This from Dr. Robarts is the chief paper, I think. He is really getting quite alarmed by the delay in flax supplies, and would like you to take it up on a high level."

The DG grunted. He did not like Robarts. A fumbling, ineffectual fellow outside his own laboratory. But there he was certainly first-class.

"Well, I'll see him in half an hour, when I've looked through these. In the meantime can you get me some tea? And will you look out the papers on Pylon yarn for the five o'clock conference? And phone London that I have decided to spend the night here, not in Bristol. Sir Walter Gilpin has asked me to dinner, so will you phone and accept? And see about getting the flat ready, please."

Miss White hastened off about these duties, but as she ran down the corridor on the way to the canteen she had a good excuse to drop in to see her friend, Charity Brown. She burst dramatically into Chatty's little room, once a writing-room off the library.

"He's come, my dear! And I had been praying he wouldn't, this Wednesday. No flicks for me tonight, I'm afraid. Isn't it *beastly*? When you think we're one little department out of hundreds, and yet he comes down here every week. I'm sure he does it just to make me break my dates. It's just like him."

Charity murmured. She was trying to draw up a rota schedule for the staff's summer holidays, and it demanded a lot of concentration.

"That must be it," she said absently. "He probably pays one of the messengers to spy on you, and then when he hears you're going out he says to the Minister, 'You'll have to handle that Press Conference yourself, Minister. I hear Betty White has a date, and I've got to go down to Wassel House and stop it.'Very likely!"

"Well, why *does* he come down so much?" countered Betty, still unconvinced.

"Because he likes to see the one research station in the Ministry which really works and gets results. The other MSR stations are just ticking over waiting for someone to tell them what exactly they *are* supposed to be doing in peacetime. But we've got a job to do—we've got some justification. I suppose the DG likes to see people with something else on their desk besides their feet!"

Betty laughed, although she shared Charity's conviction that theirs was the office which bore the whole weight of world affairs upon its shoulders.

"Anyway, tell Robby he is wanted in half an hour. And, by the way, if the DG loves our department so much it's funny he doesn't like its head and inspiration more.You ought to tell Robby not to look so alarmed when he sees him. It must be rather off-putting even for a Director-General, you know."

"If he didn't work harder than anyone else in the department he might not look so anxious." Charity did not like anyone else to patronise her chief. That was her prerogative. "What is he wanted about? The flax supply?"

"That's right. He is crying for his tea. I must rush. And I did want to see that picture!"

She dashed off, leaving a fleeting impression of pleasure sacrificed to the Moloch of Government service. As Charity knew that she spent most of the day when the DG was absent writing long letters to boy friends, explaining to them as they returned from service overseas why she could not redeem the promises made to them in the heat of war, she was not convinced. The DG had two other secretaries in London, but he found it convenient to have another at Wassel House so that he did not have to bring one with him on his frequent visits. Charity wondered with awe whether

4

he had a dozen others scattered over England in the other Ministry of Scientific Research stations. Fifteen secretaries! It sounded vaguely immoral. To her mind the DG was the symbol of omnipotence. Within his world of the Ministry of Scientific Research he was all-powerful, and he exercised his power daily over the lives of his subordinates. True there was an even loftier figure—the Minister—towering in the background. But the Minister of the moment was a transitory figure. Everyone knew that he was simply awaiting translation to a more important department. And during the interregnum the reins of power had slipped to the tight and capable grip of the DG.

Charity pushed aside the rota, about which her only certainty was that it would exasperate and offend every member of the staff, and went into the ex-library next door. Robby must have slipped out by the corridor door, because the room was empty. Crossing to the desk, she sighed over the confusion amongst the correspondence she had so neatly arranged. Everything had looked so business-like when placed in a neat pile of descending order of importance, with little priority slips just showing and reference tabs peeping from the tan covers of the files. Other secretaries, she was proudly aware, left their chiefs to wreak what havoc they wished in their pending-tray, but not she. Every evening she went laboriously through it and brought up again to the top the letters which Robby had attempted vainly to slip to the bottom. She was not at all sure that this zeal was appreciated. Sometimes Robby seemed quite resentful when an unanswered letter appeared day after day on the top of his tray. But whether he liked it or not she knew it helped him to keep a semblance of order in the administrative side of his work. As his secretary, Charity had no illusions about Robert Robarts. He was a brilliant scientist, but he didn't know the first thing about keeping a department in order. Fortunately she did, she congratulated herself. And without Robby ever being aware of the transfer, she had managed to take over a great deal of the routine administrative work, leaving him freer for his weird experiments and prototypes, about which she was blissfully ignorant.

Walking across the room, she took the internal phone from its hook on the wall and dialled a number. Then, unwinding the long cord, she sat down on the window-seat. The view was from the back of the house, overlooking the park. She could just catch a flash of the bluebells down by the stream where they had had lunch. The rookery in the elms beyond the walled kitchen garden was having a vociferous gossip as the sun, sinking behind Wassel Peak, cast its last, long shadows through the great trees in the park. There was a good deal to be said, she thought, for the dispersal of Government departments— from the point of view of Civil Servants, anyway.

A crackly voice at the other end of the line said:

"Number two Lab."

"Is Dr. Robarts there?"

"Yes. Hold on a minute."

"Hello?"

"Dr. Robarts, the DG has arrived and would like to see you at four-thirty. About the flax supply."

She could picture poor Robby sucking his cheeks anxiously. He hated interviews with the Man.

"Ah yes. Would you get out the papers, Miss Brown, please? I'll be up in a moment."

She put down the receiver without getting up and leaned back against the window-frame. Summer time would start next week. Long, lovely evenings to walk on the hills and to work in Uncle John's garden. When she worked late here the sun would be shining through the window and bringing out the golden tints in the panelled walls. At weekends she would go cycling with Betty or Bill and drowse in beer-scented pubs. The lack of central heating, the smoky fires, the freezing draughts that penetrated every corner of the old house in winter would no longer matter. In summer the house's famous

Georgian elegance would look its best with windows open to the sunshine and curtains billowing slightly in the breeze like crinolines. Yet some people complained because it wasn't a stuffy Government office in Whitehall—noisy, dirty and confined. Well, no doubt their prayers would be answered soon enough. Wassel House was long overdue for de-requisition.

"Am I interrupting you, Miss?"

She jumped at the voice at her elbow and turned with an angry gesture. That nasty little messenger Parry had entered the room, and had crept with feline stealth as far as the desk without her hearing him. He stood with hands clasped in front of him, hypocritically anxious, and bent slightly forwards so that she could see the eight—she had counted them—oiled strands of hair that meagrely covered his flat scalp. Charity liked the messenger corps in general. They were all old enough to be her grandfather and, strong in the qualities of self-respect and good humour, they regarded themselves as the inadequately paid but essential foundations of departmental life. Most of them were ex-servicemen from World War One, and out of the wells of their experience they were glad at anytime to offer comfort, advice and warning. In fact, they were old dears. But not Parry. It was amazing how a little man with an unpleasant smell of stale beer always about him could manage to be frightening rather than contemptible.

She got up hastily, and then flushed with annoyance at such an apparent manifestation of guilt. What a little blackleg the man was! Standing simpering there with his eyes dripping curiosity and spite!

"Do you want anything, Parry?" she said abruptly, going over to the desk and ruthlessly starting to bring order amidst the confusion.

"Oh, I *am* sorry I startled you, Miss. It's a lovely evening, isn't it? No, I just wondered if Dr. Robarts would be thinking of a game tonight. I just got back from Town, you see."

He never missed an opportunity, Charity thought bitterly, to show how his special job as the Director-General's personal messenger enabled him to slip up and down to London while all the rest of the staff were obliged to hoard leave for months in order to wangle a visit.

"Well, you can see he's not here."

"Yes, Miss, I see. Thank you for your kindness, Miss."

In another moment she would have said something regrettably rude, but Robert Robarts hastened into the room, smoothing down his wiry grey hair with both long-fingered hands and trying at the same time to hold under his arm a sheaf of unruly documents. There was a little pucker between his grey eyes, and he dropped the sheaf haphazard upon a chair.

"Ah, Miss Brown, are the papers ready? I should like just to look through them before the meeting. I've got ten minutes, haven't I?"

"That's right, Dr. Robarts. Here is the main file, and I'll get your subsidiary notes at once."

Charity rushed off, penitent that the papers were not ready and doubly furious at Parry for having found her slacking. She could hear him buttering up Robby as she rustled through the files.

"If you're going to be in conference with Sir Arnold, sir, of course you'll be busy for some time. I was wondering if you would like a game, but of course . . ."

Robarts was a modest man who knew that his meetings with the DG were usually brief and business-like. But even he could not resist the subdued awe in Parry's voice and the implication that he was accustomed to confer with the DG long into the night. Charity could almost hear him purr as he replied.

"Well, I think it won't be a long conference tonight, Parry. Yes, I would like a game. We haven't had one for a fortnight, and I want my revenge. What about seven-thirty?"

"Oh yes, sir. That will suit me very well, sir. I'll meet you in the canteen then."

When Charity went back into the room the messenger had gone. Robby was pensively gazing at his in-tray. Dear man, she thought affectionately. He's wondering why the DG doesn't like him. As though that monster could like anyone! She put the notes down, and Robarts jumped nervously. He looked at her with a grateful smile. It was nice having a chief who appreciated you. That reminded her of the stupid little scene with Parry and, on the strength of the grateful smile, she spoke impulsively to Robarts.

"Dr. Robarts, I don't think you ought to trust that man too much—Parry, I mean, I hate saying this, and I wouldn't to anyone else, but I'm sure he isn't trustworthy. The other day I found him going through your in-tray, and quite often I have found him here without any real reason. Perhaps it doesn't mean a thing, but I *do* think you ought to be careful."

Robarts looked at her in some amazement. She was quite white-lipped and tense. But he recalled now that she had often been rather sharp with Parry on apparently no provocation. He found it difficult to concentrate on the subject. He was trying to remember the name of a blue flower that she somewhat resembled, leaning slightly towards the desk in her slim blue dress, with her black hair all rumpled from the pencils she must have been absent-mindedly thrusting through it. But she was waiting anxiously, so he smiled gently.

"Oh, I don't think there's anything really to worry about, Miss Brown. Parry is, unfortunately for one in his position, a man of superior intelligence—really his chess game is quite brilliant sometimes—and I suppose he takes an interest in papers which his fellows, quite rightly, merely collect and deliver. I will speak to him about it, but I'm sure he is quite reliable. After all, he wouldn't have been appointed the DG's messenger without thorough examination, would he? But I will mention it over our game tonight. That will keep it quite friendly."

Charity bit her lip. The man didn't have the faintest idea what she was talking about. And she felt a curious little undemocratic rancour that the head of the department should choose to play chess with one of the messengers—and what a messenger!

"Mr. Ratcliffe plays chess very well, I hear," she blurted out, and wished at once that she had been stricken dumb.

Robarts stiffened, and turned back to the desk with an impatient gesture.

"I have played with him," he said briefly.

It was clear that Charity was misinformed about the skill of the Deputy Administrative Director at chess, and she crept out of the room. . . .

Half an hour later, while Robarts and the DG were closeted together, Charity found time to go down to the canteen for tea. She sauntered down the front staircase, stroking the smooth mahogany of the banisters with her finger-tips and feeling for the hundredth time how bitterly the owners of this lovely house must regret their compulsory exile during the war and into the peace. With summer coming on, they must, in some stuffy City flat, be remembering all the more keenly the beauty of it. She had seen a letter in *The Times* from a Wassel, complaining about the delay in de-requisitioning private houses now that the war was over. She sympathised! Bill Ratcliffe, rushing as usual, caught her up at the turn of the stairs, skidded to a stop and took hold of her arm to prevent himself falling down the rest of the flight. He did not let go.

"Do you realise," she said severely, "that every time you skid in those great climbing boots of yours you leave an indelible mark on one of the loveliest floors in England?"

"How right you always are, Chatty; how right and how righteous! 'Sdeath, woman, would you dare to compare in importance the blemish of a few healthy scratches on a wooden floor with the blemish of an emaciated frame upon the Deputy Administrative Director! With all the burden on my head of keeping ingrates like you fed, housed and happy, it's fully fifteen minutes past my appointed tea hour, and I am still unfed. Ah, the public little knows what its servants sacrifice on the altar of duty!" He sighed gustily. "What detestable interest our Lord and Master shows in our work, eh? I foresee a long night of consultation and discussion ahead. Thank God he's got Robby to glut his maw for the moment. Can one glut a maw, by the way?"

"Not yours. Does he really *discuss* things with you, Bill, or is that just a figure of speech? He doesn't look a very discussable man to me."

Bill Ratcliffe laughed wryly. He was a candid young man, cursed by the misleadingly boyish characteristics of red hair, snub nose and freckles. In a gloomy moment he had once confided to Charity that these facial traits probably foredoomed his Civil Service career, now being taken up again after four years in the Navy. He was always on the alert for a Principal Secretary or even an Assistant Principal Secretary with similar features, but so far without success. Short of a plastic surgery operation to endow him with the regulation aquilinity he saw no hope except to join the Colonial Service and hide his appearance in some distant post of the Empire. For the present, while his betters decided on his future, he was tied to a very unsuitable administrative job working with scientists about whose mental processes he was completely mystified.

"Well, perhaps 'discuss' is drawing it a bit strong," he replied. "You see, he says to me: 'Ratcliffe, sit up and look sharp, and what are you going to do about this?' And I say to him: 'Sir, I think we ought to do that—or this, as the case may be.' That's his cue for saying: 'Nonsense, Ratcliffe, nonsense! Most unpractical. Now you do as I tell you. . . .' And so that's that. If he were only wrong sometimes it might be more instructive, but he never is. They always say: 'Learn by your mistakes', and if he would only give me a chance I'm sure I could learn a lot that way!"

Charity was laughing as they entered the canteen, and Graham Stone, sitting by himself at the table before the fire, scowled into his murky tea. He detested these noisy secretary types, with their short hair, narrow figures and rowdy laughter. Full-figured women—women, not girls—with placid, womanly dispositions and not much interest in anything outside their home and their man were more to his taste. But nowadays they just didn't exist in England. Even women who were naturally that way dieted until they ruined their tempers and cultivated a passion for Current Affairs—Current Affairs, forsooth!—just to show how intellectual they were. What creatures to come home to! After six years of war a man wanted something warm and soft in his arms, not something scraggy and pert and chattering about the problems of the post-war world. Although he determinedly did not look up, the couple came to the fire and joined him at the table. He supposed, bitterly, that they thought it was the least they could do for a war hero.

"Mind if we sit here, old man?" Bill said brightly.

"It's quite cold out of the sun, isn't it? 'These treacherous spring days,' my aunt used to say. 'Ne'er cast a clout till May be out,' and similar words of wisdom. What'll you have, Chatty? Char and cake? Right!"

He wound his way through chairs and tables to the hatch at the other side, from which kitchen noises proceeded. The breakfast-room adjoining the dining-room at Wassel House had been converted into an up-to-date kitchen. The dining-room itself, equipped with painted green chairs and tables and stripped of the Regency furniture which had been its pre-war glory, made a comfortable canteen. The eternal character of the Government office was determined by a green-baize notice-board hanging on the wall at one end, covered with fluttering leaflets announcing village entertainments; the cast for the next staff play; the times of buses to Stroud and Gloucester; an order that canteen cutlery and crockery should not be removed from

12

the room; a printed notice appealing for fuel economy; details of new rates of pay for clerical grades. Most of these were dog-eared and bedraggled, symbolic of the weariness of exile which pervaded the staff of Wassel House—a weariness made more exasperating by the knowledge that other Government departments had already returned to their urban homes. At the other end of the room were three great windows set deep into the wall with ample window-seats. Heavy green curtains were pulled to one side. There were no carpets, but the panelling half covering the walls gave the room an appearance of warm furnishing.

Charity was not unconscious of Graham Stone's dislike. In fact, he had never tried to hide his conviction that most of his associates were lotus-eaters, or worse, for whom the war had been vainly fought. She sat rather uncomfortably while he took a sip of tea. A good secretary, she thought, sternly, should try to be on good terms with her chief's principal assistant. A stab at light chatter could hurt no one.

"So the DG is down again," she ventured.

Stone glowered at her: "Yes, pompous old fool!"

Charity was intrigued. No one was particularly fond of the DG, but few were passionate in their dislike. His scientific staff agreed that he was only a second-rate scientist, but they were amazed that he knew anything at all. After all, his long and distinguished Civil Service career had been largely in the Post Office and the Treasury. But the DG had proved again the Civil Service axiom that a trained administrator can administrate and understand anything. In conference he was able to discuss fluently the scientific problems of the moment, without a flicker of his eyelids to show that he was not discoursing on his own subject. His expert subordinates were amazed and a trifle suspicious. First-class honours in Greats do not win a man the admiration of all scientists. His achievement, therefore, in winning the coveted post of head of the wartime Ministry of Scientific Research was not generally welcomed. But the appointment had been justified. Suspicious or not, all the MSR staff were agreed that it was the DG's brilliant administrative powers which had put the infant Ministry on its feet. A succession of good and bad Ministers had had astonishingly little influence on the smooth running of the department. The MSR had been made by its DG—and, in turn, it had certainly made his own reputation. It weighed little against this that Sir Arnold Conway was an unpleasant individual. His personal characteristics affected few, because he actually came into contact with only a handful of the staff.

"I've only seen him once or twice," Charity temporised. "He looks rather unapproachable and rigid."

"Rigid!" Stone laughed abruptly. "I upset his rigidity this afternoon. Almost knocked him downstairs. At least, he almost knocked himself, flying round corners like a night-prowling cat! I suppose I should have thanked him for touching me; not a word of apology, of course. By God, I should like to have had him under me in the Army!"

Charity almost giggled at the thought of a massive Sergeant Conway taking orders from the black-browed Captain Stone, but a peal of laughter from a table full of Registry girls in the corner distracted her. Parry was there, leaning over the table, his arms familiarly round the necks of two typists, telling them some dirty story probably. She could not restrain a grimace of dislike, and Graham Stone noticed it. He followed her glance and laughed.

"Are you in the anti-Parry brigade? What's the matter with the man? Wherever I look I see black looks towards him."

"I detest the creature! Always sneaking around spying. You don't like him, do you? I thought I heard you ticking him off the other day."

"Monday? Yes, he came to me with a long story about your friend Ratcliffe having threatened him. I told him I didn't want to hear office gossip. My God!" —Stone seemed

14

suddenly shaken by anger—"what's the matter with all you people? Isn't it enough to have won the war, without making miniature ones in your rotten little offices?"

Charity flushed. She knew Stone's history, and could appreciate his reasons for cross-grained bitterness, but he had a scathing, searing way of speaking, quite out of tune with her own rather tranquil temperament.

"It's only people like Parry who cause trouble," she said coldly. "On the whole we don't get on too badly. Of course you wouldn't know, but six years shut up in a village with nobody's companionship except the other prisoners is pretty wearing on people's good nature."

Stone looked at her quizzically, and Charity realised she had made the *faux-pas* of the century. She was still searching for words when Bill fortunately came back at that point and burst into conversation about the possibility of motoring over to Stinchcombe Hill golf course for a game next Saturday. He was longing for a chance to stretch his legs. Charity was busy, but Stone agreed in an off-hand manner—the gentlemanly version of "I don't mind if I do"—and wandered off, back to the laboratory. As he reached the door, Parry, who had been going out, stood aside with elaborate courtesy only marred by an unpleasant sneer. Stone ignored him and stumped out, leaning heavily on his stick.

"That man," said Bill seriously, "is heading for his come-uppance, in the parlance of the cleaners' room."

"Stone?" exclaimed Charity. "But he is an excellent worker, Robby says. And he has reason enough to be sour, a P.O.W. five years!"

"Not Stone, you sweet ass! Parry, the messenger, the Quilp type. Or don't you read Dickens, you modern hussy? He seems to have appointed himself *agent-provocateur* extraordinary. Yesterday he was trying to threaten me about some papers which were found lying on my desk—very hush-hush and God knows how they got there. Said he didn't want to report me, but. . .! *Mea culpa* all right. But how the devil did *he* know without reading them pretty carefully that they were important? Stone came in while I was telling him off, and, by Jove! he seemed quite impressed by my dialectical effort. But we don't want the spy atmosphere to develop here. Somehow I thought that sort of thing had ended with the war. I told Robby about it actually and, while he administered suitable reproof for my sins, he didn't seem to see the point that messengers aren't supposed to do research work on their rounds. Then there have been other things. Fellows like that deserve all they get, and I'd like to be the one to deliver it."

"I couldn't agree more," said Charity feelingly. "He always makes me feel as though I were embezzling tax-payers' money. But Robby won't do anything about him as long as his chess game keeps up to par. That reminds me! I thought you said *you* were a wizard chess player?"

They left the room in cheerful argument about whether the ability to invent unusual though unsuccessful gambits was the criterion by which to judge a chess player.

Upstairs Robarts was leaving the DG, tripping unhappily over a chair as he sidled towards the door. Sir Arnold sighed impatiently.

"We shall be discussing Pylon yam's progress at six, Dr. Robarts. So I shall see you then. Stone's working on that, isn't he?"

"That's right. He is doing most of the practical work now. He gets better all the time."

"I hear he's drinking a lot. Is that true?"

Robarts gasped. It was uncanny the way the DG appeared to find out things about his staff of which Robarts himself was only just conscious.

"Well. . . yes, I have noticed a slight heaviness some mornings, though I've never actually seen him under the weather. Of course he's a difficult man to speak to. After so many years as a prisoner I think even the best people get a bit unbalanced. Not dangerously, I mean—just touchy."

"I don't quite see your point, Dr. Robarts. It seems to me that Mr. Stone is a very fortunate young man. There aren't many chemists of his age who have such responsible positions—and such a good beginning to a career. I don't believe in pampering these ex-service-men too much. Give them their gratuity and then let them remember they are now ordinary citizens with ordinary responsibilities. Speak to him about the drinking. It is deplorable that a man in his position should risk having his tongue loosened in a village pub." He paused coldly. "I'm surprised, Dr. Robarts, that you hesitate to raise the matter. It is your personal responsibility to have only the most reliable men here, as well as the most technically accomplished. Speak to him tonight if you have time."

Robarts retired from the room feeling flushed and incompetent. Although he had only a handful of men under him, all but two or three being callow, young assistants ready to obey his slightest word, he seemed to have more mental worry about them than the DG had, with many hundreds to control. How he detested these administrative responsibilities! During the war he had longed for the day when he could reclaim the privilege of doing his own laboratory work. But the peace had brought no respite. Most of his colleagues, quicker off the mark, had returned to their universities and their private firms. Robarts had lingered on, becoming more essential with each colleague who drifted away. He shied away from the intuitive Miss White, who was trying to soothe him with the weather news, and rushed back to his room. Better get it over with. He could hardly ignore instructions from the DG himself.

Charity was not there, so he rang Stone himself and asked him to come up. His assistant arrived in a white lab-coat, looking thoroughly peeved at the interruption.

"Ah, Stone, just sit down for a moment, will you? Sorry to interrupt you, but I just wanted to have a word with you. First

I want to congratulate you on the work you have done here. Obviously you're on your way to the top. If you had been working the past five years, instead of kicking your heels in a prison camp, you couldn't have a more responsible post."

He paused for a moment, uncertain how to continue. Stone looked unhelpfully at his boots, obviously aware that he was not summoned only for congratulation.

"Now, I don't have to mention, Stone, that you and I have a rather special responsibility here. In regard to much of the work we are the only ones who know what the miscellaneous experiments going on are, we hope, leading up to. The other fellows know what result they're expected to get from a particular experiment, but they don't always know to what use that result will be put. I don't pretend we have to cope with anything as serious as the German spy system, but the value of our work does depend partly on secrecy. The DG—and the Minister, too—think that this discovery of ours will prove of vital importance in the textile export drive. Sir Arnold told me only today that he thinks it will make nylon old-fashioned. Anyway, there are plenty of commercial firms overseas which would like to get hold of the secret for their own textile plants. Well, naturally a very great deal depends on our discretion, Stone. That's why I wanted to mention to you quietly that it might be well to be a little more careful about the amount you drink in the evening. I do assure you I quite understand the temptation—after five years in Germany, real beer must look attractive. But just bear in mind, when in future you are inclined to take a little more than you can conveniently hold, that a moment of carelessness may render the research of years value-less."

The last part of the speech was delivered in something of a rush, as Stone had jumped to his feet and was panting to interrupt long before the end of the mild reproof.

"What the devil is this?" he burst out vehemently. "Can't a fellow get quietly tight sometimes without being treated like a naughty schoolboy? Why the devil shouldn't I get drunk? I'm not the talking-drunk type, anyway—just the moody-drunk. I sit in a corner and get closer than usual. But if you don't believe me, that's fine. Get me fired as soon as you like. I've had plenty of offers from outside, and at least I wouldn't be stuck away in a mouldy village. It's as bad as the prison camp, but at least we trusted each other there."

Robarts was on his feet now, his face dead-white in contrast to the other's heat and his voice controlled but intense.

"I don't like your tone, Stone. You must be mad to suggest that I don't trust my staff implicitly—perhaps too much so in a few cases. It was your own unpleasant smell of whisky one morning which first brought the matter to my attention—and your headaches several mornings. It's about time, Stone, you started counting your blessings. Nobody likes being stuck out here in the country now that the war is over. I hope we shall move before long, as soon as we have finished the present series of experiments. But most of the staff manage to control their feelings more successfully than you, in order to maintain a cheerful atmosphere here under rather trying conditions. I hope in the prison camp you were not such a depressing influence as you are here! The conditions are not unlike, and I must request that you endeavour to adjust yourself to what is unavoidable, and cease inflicting your miseries upon other members of the staff. You may go now. Thank you."

"This is the second time," Stone said tensely after a soundless moment, "that I have been told this place is like a prison camp. My God, if you only knew!"

Charity had come to her office from the corridor in the midst of this conversation, and she listened with delight as the door slammed on Stone and Robarts slumped down in his chair. It was a pleasure to hear little Robby really laying down the law. A bit pompous, perhaps, but he needed practice. If only he would do it more often. She picked up her shorthand book, smoothed her hair and went in.

"Will there be any more letters today, Dr. Robarts?"

Robarts was huddled in his chair, looking quite savage, and his expression did not change as he looked at her. She stepped back a pace, amazed to see her gentle chief with such a lowering face.

"I am meeting the Director-General at six again. Kindly wait until I come out, in case there is any urgent work. Unfortunately Mr. Ratcliffe will also be at the meeting and not available to amuse you. In his stead you might mimeograph those staff leave instructions."

Charity was so staggered that she walked slowly back to her room and sat there for two minutes before she could really comprehend that Robby had actually been rude to her. Rude, and with intention to hurt! And without any provocation! How had it ever concerned him that she and Bill were friendly? And when had it ever interfered with her work? It was unbelievable.

She had had employers who had been consistently rude, but she couldn't take it from Dr. Robarts. She felt as though the whole foundations of her job had collapsed. If he really felt like that she couldn't—she couldn't go on working for him. And she had thought she was such a good secretary! But she would rather be in the Typing Pool. She would apply for a transfer tomorrow!

She got out the notes and started copying them, her fingers working slowly under the paralysing impact of this blow. For half an hour there was no sound except the rattle of her typewriter. The room darkened and she, needed a light, but she worked solemnly on. The door between the two offices opened slowly, but she did not look up. Robarts came in, his normal expression of gentle anxiety deepened by melancholy.

"Miss Brown. I must apologise most sincerely. I don't know why I said that. It is none of my business, and certainly I have no complaint about your work."

"That's quite all right," said Charity stiffly, "but of course if my work is unsatisfactory——"

"Oh, no, no, no! Really I think you're an excellent secretary. I am most fortunate. . . ." Robarts still lingered, looking doubtfully towards her.

She softened.

Well, I should be very sorry to leave you, Dr. Robarts. I like the work."

They smiled at each other in a friendly way and, as if to seal the pact, Robarts burst out:

"I say, I'm going to Gloucester shopping on Saturday. Do you think you could come, too—if you would like to, I mean?"

Charity had a date, but, she assured herself, she could hardly refuse this pipe of peace.

"I'd love to," she said.

★★★

It was seven-fifteen when the DG left his room on the way to dine in Stroud.

"I shall be back about eleven," he said to Miss White. "Warn the porter to be ready to let me in. Good night."

He strode along the hall, nodding briefly to Ratcliffe, whom he passed on the way, turned down the stairs and descended them two at a time, flashing past Stone, who was hopping down with the help of the banister. Martins was off duty at the front door, but Parry was on watch. He leaped forward, all eager service, and opened the door obsequiously. The Director-General, tired after the afternoon's meetings, stiffly ignored the cordial "good night" and went silently down the steps and into the car. The limousine slipped away, watched by many of the staff from behind curtained windows. A light breath of wind stirred the rookery to brief comment. In every office typewriters were being covered up, the last letters sealed, files locked away and noses powdered. Down in the labs equipment was being cleaned and experimental material locked away in the great safe in Lab 2. The breath of wind ran through the building like a sigh of release. The working day was over. Now for some fun at last.

CHAPTER II

PEACE had come to the whole world except Little Biggling. But there the rival armies still surveyed each other with mutual distrust and increasing dislike. It had been a long war, and Little Biggling felt it had borne the brunt. The compulsory honour of being war-time host of a Government department had been accepted at first with uncritical enthusiasm. The village had lived to learn that the honours of Governments are not to be sought, and that the singularly painful version of war-time austerity known as Dispersal of Government Departments was an instrument of torture for quiet country folk not surpassed since the enclosures.

The necessity of the invasion Little Biggling could not deny during the war (though it might wistfully describe the superior attractions and claims of Great Biggling). A certain pleasure could, indeed, be derived from the fact that the Ministry of Scientific Research department selected for the occupation was Highly Secret, and a rich mine of rumours about what Went On There could be worked surreptitiously by local gossips. But no one could believe any longer that the work of the department was important. The war was over, and secret weapons were two a penny. Yet still the baleful masters of the Ministry of Scientific Research pretended that they needed Little Biggling's stateliest home as a research centre, and still they maintained a company of locusts to staff it. The villagers were not to know that war-time research had led this station on to a discovery of even more importance for the purposes of peace. They only knew that peace brought no relief from Little Biggling's heaviest war-time cross.

The groans of the villagers were all the more bitter for the high hopes they had previously entertained in the innocent days of 1940. The tradespeople had rejoiced in the selection of their village as a Government evacuation centre as an Act of God designed to provide them all with ample retirement pensions. Instead they discovered that the shortage of supplies was made no easier by the influx of some hundred active men and women, well supplied with spare cash, and that their lives were made miserable by the conflicting suspicions of local and Government customers that each was being denied supplies for the benefit of the other. The publicans' dreams had also been shattered in the discovery that the newcomers' powerful thirsts could hardly be assuaged by their meagre beer supplies and that settlement of heated arguments between locals and strangers made an innkeeper's life a permanent tight-rope performance. The Little Biggling girls had looked forward to the invasion with high hopes, but, if some of them were rewarded for their faith, the majority found that the main result was the defection of all eligible and enterprising Little Biggling youths to the glamorous typists and clerks, new-painted from the metropolis. And as for the disillusionment of the Little Biggling boys, especially those returning from the wars, about their local sweethearts, their opinion can hardly be repeated.

Nor was this the worst. Not only had Little Biggling been expected to be polite to the locust strangers, but to live with them. Even Government officials, they were assured, had to live in houses. But there were already people living in the Little Biggling houses. "No matter," they were told, "we can fit them in somehow." And fitted in they were, by dint of commandeering every spare room in the village and surrounding farms, by saying sternly to reluctant householders, "So many shall you have, no more, no less; and any complaints shall be presented on Form B6 Z." Without respect for rank or station, the billeting officers cut a swathe through the village, dropping here a single female, there four single males, in one place a married couple, in another a departmental head whose wife visited weekends. In theory only a bed, bare room and the usual facilities need be provided for the half-guinea paid the householder. In fact the soft-hearted housewives had found themselves, during six years, for suitable recompense, providing one or two meals and innumerable cups of tea every day. In fact, also, they often became quite attached to the helpless pawn of the system—the billetee. Many a warm friendship started when a hostile figure opened the door with every manifestation of distaste to the innocent and timid soul being shepherded to its special place in the Little Biggling fold by a determinedly cheerful and unsnubbable shepherdess.

But a handsome proportion of individual successes could not convince Little Biggling housewives and, it follows, their families that they were not being put upon. And now that their own demobilised men and women were returning home the overcrowding in the village became well-nigh intolerable. Horrid stories about the private relationships of Ministry staff were the meat of local chatter. A stranger listening to talk in the 'Blue Dragon' about local crime would have deduced that the Ministry was largely staffed by the more reckless type of adventurer and brigand—whereas in fact the department was a research unit consisting mainly of aged and over-worked scientists and administrators.

On the whole, said the calmer souls in the village, under the able leadership of Dr. John MacDermot, local physician, Little Biggling had suffered not so much a disaster as a shock. It could afford to compare its blessings with those of the bombed city from which its visitors had originally come, and when the operation was over the patient might not only recover, but find itself slightly invigorated from the experience. But even the calmer souls were dismayed by the length of the operation and prayed daily for the end of this tribulation.

The Government workers also had their complaints. They found it, for instance, difficult to believe that an inhabited place in a civilised country could boast only one cinema (two shows Thursdays and Saturdays only), a village hall providing a monthly dance (to the music of one pre-World War I piano) and two public-houses. Those who were not attracted by church entertainments—and those, alas! were legion—either had to spend most of their free time riding in buses to Gloucester or Stroud, or sitting in their billets or the 'Coach and Horn', wistfully planning their next trip to London. They had perforce to make their own entertainment, and a fine selection of dramatic, discussion, art, hiking, social and other clubs had been formed. But with the will-o'-the-wisp prospect of returning to London, now that the war was well over, most of these clubs had died away, leaving nothing in their place but a great feeling of impatience. Even at the height of the war many of the department's staff still lamented as bitterly as ever the exchange of London's liveliness (air raids and all) for the primitive security of Little Biggling. Now, with peace returned, and six years after the London exodus, there was no compensation that they could see for this exile in Egypt. Their loudly expressed complaints did not contribute to harmony between the hosts and guests crowded uncomfortably in the village.

But amongst the Government staff there were also more accommodating characters, ready to admit that the incomparable beauty of the Cotswolds around Little Biggling and the country pleasures of tramping over muddy fields, fishing the local streams and chatting in remote pubs with the slow but kindly Gloucestershire workers were sufficient compensation for London's more sophisticated amusements. And after six years even the most unaccommodating persons must put down some roots into the soil where they are planted.

Later on this April evening the inhabitants of Little Biggling, old and new, were occupied about their various recreations. The vicarage, a pretentious mid-Victorian pile of a house which the Vicar's wife ran single-handed, was humming with the noise of four borrowed sewing-machines and the chatter of thirty-two village women and six Ministry typists, busy making the two hundred pairs of pink-flannel pyjamas ordered by the Red Cross for delivery next week, to clothe the children of Liberated Europe. The Vicar, young ex-padre of the RAF, perhaps anxious to escape so much concentrated femininity, had taken himself to the village hall—a rectangular brick construction on the other side of the church marked for all time over the main door with the words "John Stubbs—1926". Under the shelter of John Stubbs fifteen assorted boys of the local Scout troop were planning their first spring outing, and the Vicar was giving his blessing to the enterprise and provoking unchristian fury in the breast of the Scout-master, who was also the local greengrocer and of a botanical turn of mind, by suggesting they devote themselves this spring to visiting neighbouring aerodromes, where his R.A.F. friends would gladly advise them on how to construct a glider of their own.

At the 'Blue Dragon' Little Biggling farmers and tradesmen, with a small representation of Ministry staff, were discussing local scandal and the errors and incompetence of the Nation's leaders. At the 'Coach and Horn' Ministry staff, with a small representation of local farmers and tradesmen, were discussing Ministry gossip and the errors and incompetence of the Nation's leaders. There was a large feminine contingent at the 'Coach and Horn.' Mr. Acton, the landlord, had once disapproved of women in pubs, but having no legal right to forbid them entry, he could only show his disapprobation by serving all the men first. After six years of persistent feminine custom he had almost forgotten why he did this, but it had become an accepted tradition of the 'Coach' that men came first. In an alcove by the window Graham Stone had obviously profited from this favouritism by getting very drunk. As he had remarked earlier in the day, his was a moody drunkenness, and he sat alone in the dark corner glowering at the more gregarious members of the staff.

But the majority of the inhabitants of Little Biggling took their recreation at home. It being neither Thursday nor

Saturday, and the cinema closed, most of them were content to stay within doors about their domestic business. A few stray couples lingered dreamily beside the river, but even by eight o'clock the streets were almost deserted. A stranger wandering through the village would have understood what the Ministry staff meant when they compared it to a cathedral town without the excitement of church services.

Robert Robarts was sitting in his billet, in an upstairs back-room, exotically furnished with Indian bric-à-brac by a devout widow of Indian cavalry. Fringed curtains and table-covers embroidered with strangely proportioned animals no doubt familiar in India, four little black-and-white inlaid tables of such unsteadiness that it was dangerous, he had been sternly warned upon arrival, to place anything upon them, and a large brass bed with round knobs at each corner gave an interesting character to the room. The wallpaper was in a frenzied design of red roses and green trellis. The only seating accommodation, except the bed, which rattled, was a black rocking-chair with wicker seat and back. Robarts did not like rocking. It made him sick. But he sat there this evening with his feet hooked under the bed in order to keep it steady, gazing blankly at the wallpaper. It could not have been the wallpaper, however, which reminded him of Charity Brown. He thought of her in quiet tones of grey, shading into silver like a birch tree in the spring—nothing dazzling or striking, but gently moving, quietly penetrating the consciousness and lingering there pleasantly while more startling impressions passed through and were forgotten.

At the age of thirty-six he had not fallen in love—he had slipped there, imperceptibly gaining momentum until, with a shock, last week having tea at his desk, it had suddenly occurred to him that Charity had become an indispensable part not only of office work, but of his life. Perhaps the realisation had something to do with the coming of peace and the desire for a more settled way of it. In any case it was a shattering conclusion for a man who had accustomed himself over a period of years to living alone, and whose whole life had been built on the principle that whatever he did, thought or suffered must be experienced alone. Now this loneliness he had thought so satisfying had become intolerable. He wanted Charity to confide in, to talk to, to go out with and to come in with—in fact, to live with. Every evening it became harder to face the awful moment when he must say good night. The thought of next Saturday's outing uplifted him for a moment. But, after all, that was only for a few hours. And he would be satisfied with nothing less than a lifetime. Madness! For although there was only ten years between them—a mere decade—Charity obviously regarded him as an aged dotard, an ancient relic, whose grey hairs demanded a filial respect. She called him "Robby"—he had heard her—and with a kindly patronage which infuriated him at the same time as he adored the kindness. It was the prematurely grey hair which did it, he thought bitterly. But for those he might have looked as young as Ratcliffe, who, after all, was thirty. He distrusted Ratcliffe. An insidious, plausible fellow, obviously playing about with Charity, but incapable of any real and deep affection. Yet she seemed to like him. He had often heard their laughter coming from her office, and they seemed to go out a lot together, too. "Chatty" he called her! Ridiculous name! It was sacrilege to truncate such a charming, expressive name as Charity to something so vulgarly inappropriate to the subject. These young people had no taste. Ah, there it was again! "These young people"! Could he never remember—and if he couldn't how could they?—that he was practically of the same generation? But it was no good—fifteen solid years, and unregretted years, of study and research cut one off from the normal growth of one's generation. It was too late now to graft himself again on to the main plant. The rocking-chair moved violently under the pressure of his bitterness, and he got hurriedly to his feet. Being up, he thought, it might be as well to take a brisk walk to get these ideas out of his head. It was a nice stroll across the fields and through the churchyard and back round Dr. MacDermot's house. Charity lived there, incidentally.

The object of Robarts' hopeless passion was at that moment lying flat on her stomach with a map of the district spread before her. Uncle John, known more formally to the villagers as the Doctor, sat behind her in an armchair, leaning over and tracing with a walking-stick the paths she ought to follow in her summer walks. Aunt Mary was out at the Red Cross sewing party. It was just as well, for, although an undoubted dear, Aunt Mary's very presence tended to remind people of neglected duties. At this moment, for instance, she would probably have been surreptitiously indicating to her husband and niece that they had a guest who also deserved some entertainment.

But Inspector Cam, sitting comfortably before the fire with his pipe, was content to listen to their arguments about the respective attractions of antiquarian interests and scenic effects without participating. He and the Doctor were friends of too long standing to feel any necessity for mutual entertainment. They had been to school together—a well-known Gloucester grammar school—and had been intimate ever since they were rivals for the position of head-boy. The Inspector had won. But the Doctor won the next round, for when he left school his father, a retired Army colonel, had been able to afford to send Jack MacDermot to University and then to medical school. Bob Cam had also had a hankering after Hippocrates, but his mother was the penurious widow of a provincial lawyer, and it was necessary for him to choose work which would bring in an immediate income. His friends argued anxiously about the rival merits of business, the law, trade, the Merchant Navy for the promising but penniless young man. Cam listened politely to all their reasoning and argument and chose—the Police. If he had chosen Crime his friends and his mother could not have been more horrified. It was incomprehensible that a young man with first-class intelligence should be satisfied to walk around Gloucester on a beat, in a tall helmet. It was the helmet that upset his mother most. During those first years Cam had to leave it outside in the tool-house in order not to exacerbate her feelings. Although he never gave any other reason for his strange choice than his curiosity to see the police records of his friends, Cam threw himself into the new life with enthusiasm.

Very soon he was promoted, and in course of time he was selected for training at the Police Staff College. He passed out top of his class and was offered a post in the CID. But again Cam seemed bent on frustrating his friends' kindly ambitions, for he refused the offer, preferring to return to his own county constabulary. That was five years ago, and now Cam was an inspector; his friends were again becoming reconciled to his incorrigible lack of ambition, especially as it was known that only a superintendent who took an unconscionable time in retiring delayed his further promotion. Cam himself was not enthusiastic about the prospect. He was, to tell the truth, a lazy man. Having achieved the comforts of an adequate income, an attractive wife and family, a pleasant home in the loveliest county in England, he was suspicious of any promotion which might trespass upon the time he had to enjoy these delights. . . . But the superintendency was not to be avoided. Cam saw without vanity that he was the obvious choice for the post when it became vacant. In the meantime there was no one in the county who more sincerely urged and encouraged the present Superintendent to husband his waning strength and to continue as long as possible his services to a grateful country.

By a pleasant coincidence Jack MacDermot also returned to Little Biggling in a professional capacity. He had become a partner in a local practice mainly in order to be near his parents. By the time his parents died he had inherited the practice, and was far too happy as the most respected doctor in Wipton Rural District to reconsider his old ambitions of a Harley Street practice. So the friends remained together again—at the top of their particular trees in the small garden they chose to cultivate. With affection for each other personally they combined respect professionally, and it was their custom to pass at least two evenings a week in each other's company. Cam felt almost as much at home here in the inglenook as he would in front of his own modern tiled fireplace, and he was lost in vague contemplation of sparks flying up the chimney as the other two talked.

"What about Saturday?" the Doctor was saying. "We might walk over to Iron Acton. There's a nice little church there."

Charity shook her head. "I can't. I *was* going to do some domestic chores, but Dr. Robarts has suggested driving into Gloucester, so I thought I'd take the opportunity to see the cathedral. But the Saturday after would be all right."

"I saw Robarts the other day," volunteered Cam, suddenly coming out of his dream. "At the chemist's. Clever little chap he looks."

"Clever!" exclaimed Charity with withering scorn. "He's the most brilliant young chemist in—in the world! You remember the Banshee invention? *That* was his. And he's not so little, either—only rather slight and worn because he works so hard."

"Well, well," said Cam. "Fleeting impressions, you know. What does he do exactly in that menagerie of yours?"

Cam was unfortunately one of the anti-Ministry party— mainly on the grounds that the staff did not appreciate their good fortune in living in Little Biggling and that it was high time they left it.

"He's the acting-head of the whole establishment, really. We've some Finance and Establishment branches here serving the whole Ministry, and he only has nominal authority over them—I mean they have their own heads in London, but Robby keeps an eye on them if they need an immediate local decision. His real job, however, and what he's best at, is the scientific side of the work—the lab work. That's what he was really appointed to be head of."

"I thought Wassel House was entirely for research," said the Doctor.

"That's what it was established for during the war. But, you see, a lot of the lab staff and essential administrative and clerical staff have left recently—there are only about twenty of us altogether—and that means a lot of empty offices in the house. So as Establishments were closing some of the other research stations and had some extra Finance people they couldn't fit into the London office, they sent them here temporarily."

"Do you mean to say there are only twenty scientists up there?" said Cam with disbelief. "Why, I can't step outside my house without tripping over long beards in the shrubbery."

"There are only five scientists," Charity laughed, "and six lab assistants. For the sort of work we do there's no need for a large staff. The long beards probably belong to our messenger boys."

"And why don't they release Wassel House?" asked Cam sternly. "What have we done that they leave us until the last? Are they keeping us for the next war? Don't tell me that you're working. Personally I think your Director-General just likes to have a place like this to spend his weekends."

Charity sighed. It was an old argument.

"It takes time to close up an organisation like this, Mr. Cam. And as the work we are doing *is* of importance—whatever you say—they're not in a hurry to move us. When we've finished our present experiments they may take action."

"'We are doing'!" exclaimed the Doctor. "So Charity is now dabbling in scientific experiments, Cam! You and I had better evacuate to London, eh? She's probably working on something to out-atom the atom bomb."

Charity threw a cushion at him and suggested they listen to the nine o'clock news.

Outside Robarts was lingering unhappily in the lych gate,

wondering if she would be going out for an evening walk. But she didn't, so eventually he strolled down Bramble Street towards the 'Blue Dragon' in search of a heartening drink.

Another member of the Ministry staff had been more energetically engaged that evening. Emerging from the office about seven-thirty into clear, warm light, Ratcliffe had decided, on the spur of the moment to pay a visit to the top of Wassel Peak. This hill, unusually steep and angular for a Cotswold hill, started half a mile from Wassel House, then rose sharply for some two hundred feet. On the side facing the House it formed a perfect cone, on the opposite side it sloped more gently away into a long hill, gradually subsiding into the Wipton road, two miles away. Bill had been up it in daylight, but the thought of the view on a starlit night attracted him. It was not a difficult climb, but a slow one.

The view was rather disappointing after all the effort. A light mist had swung over from the sea, obscuring the stars. From the dark loneliness of the hill-top the lights of the cottages far below seemed as distant as stars, and he felt as isolated from humanity as if on a mountain of the moon. There was always a breeze at the top of Wassel Peak, but tonight it was very slight. Ratcliffe sat there for about half an hour, pondering about his future career, then the wind died down altogether. Solitude suddenly seemed rather unattractive, and, getting up abruptly, he started down the other side, following the path that led to the Wipton Road. It was like descending into a mild steam bath. He realised that a storm must be brewing.

Tired and rather depressed after the climb and the long walk, he came back into Little Biggling by the Wipton Road, and the thought of a drink struck him as very pleasant. The 'Coach and Horn' was his customary pub, so he did not go the quick way home via Bramble Street, but through the Market Place. At the pub the atmosphere was even fuggier than outside, the bar crowded and noisy, and as he went in Stone looked at him with drunken gloom from a corner. He stopped for one drink, but there was no one there he liked—except Stone, whom he admired, but who didn't like him. A few minutes later Ratcliffe made his way out again to the street, wondering if the 'Blue Dragon' would be more congenial, with soft Gloucestershire voices and local gossip instead of feminine shrieks and eternal talk of departmental personalities.

He turned to the right down Clover Street. Near the end of the street, as he was sauntering along, there came the sound of soft voices from an alley which he had passed a few yards back, and then a scream. He paid no attention for a few steps. Women's screams nowadays usually meant they were having a good time. But there was another more urgent cry and the sound of heavy breathing, as if a struggle were taking place. He hesitated and walked delicately back. It would be damned embarrassing to get mixed up in an affair when neither party welcomed you. On the other hand, the woman sounded as though she meant business. At last, as he turned the corner, he hesitated no longer, and, leaping into action, he sent the man flying back against the wall and helped the woman to her feet.

"What the devil's this!" he said angrily, recognising the man. "Do you know what the result of this will be, Parry? By God! I'll have you fired, if it's the last thing I do."

Parry made no move or reply for a moment, but lay apparently stunned with his head against a pile of iron railings in the alley. In the silence of the moment the woman, without another word, slipped round the corner and into the darkness. Ratcliffe pushed Parry with his foot and then pulled him up roughly by one arm. The messenger rubbed his head with a ludicrous expression of self-pity, mumbling drunkenly the while. He could hardly stand, and kept slipping against the wall and clawing at it desperately to keep on his feet.

"Nice little woman. She loves me. You run along, whoever you are. We're happy, aren't we? Where's she gone? Nice little woman loves me. Can't help it. . ."

"Oh, shut up!" said Ratcliffe disgustedly. "She's gone, anyway."

Parry made a lunge towards the street, which brought him face down in the dust. Ratcliffe picked him up again by the collar and cursed him unkindly.

"I'm taking you home, Parry. Tomorrow we shall see about firing you. Come on, you. . ."

As they went back up Clover Street, Ratcliffe had difficulty keeping Parry on his feet, and he thought ruefully to himself that any onlooker would think they were both drunk and trying to keep each other up. Parry lived over a draper's shop—Miss Penny's—on the Market Place. As ex-officio billeting officer, Ratcliffe had been responsible for placing the messenger there six months ago, and he felt a twinge of conscience now. It was a damned shame bringing a man back in this condition to a decent home. But there was certainly nowhere else he could go, except the lock-up, and Ratcliffe felt that the reputation of the department would not be improved by handing over its members to the police.

"Leave me alone, you," Parry was muttering. "I know you. Ratty Ratcliffe, that's who you are. Ratcliffe the Rat, that's you." He choked with laughter at his wit, and Ratcliffe jerked him wordlessly along. "Don't you touch me, you devil! I know about you. I can get you into trouble, I can. And you're not the only one. Oh, there isn't much that James Parry doesn't know. He's a bright fellow, James Parry is. And everybody hates him!" He slobbered repellently. "Never mind. The Chief'll look after me. He'd better. I'm well related, I am; a regular toff. Don't you hurt me, Ratty, or I'll have you up! I'm. . ."

"Shut up, I say!" Ratcliffe ordered sharply.

There was a sinister quality in the man's drunken threats which repelled him. Who did he mean by the Chief? Robarts? More probably some drunken idea of the fool's.

They reached the draper's, and he knocked sharply on the shop door, pinning Parry firmly against the wall with the other hand. He heard quick steps coming downstairs, the shop light was switched on and the door was unbolted. Miss Penny's

head appeared, peering short-sightedly into the black night.
Who was it? Mr. Ratcliffe? Oh, how nice to see him after——
Oh! The gasped exclamation resulted from Ratcliffe dragging
Parry, now voiceless and limp, into the shop. She shut the door
behind them and leaned against it while Ratcliffe explained
and apologised profusely. But no apologies could prevent Miss
Penny looking as though she would any moment burst into
tears, and clasping and unclasping her hands anxiously.

"I'll take him up, Miss Penny. You go into the shop. No, don't
worry. It's the least I can do. And we can lock the door on this
side so there's no danger of his getting out again. Not that there's
much, anyway. He's almost dead to the world. And tomorrow
morning, come hell or high water, he leaves here. We'll get you
a nice young girl next time. It's a shame you should ever have
had a fellow like this. I can't say how sorry I am."

Not all Ratcliffe's gentle handling, however, could restrain
the tears, and Miss Penny retired to a corner of the shop to
commune with her handkerchief while he persuaded and
forced Parry upstairs.

The draper's shop was on the corner of Cat Lane and the
Market Place. At one time it had been two shops, one facing
the Market and the other the lane. Their union had never been
fully consummated upstairs, although the two show-rooms had
been thrown into one. There were therefore two flats above the
shop, each with its own stairs leading up from one of the two
street entrances. Besides the show-room's main door, across the
angle of the corner of the building, it could also be entered
from the foot of each of these staircases. Miss Penny found
the division of the entrances an ideal way of having lodgers
without being aware of their existence. The lodger's flat, now
occupied by Parry, was at the top of the Cat Lane stair, while
her own had the more interesting outlook of the Market.

Miss Penny, sobbing quietly to herself, heard young Mr.
Ratcliffe push and pull the inert Mr. Parry upstairs. After a
few minutes, during which she breathlessly heard bedsprings

squeak, a window slammed shut and, after a pause, coal shovelled out of the scuttle, Ratcliffe came down, rubbing his hands with distaste.

He laughed at her white, upturned face, for by now she had fearfully approached the foot of the stair and was gazing up in apprehension.

"There now, Miss Penny," he said gently. "You mustn't worry yourself like this. I've put him to bed, shut the window, put coal on his fire to keep him warm and locked the door with his own key. I'd really make an excellent valet! Just put the key away and you're perfectly safe until morning. Lock your own door, too, if it makes you feel better. Anyway, he'll sleep soundly, don't you fear."

"It's so horrible!" Miss Penny murmured brokenly. "I've always had a horror of drunkenness. My father sometimes used to—oh dear, dear, dear! I'm sure it will be all right, but it's most upsetting. It's not the first time, you know, but I didn't like to complain. He's rather fright—*Do* you think, Mr. Ratcliffe, you could find him somewhere very nice where he'd like to go? I *would* like a nice young girl if it could be arranged. But it won't do any good; no good at all. It's so horrible."

"I'll get you a nice young girl if I have to marry her to do it!" Ratcliffe swore.

He reassured her, comforted her, flattered her, and finally, after placing the key for her in the third empty box from the left on the top shelf behind the notions counter, he took his leave.

Coming out into the dark street he was overwhelmed for a moment by the raucous sound of voices singing "Roll out the Barrel" in the 'Coach and Horn.' But he had lost his taste for a drink after handling the drunken messenger and was in no way anxious for company. So, feeling cold and weary, he passed across the Market Place and down the shuttered street to his own lodgings and a warm bed.

CHAPTER III

"BIRR-RR-RR!" A shrill, high-pitched note of alarm broke into the peace of Dr. MacDermot and cut abruptly the crescendo of a snore. He humped over angrily to his other side and fumbled blindly for the alarm switch. When he had found it and pressed it down he clutched the sheets warmly round him again and relaxed. Mary had not woken. He would have two or three more minutes nap.

"Birr-rr-rr!" The alarm again calling with a desperate note.

"Saints and aunts!" he exclaimed bitterly, and, groping wildly, switched on the light.

According to the clock it was only six o'clock, and his alarm was set for seven. What the blazes! With the slow comprehension of the sleepy he realised that the ringing was the phone. The operator must have put the plug in and left it there, because the bell was sounding shrilly now, without a break.

Mary was awake, sitting up in alarm and exclaiming, "What is it, John? Turn off the alarm, for heaven's sake! Oh, it's the phone. Good heavens, what a racket! My heart stopped beating, I'm sure——"

Dr. MacDermot slipped his feet into slippers and his arms into a dressing-gown. For the hundredth time he swore that he would see about having a telephone extension to his bedside the very next day. He couldn't find the light-switch in the hall, and the bell rang relentlessly. What was the girl about! At last he got to the telephone and, lifting the receiver, barked snappily:

"Hello! Who is it? Who's that? Speak slower, for heaven's sake!"

Mrs. MacDermot listened anxiously. She hoped John was not going to be called out early, when he was just recovering from his exhaustion after the 'flu epidemic. In his side of the conversation she heard rising alarm.

"What? Yes, yes. What! My God! Are you sure? No, no! Now you go and sit down and take a sniff of smelling-salts. At once, do you hear! I'll come immediately. Have you phoned the police? All right, I'll see to it. Now, smelling-salts, mind you! And don't go up again, on your life! I'll be there in three minutes."

His footsteps pounded up the stairs again, three at a time. He looked white and rather frightened as he came into the room.

"Mary! Something rather nasty has happened at Miss Penny's. Keep calm, my dear, and phone the police that they should go there at once. Her lodger has had his head knocked in. Maybe an accident, but Miss Penny sounded as though it were a bit stronger than that. Now keep calm, dear, keep calm!"

He threw off his dressing-gown and pyjamas with abandon and started putting on his shirt inside out, while Mary, pale but collected, called the police. When she had put the call through and briefly repeated the message, she got up and patiently helped him get all his clothes on right way out. Five minutes later, surgery kit under his arm, feverishly trying to knot his tie, he was flying downstairs while she called after him:

"Now, bring Miss Penny back to breakfast if she's upset, John. Don't forget."

A few early risers were about the Market Place as he fled through, and looked after him with interest. "Some poor girl's baby all in a hurry," Mrs. Cox suggested to Mrs. Rattan as they cycled past on their way to do cleaning at Wassel House. But her conjecture, appeared improbable, as he hastily entered Miss Penny's shop door.

She had not lain down, but was feverishly pacing the shop, with one hand clutching a bottle of smelling-salts, in the other a damp handkerchief. She was dressed in a faded kimono, with flowing sleeves adorned by fiery embroidered dragons, and old cloth slippers. A frenzied attempt to pin up her hair in its usual top-knot bun had resulted in a grotesque cockscomb effect, with the grey hair falling away in loose strands from the few pins which secured it. She leaped upon the Doctor as he pushed open the door.

"Oh, Doctor, Doctor! Thank heaven you've come! I don't know when I've been so upset. Such a thing never happened to me before. What will people say? It's horrible, Doctor! And the police! Oh!"

With a wail, which still managed to be refined rather than abandoned, she took another sniff of smelling-salts and was rendered speechless for a moment.

"Sit down!" said Dr. MacDermot, taking advantage of the pause. "Keep quite quiet, don't get excited, and tell the police when they arrive that I'm upstairs with him."

He felt calmer now. Other people's excitement always steadied his own nerves. With his wife he was sometimes conscious that he was by nature a timid soul. She was so magnificently self-contained herself. But with his patients, who, in their ignorance and trouble, looked to him as a rock of reliability, he found it easier to appear imperturbable.

He walked up the flight of stairs leading to the lodger's room. The door was ajar, and as he turned the corner of the banisters to enter he was struck by the warmth of the air coming out of the room. He pushed the door gingerly with the tips of his fingers. It swung back, revealing before the fireplace the crumpled body of the lodger Parry. Even from the door the Doctor knew he was dead. Surely no one could lie, even in unconsciousness, with such rigid distortion. He lay on his back, and both arms were twisted beneath his body. His face was turned towards the fire and half lay upon the brass guard-rail. Stepping carefully, MacDermot approached the body. He bent over it a few minutes and then straightened himself. No doubt at all! Dead as a poker. With slight repugnance he stooped again and drew the hair away from the scalp wound. It was sticky with perspiration as well as with blood. A little brown pool had been formed on the whitewashed hearth by the blood dripping from the wound. It was a deep cleft in the skull, fairly long, but narrow. The edges were rather uneven, and it slanted from the temple across the brow above the right eye.

He looked round the room. It was so warm that a slight mist hung in it, drifting slowly towards the door, as if making a reluctant escape from the scene. The window was misted over like frosted glass. The room was a mess, but more with the accumulated carelessness of weeks than with any sign of a struggle. Still, that was the job of the police—to bother about struggles. He wondered nervously whether it would be in order to open the window and relieve the nauseating fug, but decided that discretion forbade. A cigarette would perhaps be permissible, corpse or no corpse. But at that moment there was the clattering of police boots upon the stairs, and he put the case hastily away.

With Miss Penny dodging nervously behind, like a rather timid sheep-dog behind some very formidable sheep, the police entered. Inspector Cam came first, filling the doorway with his burly strength. He stood there motionless for a few seconds, his blue eyes, shadowed by shaggy, greying eyebrows, taking in the whole room section by section, left to right. As he covered the section in which the Doctor stood he nodded kindly, said "Morning, Doctor," and allowed his gaze to move on to the next exhibit. Dr. MacDermot felt nervously that the Inspector was visualising the whole scene of the murder and that his own presence would somehow involve him inextricably in that scene. But with the same respect for an expert which he liked his patients to feel for his own professional methods he remained courteously silent until the Inspector had surveyed from his vantage point the last corner of the room. Then the great man moved forward, followed eagerly by the heads of Sergeant Rowley and Miss Penny. The latter seemed to have recovered from her first horror, and lingered in the door with an expression of fascinated disgust.

"So!" said the Inspector genially. "This is the corpse, is it?"

He walked over to the body and stood looking down at it with a kind, if patronising air. His attitude suggested that the body was now in safe hands and need worry no more about itself. Without investigating closer, he looked round at the Doctor.

"Well, Doctor? It's a bit early, I know, but have you any ideas about how and when?"

Dr. MacDermot ran his fingers through his hair with an impatient gesture.

"You know, Cam, this is a little off my beat. I honestly think you ought to get a police-surgeon from Gloucester, if you can. I'll do my best, of course, but apart from saying he's dead I can't swear to anything."

"Ah," said the Inspector kindly. "Well, if you can swear to that it's a beginning, isn't it? But just rough guesses are all I want. We can get our own man later, as you suggest, and an autopsy will be necessary."

"Well, then, I'd say he's been dead about eight hours—since about ten last night. But his right arm is still quite loose and the rigor is by no means complete. The heat of the room might have affected the time taken for it to set in. Eight hours, however, would about cover it, I think. And as for the weapon, I won't even guess what it was; but something narrow, rounded, and the part that hit the head was about four inches long. There were two, perhaps three, strokes."

The Inspector nodded slowly and got down cumbrously to his knees. He leant over the body, and the room was silent for a minute or two except for his heavy breathing and Miss Penny's occasional gasps. The Doctor leant over him, watching his deft investigation with professional interest. He had never seen Cam at work before on a case of this kind, and was impressed by the confident competence with which he approached the problem. He was quite flattered when the Inspector looked up into his face and nodded.

"I think you're about right about the time. As for the weapon, this is the type of thing, don't you agree?" He touched gingerly the brass guard-rail upon which the head was resting and tried to move it with two fingers. The Doctor nodded.

"But it can't have been that," he commented, as the rod seemed stuck fast in its brass joints.

The Inspector grunted, and with the help of a chair clambered to his feet again. His broad, ruddy face puckered as he sniffed the air, and, looking round again, he noticed Miss Penny.

"Hot in here," he remarked. "Was it always like this?"

Miss Penny was delighted to break silence.

"Oh, I know, Mr. Cam. Mr. Parry felt the cold so much—he was such a little man—and he kept his room much warmer than *I* would like it. And coal was included in his rent, you know. Why, he sometimes used two scuttles a day! But I didn't grudge it, Mr. Cam. The thought never crossed my mind, even though I may have grumbled jokingly to Mr. Witherspoon occasionally. But when I came up this morning——"

"Now, now," said the Inspector reprovingly. "All in good time, Miss Penny. I shall take a full statement in due course. Just let me finish here, *if* you please."

He turned to the fireplace. There was a heap of still-smoking ashes in the grate. Although now almost out, there must have been a considerable fire earlier in the night. Kneeling down again—a slow process—Cam gently inserted both hands, wincing as they contacted some hot coals, and as he brought them slowly to the surface he brought with them a layer of flaky grey ashes which even an amateur could recognise as burnt paper. Then, peering round the edges of the grate, Cam probed a finger behind a fire-brick and with a grunt of satisfaction brought out a charred scrap of white paper. Further inspection revealed no more treasures, and Cam, after a brief look at it, placed the paper in a small box from his waistcoat pocket.

Dr. MacDermot shuffled impatiently. He would have liked to have seen that paper, and, after all, they were old friends. Cam wasn't getting on very fast.

"Do you notice," he said pointedly, "that the window is locked inside?"

"Yes," said the Inspector, "I notice," and Sergeant Rowley looked reproachfully at the Doctor.

Profiting by the general docility his gentle snub provoked, Cam proceeded to walk delicately around the room. He did not seem to mind an audience—even to be aware of it—as long as he was not interrupted. To MacDermot's disappointment, he collected no stray buttons or wisps of thread caught on nails, but he looked everywhere. Starting at the left of the door, he examined the wardrobe which stood there, taking out the two old suits which hung there and going through their pockets; trying the lock; inserting his head through the door and examining the floor with the help of a flashlight. Re-emerging, red-faced, he leafed through a pile of old and dog-eared magazines in the corner of the room. Most of them were of the penny-thriller type, and he left them with disgust. A table beside the bed had upon it a chessboard and the pieces arrayed as for the beginning of a game. Cam looked at them for a few seconds and fingered one or two in a desultory way. But the bed interested him more. There were brown stains upon the faded bed-cover which seemed to be newly made, and he felt and smelt these with care. With his pen-knife he scraped some of the dirt into a glass phial which Sergeant Rowley leaped eagerly to present. Then he turned to the window. Without touching it, he looked at the lock with close attention for some seconds. Finally, with a last inspection of the window-sill, he returned to the body. Kneeling down again, he deftly removed the contents of the pockets and placed them in a box provided by the constable—a key-ring with two keys, a letter date-marked Bolton, a very grubby handkerchief, a Ministry pass with photograph of the deceased, his identity card, some stale crumbs, loose change amounting to eight shillings and tenpence-halfpenny, a pocket-book with two pounds and the return half of a ticket to London. To the Doctor these seemed poor treasure trove, but the Inspector looked at them with some pride and put the letter in his own pocket-book. In the same ponderous way, he lumbered to his feet again.

"Now, Rowley," he said to the young sergeant, newly promoted and obviously burning with ambition to show his mettle. "You know what to do. Make the most of the job. Go through this room, touching as little as possible and making a list of what the fingerprint boys ought to cover. I'll check it before I go. And look out for anything I may have missed. Make a rough sketch of the room and its contents for me. I'll be having a message sent for the photographers, Dr. Prescott and the rest of the Gloucester gang, so help them as much as you can when they arrive. And finally, don't let anyone— anyone—in here without my written permission."

"Oh-h!" A long, pent-up cry burst from Miss Penny. Clearly she had been restraining herself too long and the dam had broken. She turned a tear-stained face to the men. "Oh, Inspector, Doctor, has it got to be mur—— Can't it possibly be an accident? Perhaps the poor man fell. Couldn't he, please? I've never had anything like this before, and it does give a place a bad name."

Cam looked at MacDermot, and the Doctor shook his head.

"I'm sorry, Miss Penny. It's terrible for you, but personally I don't see how it could have been an accident. The Inspector will correct me. At first I thought he might have done it on the hearth-guard. But no man, Miss Penny, no man breaks his head on a bar and then gets up and does it again in the same place. There is certainly the mark of more than one stroke there!"

He looked enquiringly at the Inspector, who nodded.

"That's right. Moreover, those stains on the bed are certainly blood. It looks as though he were killed there and then dragged on to the floor. No, Miss Penny, we'll just have to make the best of it. So don't worry. Suppose you get dressed now, while Doctor and I go over his story. Then I'd like a statement from you, please."

Miss Penny apparently realised for the first time that she was in a state of undress in the presence of three men. She turned as pale as if another corpse had been discovered in her own bedroom and gasping, "A statement—yes, of course, a statement," rushed out of the room and down the stairs.

Dr. MacDermot cast a sly look at the Inspector as they followed, but Cam was on duty today, and refused to be amused. At the foot of the stairs he went out of the street door for a moment and rescued Constable Peak from a commission of inquisitive boys by sending him off to summon the County Constabulary from Gloucester. Returning, he led MacDermot into the shop and seated himself precariously upon one of the high chairs on which Little Biggling matrons were accustomed to select their dry goods. Dr. MacDermot found himself another and brought it over. The top half of the door was glass, and through it they could see a little group of villagers already assembled on the next corner and gazing on the shop with interest. Obviously the news was already out. MacDermot suspected the telephone operator, while Cam thought grimly of the police-station staff, but in any case there had never been any chance of keeping a sensation like this secret in such a small and close-knitted village.

"We shall have to close the shop," said Cam to himself, and then turned to the Doctor. "Now, MacDermot, I shall want a proper statement from you later at the police-station, but it would be helpful if you'd just run over what you know about this."

"Practically nothing," said the Doctor unhelpfully. "I'm afraid I won't be a star witness, Cam. Nor a principal mourner. From all I hear, the man was a nasty bit of work."

"Oh, you knew of him?"

"Something of him. Parry was a messenger at Wassel House, and Charity has mentioned him to me. Rather unpleasant, sneaking sort of fellow, I gather. Also I attended Miss Penny last month for influenza, and she told me what a difficult lodger he was—but you'll find out all about that from her, I suppose."

"Just tell me briefly what she said."

"Oh. Well, he wouldn't let her in his room, and from the glimpses she'd had it was a mess—that was the gist of it. You know what a neat little piece she is—apart from that kimono thing!—and it was mild torture to have such a glory-hole in her establishment. Then he got drunk sometimes, and that frightened her. Their sleeping quarters are only separated by a wall, and he would thump about all night, I gather. She was quite hysterical about the noises. Then he pried into her private affairs (prying seems to have been everyone's complaint about him), and though I cannot conceive that he found much to interest him, you can understand that it was annoying. I was a fool not to get him moved at once, but that 'flu epidemic has kept me pretty busy, and I admit it slipped my mind. Practically all my local patients want to tell me the iniquities of their billetees, and it's difficult keeping them all straight."

"Right," said the Inspector absently. "Well, now for your own part in the affair."

The Doctor briefly told his activities since first waking this morning, and was rewarded by a word of commendation: "Very workmanlike report. I shall enjoy hearing you in the witness box."

MacDermot shuddered a little at such praise, but obviously that would have to come, and it was as well to know that he would not make a fool of himself.

A patter on the stairs announced that Miss Penny had finished her toilet. She appeared, tidy and prim as an antimacassar, her hair tightly wound in an elaborate bun on the crown of her head, her grey dress buttoned to the neck and decorously hanging to surprisingly neat ankles, a steel bead necklace looped several times across her narrow bosom. Her more collected appearance was reflected in her manner. With nervous but conscientious hospitality she suggested a cup of tea for the gentlemen. Even Cam relaxed his official solemnity. Like MacDermot, he was accustomed to an early-morning cup in bed, and it was getting on for seven-fifteen now. Over the tea they resolutely avoided the subject of the corpse upstairs. This meant that Miss Penny remained speechless, but the two men chatted cheerfully about the impending thunderstorm and the farmers' complaints of drought.

Finally Cam put aside his cup and his cheerfulness with a firm gesture and turned to Miss Penny.

"Now, Miss Penny, I haven't got a shorthand writer here, and you will have to make an official statement later at the station, but it would help me if you could describe to me, as the Doctor has, just what you know about Parry and what happened last night."

Unexpectedly Miss Penny's restraint broke, and instead of replying she burst into hysterical sobs, burying her face in her hands and speaking in muffled tones.

"I know what you think; but I didn't, I *didn't*! And you know you'll never believe me! You know you won't! Ask anyone; they'll say I couldn't. Even if you do think. . ."

"Come, come," exclaimed the Inspector, bewildered but patient, "there's no reason for this, Miss Penny. I only want your statement. Of course I'll believe you." He checked himself doubtfully. That was human, but not official. "Well, I'll check everything, of course; but if you've done nothing wrong there's no cause at all to get excited."

This caused renewed sobs and protestations and exclamations of despair. The Doctor stepped into the breach.

"Now, now, Miss Penny. I've given my statement, and I can assure you it didn't hurt at all. It's the normal procedure in cases like this, you know, and there's no sinister implication. Cam can't say it, because he's on duty, and that makes him very careful, but *I'll* tell you that he as soon suspects you of being mixed up in this affair, except indirectly, as—as—as *me*. So cheer up, there's a sensible woman."

Cam looked a bit taken aback at this carefree pledge of his views, but Miss Penny's sobs became sniffs, and eventually she dried enough of her tears to speak.

"I know it's silly of me, Doctor and Inspector, but I've been so upset! You see, I *know* about things like this. I—I read stories about it—detective stories, you know—and the moment I saw that man lying there I thought to myself, in a flash, 'Death in a Boarding House'! That's where all the lodgers got poisoned by the landlady in the soup, you know—or was it the gravy? Anyway, it was poison. And the moment I saw that upstairs I thought, 'They'll think it was me,' because although it's not poison this time, still, I thought, Mr. Cam may not think of that; and me having the key and having said I didn't like Mr. Parry—although I'm sure it was just that he was so inconvenient, and not that I ever thought of him like *this,* they might think *I* did it, like Mrs. Bramblehurst."

At the thought of this powerful evidence Miss Penny was again overcome and took refuge in her handkerchief. The two men looked helplessly at each other.

"Mrs. Bramblehurst would be the landlady," said MacDermot at last, trying grimly to get hold of one item of sense in the outburst.

"Ah," said Cam, as though that solved one difficulty, anyway.

He turned again to the unhappy woman, and after several minutes of assurance that the request for a statement was not preliminary to the issue of a warrant, persuaded Miss Penny to speak.

The Doctor listened with interest, conscious that his presence was not strictly necessary, but determined to carry home as much news as possible to Mary and Charity.

Apparently Miss Penny, upon rising at her normal hour of five-thirty to make clean the house and shop, had recalled that her lodger was locked in his room. (This necessitated a long digression to describe Parry's return the previous night with the assistance of Ratcliffe, and the hiding of the key. Cam questioned her with interest about the sequence of events, and took a few notes on the back of an envelope.)

Returning to the morning's events, Miss Penny described how she had gone upstairs fearfully, having retrieved the key from its hiding-place. Outside the door she hesitated a moment. She had a feeling that as she unlocked the door Parry might leap out on her. So she called through to him, but there was no answer. Stiffening herself, she inserted the key and turned it. But still there was no sound from the room, and the thought crossed her mind that perhaps Mr. Parry had been taken ill in the night and, unable to find his key, had died there alone. Really alarmed, she cautiously opened the door and peeped in. The room was misty with heat, and through it she saw the lodger lying on the hearth. She screamed, needless to say, and then went tentatively across to see if she could do anything. It was obvious she could not, so without touching anything she ran downstairs and phoned Dr. MacDermot.

At the close of her story she looked fearfully at the Inspector as though expecting summary judgment as to whether she should now be arrested. He, however, was biting his finger thoughtfully.

"Now, Miss Penny," he said eventually, "did you go up with Mr. Ratcliffe to put Parry to bed?"

Miss Penny looked shocked.

"Certainly not. That was a man's work. And indeed Mr. Ratcliffe couldn't have been more obliging. But then he is a nice young man."

"Did you hear any sounds from Parry's room during the night?"

"N-no. Of course I took a little sleeping pill because I was so upset, and was asleep in about half an hour, and didn't wake again until just before five. So perhaps I wouldn't hear anything, would I?"

"Hmph!"The Inspector seemed disappointed."But so far as *you* know Parry was not disturbed from the time Ratcliffe left him until you went up this morning?"

"No; but of course he must have been, mustn't he? I mean . . ."

Miss Penny fluttered vaguely with her hands to indicate the Inspector must not base his case entirely on her evidence, flattering though that was.The Doctor, on the other hand, cast Cam an alarmed glance.

"What was your opinion of Parry?"The Inspector changed the subject abruptly.

"It's very difficult, isn't it? I mean, I suppose you want me to tell the truth, but one isn't supposed to speak ill of the dead."

She shook her head perplexedly.

"In a police case," explained Cam patiently, "the character of the deceased is open for discussion."

Miss Penny was relieved.

"Well, I can't say that I really liked him. He was so difficult. He wouldn't let me clean his room, for instance. And though that saved trouble, some people might say, it was very upsetting to think of that room being so untidy. I always say that one untidy room in a house makes for dust and dirt everywhere. My dear mother used to say that, too. But Mr. Parry was very secretive. He always kept his door locked, too, and held the only key. He *said* he had important documents that must be kept under lock and key. But, then, he always pretended he knew everybody's secrets. Mr. Witherspoon thought it was quite *reckless* of me to have a man like that in the house! Mr. Witherspoon didn't think he was exactly honest.And last night wasn't the first time he had been affected by drink either. Quite often it happened. And then he used to get so aggressive and threatening it quite frightened me—not that I had anything to be frightened of, naturally; but it was unsettling. He was away a lot taking messages to London; but then I never knew when he would turn up. It was a great strain having a man in the house, anyway, even though not *quite* the same house, because of the different stairs, as I used to tell Mr. Witherspoon, and I really don't know what the billeting officers were about, though Mr. Ratcliffe did assure me that he would go today. He was quite unsuitable. But it's too late today, isn't it?"

"What sorts of threats?" asked Cam, staving off tears by the unexpected enquiry.

"Threats? Oh, yes. Oh, nothing really. I don't really remember. Silly things like the Ministry turning me out of the shop if I didn't treat him well."

Miss Penny laughed nervously.

"Did he have any visitors—any friends, that you know of?"

"No friends, I'm sure. He used to boast that a man in his position couldn't afford friends—that he couldn't share his secrets. . . . And he hated the village men. He said once none of them was rich enough to interest him; and I really believe he meant it! He did have a visitor about two months ago. I remember because it was the only time anyone asked for him. A grey-haired gentleman called to see him when he was out—really quite a gentleman. He didn't leave a name, but said he would see him next day at the Ministry, so I gathered he worked there. But a very superior man—not at all like Mr. Parry."

"Any other description?"

"Oh, medium tall, I should think, and about forty. Quite a plain gentleman, but very pleasant indeed."

"Hmmm." The Inspector thought for a moment. "You say there was only one key. Isn't it usual to have another for lodgers?"

"Yes, but the second was lost some time ago. And Mr. Parry said he preferred not to have another in existence."

"And the only key in existence, therefore, was the one that Mr. Ratcliffe put away for you?"

The little woman agreed, and Cam got up and walked to the shop door. There were firm bolts at the top of the door and beside the Yale lock. He tried them both, and they slipped easily into place.

"Did you secure these last night?" he asked.

"Oh, yes," said Miss Penny. "And the door on to Mr. Parry's stairs from the shop. I always lock that. And the door on to *my* stairs. I'm very careful. Not that there's ever been a robbery, but I don't believe in putting temptation in poor people's way."

"What about the other street doors—from the two staircases on to the street?"

"They are always open, Mr. Cam. It's quite safe, because the flat doors are locked. Then the milkman can come right up and leave the bottles outside the flats. Only he *doesn't,* you know. I've complained I don't know how many times, but he will leave them . . ."

Cam interrupted hastily.

"Well, the doors seem all secure, anyway—the doors into the shop, I mean."

"Oh yes, there was no way in at all. Except through the window, of course."

"'Of course'?" said Cam with some amazement. "Is that a usual entry?"

"Naturally not, but the lock has been broken for months. I've been meaning to have it mended, but one thing after another . . ."

"Well, have you mentioned this to anyone?"

"Oh, several people, I should think. Well, you know how one talks. But I always keep it shut, of course, so no one outside would know it could be opened."

Cam got up and walked over to the window she pointed out. It was not a real display window, but an ordinary sash window beside the shop door and facing upon Cat Lane. The window on the other side of the door facing the Market had been converted into a bow display window and several bolts of cloth and children's dresses advertised the nature of the shop; but this one had been left to its original purpose of admitting light. Half the catch which held the two parts of the window together had been broken away and Cam saw that this defect would be apparent to any reasonably tall person examining the window from outside. He looked at the window-sill, but it was so scratched and worn with age that any new marks would be invisible. In any case, the window was so low that it would be perfectly possible to step through it from the street to the floor without touching the sill. He observed aloud that there were no blinds or curtains.

"No," Miss Penny said. "I took down that horrid black-out stuff on the day war ended. But I haven't had time to make new ones since."

The Doctor was clearing his throat impatiently.

"I don't see where that gets you," he protested. "Surely it's the entrance to Parry's room which is the question."

"And I don't think we'll find the answer to that upstairs," answered Cam. He turned to Miss Penny. "Thank you, Miss Penny. That's all for now. It wasn't so bad, was it? But I'm afraid I shall have to request that you don't open your shop today. I have fingerprint men coming from Gloucester, and we can't have the shop crowded with sightseers."

He glanced through the door at the sizeable crowd which was now inspecting the shop from the other side of the Market Place. Some of the bolder boys were actually standing by the door, peeping over the lower wooden half, with their noses pressed against the glass. He frowned mightily at them and they disappeared.

"Naturally," said Miss Penny with dignity, "I shouldn't dream of opening the shop today. I hope I know what is proper. Even though he wasn't a relative, or even a friend, he died under this roof, and I shall act accordingly."

She refused MacDermot's invitation to breakfast on the grounds that she couldn't eat a bite and would prefer to spend a quiet hour in her own room, but the Doctor suspected that part of the reason was dislike of facing the battery of curiosity which awaited her outside the shelter of the shop.

As the Inspector and Dr. MacDermot left there was a hush in the murmuring crowd, and they were fixed by some thirty pairs of eyes. Cam eyed them disapprovingly, while the Doctor felt rather self-conscious.

"Wouldn't you think people had enough to do at eight o'clock of a morning without loitering about the pavements?" Cam turned away, and with his old friendly manner said:"Well, Jack, this is a pretty mess, isn't it? I'm afraid it means I'll have to do some work for a change."

"A fine chance for glory and promotion?" said the Doctor mischievously.

Cam shook his head doubtfully.

"Or for failure and general bad feeling throughout the village. I'm quite happy as I am, and a case like this stirs up a lot of mud."

"Well, there can't be many people with a motive for killing a man like that. The field of investigation should be small."

"The question is where to start," Cam ruminated. "I like to strike at the most likely point first, so as to put the fear of God into any malefactor who may happen to be within range of my pot shot." He considered for a moment. "Well, there's not much doubt. I'll go up to the Ministry after breakfast."

The Doctor looked at him sharply. He held no brief for the Ministry, but he was a fair man.

"That's a bit hasty, isn't it? What about the village—the pub where Parry got drunk—some of our local bad lads who may have thought he had piles of hidden treasure in his locked room? Are you ruling them out?"

"Not yet," Cam said calmly. "But I should like to speak to Mr. Ratcliffe, who was the last person to see Parry alive. . . ."

"Last but one," interrupted the Doctor emphatically. "Ratcliffe is a pleasant young friend of Charity's."

Cam nodded agreeably and continued.

"And I want to see what all this talk about his 'influence' boils down to. Nothing, I should guess; but Parry sounds to me like a good potential blackmailer, and the Ministry would offer more scope, and more money, than the village."

"Hmph," grunted the Doctor. "I could set up a profitable blackmail business myself in this village."

"But Parry, so far as we know, had no interest or connections in the village. But there's one other little thing I'd like to ask about up at Wassel House."

He took out of his pocket the box containing the scrap of paper he had found in Parry's fireplace, and opened it so that MacDermot could see the paper inside.

It appeared to be a corner of some printed paper. All of the stamped address had been charred away except for the letters '. . . earch' and beneath that '. . . eet' and beneath that again, '. . . . I'. The Doctor looked at it blankly.

Cam shut the lid of the box with a snap.

"That," he said with satisfaction," is pretty clear.

'Ministry of Scientific Research, Walton Street, London, W.C.I.' Obvious! Now why should a villager have been interested in burning Ministry papers in the fireplace?"

"Perhaps Parry used it for laying the fire," said MacDermot glumly." He could have got it, I suppose."

"Paper of this quality? Unlikely, I should say. This is first-quality Ministry paper, I should think—used for writing to Cabinet Ministers and ambassadors and things like that. If Parry had any, I think he would have used it more carefully. Anyway, I wouldn't be surprised if analysis of the ashes didn't show that the fire was practically built out of paper of this type."

"Well, you may get someone for wasting paper, even if you don't catch the murderer," Dr. MacDermot exclaimed bitterly.

"That's right," Cam laughed. "A year's imprisonment is the maximum, I think! But if we pressed that war-time law.

Doctor, the whole Ministry would be under lock and key, to my way of thinking." He clapped his friend upon the back in farewell. "Goodbye now. Tell Charity I'll pick her up in forty-five minutes on my way to Wassel House, if she can get herself fixed up by then."

CHAPTER IV

A S the sun rose higher that morning the air grew thick with un-springlike heat. Driving at a cautious speed through the market an hour later, Cam and Charity saw the villagers going about coatless in the unseasonable heat. The green shoots, just ready yesterday to burst into leaf, hung limp upon the trees and hedges. Cam mopped his brow as the car turned downhill out of the village. The road at this point was dug deep out of the side of the hill, and the close-netted branches of the elms which topped its ten-foot banks made an eternal twilight in the roadway.

"Can't remember anything like this for thirty years," Cam exclaimed, half to Charity and half to the constable sitting woodenly in the exact centre of the back seat. "Now, when I was about fifteen—that'd be about 1902, I guess—we had an August in April. Makes you feel uncomfortable, doesn't it? It's unnatural, such heat!"

Charity, leaning back beside him, was gazing unseeing at the passing banks. Her naturally placid expression was clouded with unhappy thought. Cam, glancing at her sideways, noticed that she had lost her usual fresh colour.

"Yes," she agreed, "it is unnatural. And the whole atmosphere is unnatural, don't you think? I mean the department being here, and our relations with the village, and all the bad feeling of the last few months. I've been feeling awful," she confided, turning to the Inspector. "You see, I've got a foot on both sides of the fence, and I could see how tense everyone was getting. Even you, Mr. Cam. This—this accident just seems the climax."

Cam nodded slowly.

"Yes, I see what you mean. I wouldn't have been surprised at a few pub fights recently, Charity. But they haven't materialised. And I think that all of us—Ministry and village both—are too sensible not to make the best of a raw deal. Grumbling—yes.

But not violence. And I didn't think it would ever have come to murder. Even *I* never thought of killing the Ministry staff to get rid of them!"

Charity laughed politely, and there was silence for a few minutes. Then Charity stirred herself again.

"I never liked him, you know. He was a horrid little man. But it's hateful thinking of him being so lonely, and living in a dirty little back room, and someone hating him so much he—he could do this."

"Yes," said the Inspector shortly.

The road suddenly lifted out of its high-banked shelter and burst into the dusty sunshine. Ahead of them the long vista of a straight brown road across the top of the hills stretched alluringly. Uninspired, Cam's old Morris chugged deliberately along at a modest twenty miles an hour.

"Was he generally liked?" asked Cam suddenly.

"Parry? Oh, no! Generally detested, I should say."

"By whom? Didn't he have any special friends or cronies?"

"Certainly not among the messengers. He never mixed with them. Sometimes he used to flirt with the clerks, but it was quite one-sided. He was an unattractive old man. Robby—Dr. Robarts—was the only person I ever saw really chatting with him. And Stone quite liked him, but didn't have much to do with him. I think he pitied him more than anything."

"Who did he come in contact with, then?"

"The people he took messages for, I suppose. He was the DG's special messenger, really. He used to run up and down to Town with messages for him. Quite a lot of the time he was in London. Dr. Robarts and Graham Stone and Bill Ratcliffe used to use him as a courier, too; but he was a bit of a free -lance, and wasn't on a regular route, like most messengers. He had special access to the laboratories where the others never go, in order to take the DG's messages straight to anyone who might be working there. That gave him the idea, I suppose, that he was a cut above the regular messengers."

"Was his work satisfactory?"

"I don't know, really. He used to collect and deliver what he was supposed to. But I've had several rows with him about reading secret correspondence."

"Have you indeed?" Cam commented with interest, and Charity flushed.

"Well, I'm not the only one," she said defensively. "Bill Ratcliffe complained about it, too—to him and to Dr. Robarts."

"Any result?"

"Well, not so far."

Cam laughed.

"I don't suppose you'll have cause for complaint any more."

"I'm still sorry," Charity said seriously.

The Inspector nodded briefly and became official.

"Now, when we get to the house I'd like to see Dr. Robarts first. Will he be there by this time?"

"Of course. He usually gets there about eight, and works in the labs until ten. I can ring down for him."

"Thank you. Blast your hide!"

This latter cry was addressed, not to Charity, but to a cyclist who, in an absent-minded manner, had swerved wildly into the middle of the road and back again to safety under the very nose of the cautiously driven car.

"Oh, it's Bill, of course," cried Charity. "He is a fool. But do stop, Mr. Cam. He's the one who took Parry home, and you'll want to see him. He probably doesn't even know about it yet."

But the Inspector drove steadily on.

"Sorry, Charity, but I haven't much time, and we'll see Mr. Ratcliffe later this morning," So Charity had to be content with turning in her seat and making violent gestures at Ratcliffe, to which he replied with a cheerful wave and the cry "Road hog!"

The car now turned off the road to a drive entrance guarded by handsome iron gates and two porters. They were waved through on the strength of Charity's Ministry pass and Cam's police card. An avenue of magnificent chestnuts shaded the drive, casting a mottled pattern of sunlight and shadow through the network of twigs and sticky buds. The avenue curved to the left for a quarter of a mile and then the two lines of trees veered away from each other in a wide sweep to form a circle. On the farther edge of the circle was framed the handsome Georgian façade of Wassel House. Thickly grown ivy somewhat marred its classic elegance, but gave to the house a comfortable and homely look. It was a place for children's games and house-parties and open hospitality. The outstretched arms of the chestnut avenue seemed anxiously awaiting a new influx of guests and gaiety. The scene always filled Cam, who could remember the good old days, with an intense nostalgia.

The drive curved round the perimeter of an immaculate round lawn and, following this, Cam approached the front door. A small assemblage of Ministry staff were chattering there around the two impassioned lions which a misguided Victorian had placed on guard before the Georgian door. Cam guessed from the excited conversation that the news had come before him, and his guess was proved by the silence which fell when he got out of the car. "The police!" he heard whispered in awed tones, and the appearance of his helmeted attendant caused a mild sensation. A pretty blonde girl broke away from the group and came running down to meet Charity.

"Is it true, Chatty? You've heard, of course. Isn't it terrible? What does your uncle say?"

"Hello, Betty. Yes, I've heard. This is Inspector Cam. Look, dear, I'll see you later. I've got to find Robby now."

With a glance at the Inspector she ran in front of him up the steps. He noticed she seemed more annoyed than pleased at the attention they were receiving. Unusual in a girl, he thought, with male satisfaction.

She led him upstairs into Robart's office. As she had predicted, he was not there. While Cam seated himself comfortably in the visitor's chair she rang downstairs.

"Hello, Mr. Stone? Is Dr. Robarts there? No, that's all right; but will you tell him he's wanted up here? No, just that. Thank you."

In the interval of waiting for Robarts, Charity took off her hat and coat, opened the corner safe and took out the correspondence trays. A messenger brought in the morning mail, steering an apprehensive course around the Inspector, and Charity started going through the letters.

The delay and the silence became oppressive.

"He's probably finishing off an experiment," Charity explained.

"Does he direct all the experimental work?" asked Cam.

"That's his main work, and that's what he's best at. But now that Establishments have saddled him with a lot of administrative work, Stone shares a good deal of responsibility in the labs. Stone knows Dr. Robarts' methods, fortunately. They studied under the same professor at Bonn. That's why Dr. Robarts was so keen to have him, I think."

"Germany, eh?" Cam muttered.

Charity looked at him with disgust.

"Oh, you're not one of *those*, are you? Scientific training in Germany before the war was about the best in the world, and living in Germany for a few years doesn't make a man a Nazi—quite the reverse, I should think. Anyway, both their war records prove that!"

Cam got up abruptly, as though he had just remembered something.

"May I look through your stationery files?" he asked.

Charity was surprised, but took him into her room. In a large steel cupboard were stacked the dozens of different types and shapes of notepaper and envelopes which are necessary to keep Civil Service correspondence going. To Charity's astonishment, Cam brought up a chair and started methodically collecting one sheet of each different type of paper. He was still at it five minutes later, when Robert Robarts came in.

"Sorry to be so long. Oh, how d'ye do?"

Cam had pulled himself up, and stood regarding him with ponderous solemnity.

"Good morning, sir." With a glance he quelled Charity, who was about to burst into explanations. "I understand you were acquainted with the late James Parry, sir."

"Parry?" Robarts looked blank. "Parry! The messenger? Why 'late'? What on earth *are* you talking about, sir?"

He looked at Cam with unconcealed impatience and bewilderment, but with an undertone of uneasiness.

"That's right, sir. The messenger. He was murdered last night by some person or persons unknown, and I am now engaged on investigations connected with the arrest of the criminal."

Cam rolled the official phrases roundly on his tongue, and Charity shot him an angry glance. It was indecent to take such pleasure in making people unhappy, and poor Robby was looking decidedly unhappy. Dropping into Charity's chair, he stared at the Inspector in stupefaction. When he found words they were curiously inadequate.

"But you must be mistaken! How strange—unfortunate!"

"Unfortunate indeed, sir. I understand you knew the deceased."

"Parry, you mean." Robarts seemed to recover himself in annoyance at the trivial phrase. "I do wish people wouldn't use officialese like that. 'The deceased'! Yes, of course I knew him. He was a messenger here. But—had he any relatives, do you know? Anyone to tell? This is really shocking." Robarts seemed to think this last word more satisfactory than any he had yet used to describe the tragedy, and he repeated it. "Shocking!"

During his breakfast Cam had had time to go into this question briefly.

"Yes, sir. There was a letter in his pocket from a brother in Bolton, and I have instructed the police there to inform him of the affair. He probably knows by now. To get back to you, sir. I'm afraid it will be necessary to take a statement, and in order to save you the trouble of going to the police-station, I've brought my shorthand writer. Is that all right?"

"Oh certainly. Of course. Now where shall we sit?"

Robarts leapt up and ushered the Inspector into his own office, where the constable who had been waiting in the corridor joined them. Charity, with a murmured "If I can help you . . .", remained where she was.

"Now," said Cam comfortably, letting himself down to his chair, "if you would just tell us in your own words, sir, what you know of Parry and when you last saw him."

Robarts ran nervous fingers through his hair.

"Well, as to the first, there's little I can say. I suppose I knew Parry better than I did most of the messengers, but that's not saying much. He always seemed to me an unusually intelligent man—in some lines, anyway. He had a positive genius for chess, and we have had many intensely interesting games together. We usually used to play after work here at the office. Apart from chess I didn't have much to do with him. As for knowing anything about his private affairs—well, I'm afraid I'm a broken reed. He spoke occasionally as though there were some dark secret in his life—some disappointment; but, then, he was a rather sour old man, I suppose. I suggest that we ask for his personal file to be sent down from London. That will contain all that the Ministry knows about him."

"Yes, that would be useful. Thank you."

Cam had the impression that Robarts rather hastily suggested the Ministry file in order to save himself from going into more detail.

"Then when did I see him last? Well, we had a game of chess last night, starting about seven-thirty. Parry was White, and played a Sicilian Defence game. Very skilful play. I had a job forcing a draw, I can tell you. It was a short, sharp game. Anyway, we finished about a quarter past eight, and I offered to drive him down to the village. We have a shooting-brake travelling between the house and the village every hour on the hour up to ten p.m., but I'm often here later, so I use a car. Anyway, he came with me, and I dropped him at the 'Coach and Horn'. If you want a witness, Graham Stone, my principal assistant, was with us. He'd been working late in the labs. I dropped him at the 'Coach', too. Well, really that's all, I think, Inspector. I just said good night and left them."

The Inspector shifted his gaze from Robarts' face to the ceiling.

"Thank you, sir. What time did you drop Parry at the 'Coach and Horn'?"

"It must have been about eight-twenty. It's a ten-minute drive."

"Not the way I drive it," said the Inspector severely, and Robarts looked suitably chastened. "Eight-twenty. Had you and Parry had anything to eat over your game?"

"No. We played in the canteen, as usual, and I had coffee, but I find eating and chess are not a harmonious pair. Parry had some beer."

"What did you do after dropping Parry?"

"Oh, I went back to my billet and had supper there. About ten past nine I went out to have a drink at the 'Blue Dragon', and then went along to the 'Coach and Horn' for another. At closing time—ten o'clock (but there, you know that better than I!)—I returned home and went to bed. Not very exciting, I'm afraid."

"You seem to have kept on the move, however." Robarts flushed, but made no reply, and the Inspector pressed him.

"Are you quite sure about those times, sir?"

"Yes. It's scientific training, I suppose. Anyway, I have a good time sense."

"What time did you get to the 'Blue Dragon'?"

"About a quarter to ten."

"Was Parry still there?"

"I didn't see him, but he would be in the public bar, and I was in the saloon."

"Anyone you know—and who knows you?"

"Graham Stone was still there. And Mr. Acton is an old friend. Also a chess-player, you know. One meets them in odd places. It's part of the charm of the game."

"Criminals are like that, too, sir. Ha!"

Cam looked sharply at his busy scribe to see that that flash of wit had got safely into the records. But Robarts only smiled wanly. Evidently the Inspector's good humour was not infectious. Lapsing again to proper recognition of the solemnity of the occasion, Cam returned to his questioning.

"Have you on any occasion visited Parry's lodgings, Dr. Robarts?"

"I don't— No, no. I haven't actually."

"Miss Penny, his landlady, described to me a man who enquired for Parry about two months ago. The description was not unlike yourself, sir."

Robarts clapped his hand to his chin, as though to erase the treacherous features.

"Wait a minute! About two months ago I *did* visit Parry. He had borrowed my chess set, and I wanted it back. But he was out, and I must admit the occasion had completely slipped my mind. I certainly never called on him any other time."

The Inspector grunted, and Robarts felt as if he had walked in the very shadow of the gallows. It was fantastic the way you were expected to remember your most trivial actions after the event. He mopped his brow gloomily.

"And now," continued Cam relentlessly, "can you cast any light, sir, upon Parry's talk of a mystery in his life? You are not the only one to whom he talked in the same strain. Have you any idea to what he referred?"

To Cam's surprise, Robarts burst out laughing, and for the first time that morning the little wrinkles of anxiety left his forehead.

"You too, Inspector? Parry certainly seems to have been successful in creating an aura of mystery about himself! No, I can't help you, and, if you ask me, I think it was just the man's own form of exhibitionism. He wanted people to think he was interesting—and he succeeded! I'm sure he would be pleased that you thought there was a secret in his past. No, Inspector, I think Parry was just an unhappy old man who might have made something of life if he had had the right opportunities. But he hadn't the gumption to do anything but talk—and play chess."

"Humph," Cam grunted unwillingly. "You're very sure, sir. Who are those other people who *did* believe Parry wasn't all above board?"

"Oh, Ratcliffe. Even Miss Brown, who is a most kindly person usually. There was a general feeling, to be Irish, that he took too much interest in his work. He had been caught reading secret correspondence. But I think that was just misplaced intelligence. And, after all, the sort of work we're doing—it's not war weapons, you know! Parry couldn't have done much harm even if he had read most of our papers. Not that we want our work publicised, of course, but you would need some technical training to be able to understand the significance. Still, I did promise to speak to him about it."

"And did you?"

"Yes, I did, as a matter of fact. Last night, after our chess game. Parry was naturally upset, and inclined to be truculent. He claimed, and with some justice, that his conduct was a matter for the Director-General, not for me."

"Surely not!" Cam was astonished. "Do you mean the Director-General is the direct supervisor of the messengers?"

"No, no. But Parry was his personal courier, so in a way he was part of the DG's personal staff. Anyway, Parry was very emphatic about this direct link, and went so far as to imply that I had overstepped my authority."

"A bit presumptuous," commented Cam.

Robarts shrugged.

"Oh, well, I'd hurt his *amour propre,* you see."

"Well, that's about all, then, Dr. Robarts. I may have some more questions later. In the meantime can you tell me anything about the other two members of your staff who are known to have seen Parry last night—Stone and Ratcliffe? Who are they? What do they do?"

"Did Ratcliffe see him? Oh, well, Stone is about twenty-eight, and he joined us about six months ago. He was a nervous wreck then, and though he's still somewhat moody, he's greatly improved. The previous five years he had spent in a German prison camp, you see. He was captured in 1940, and was reported killed. His wife died of the shock, I'm afraid. Then when our troops were advancing through Germany they found him in a terrible state in one of the worst of the camps. He came back to find all his old life and family gone. His mother had been killed in an air-raid. I had heard of him before the war as a promising young chemist from my old teacher, Professor Zeissen at Bonn, who was his instructor. So when I heard he was back and rather drifting I tried to get him for us, and succeeded. He has done very good work. But whether he will ever recover mentally I don't know. What he needs is an anchor, a wife—something like that."

Robarts shook his head moodily.

"He must be pretty grateful to you," Cam ventured. The scientist laughed.

"He's not the grateful kind. And anyway that is hardly the point. I wouldn't have got him here unless I knew that he could be very useful to me." He paused a moment, and then went on: "Ratcliffe has a more cheerful career. He was at Oxford when war broke out, and went straight into the Navy. There he worked on MTBs throughout the war. When he was demobbed—also six months ago—he came back to join the Civil Service, and they put him here to do administrative work until he's taken his exams. He helps me run this place— catering, transport and the like. It's as complicated as running a big hotel, with the added inconvenience that all your guests live in odd rooms in other people's houses. Ratcliffe likes the social problems involved. But he only regards this place as a stop-gap."

Cam thought he detected a note of derogation running through Robarts' attempt to describe Ratcliffe, but he did not follow it up, as he wanted to avoid prejudice before meeting the young man.

"Thank you, Dr. Robarts. And now, if you please, I should like to see them in their offices."

Robarts nodded.

"I'll have Stone sent for. He's in Lab 2, I think."

"Could I go down?" asked Cam.

"Well, of course," Robarts hesitated. "You are the police, I suppose. But rather than create a precedent I should be glad if you would see him upstairs."

Cam nodded understandingly. He had been over the laboratories at Wassel House when they were constructed early in the war, and knew, and respected, the elaborate precautions for their secrecy which had been taken. Even today there was no publicity allowed in the Press about them, although a wide circle of scientists and technicians were well aware of the research going on at Wassel House station. The laboratories were not part of the house, although the only entrance was through the cellar and a closely guarded door. They had been hollowed out of the foothills leading to Wassel Peak, and so secretly was the work done that the earth dug out of the hills had been carried ten miles away for dumping in order that there should be no indication to enemy air reconnaissance that excavation had taken place. The great majority of the departmental staff never saw the laboratories. Antique scientists were rumoured to live there like troglodytes, so engrossed in their researches that they had not ventured into the sunlight for six years. But this was mere, legend. Successive generations of laboratory workers, like Stone and Robarts, in this latter day, had moved freely in and out of their billets in the village. For any stranger to enter the laboratories was, however, the police had convinced themselves, and time had proved, impossible. The villagers knew about them, but only from rumour and imagination. The imported labourers who had dug them out of the hillside so cunningly that even a stranger actually standing over them could not guess what lay beneath the pleasant meadow, had left fine legends of Ali Baba caves. But for lack of corroboration these legends were now repeated as something out of the far past. They were one with the legends of highwaymen and sheep-stealing—exciting, but unwitnessed. There was a body of opinion in the village which claimed that the whole story was an invention of the North-Country foreigners who had dug—or claimed to have dug— the caves, and that it was unbefitting a Gloucestershire man to believe such arrant nonsense about secret work going on under their native hills.

Inspector Cam had seen the laboratories, but he had never mentioned this fact. When he had inspected the security precautions in 1940, together with an awe-inspiring group of CID and MI5 officers, the long, windowless, whitewashed rooms had been empty and still, except for one cellar where the great gleaming engines which operated the air-conditioning machinery hummed desperately at their unceasing work. It would look very different now, he expected. Filled with benches and experiments and scientific paraphernalia—well, it wouldn't mean a thing to him if he saw it. He understood they were working on textiles these days, which seemed rather dull after secret weapons.

Robarts had phoned down for Stone and now he came back to his desk.

"Miss Brown will show you the way, Inspector. There's just one thing, though. The DG is down. He spent the night. Your London people probably told you. Anyway, he may want to see you, so if you'd come back here before you go I shall have spoken to him about it."

Cam swore secretly but powerfully to himself. Someone had slipped at the police-station, and he had not heard about the DG. It was part of the security system that the local police should know when a VIP was in their area. But the Director-General had been coming down so often recently that Cam's staff had been getting a bit careless. Nice job if he'd been caught in ignorance. But his face showed only polite acknowledgment.

"Yes, I should like to see him if it could be arranged. He was in the flat last night, I suppose?"

Robarts nodded. The Inspector had been much struck by the flat—a self-contained little apartment, with bed-sitting room, kitchen and bathroom, constructed within the laboratories. It had been designed for the use of the laboratories' head—Robarts—but as the Director-General came down so often he had taken to staying there, and Robarts had had to find a billet in the village. Cam had his eye on some of the fittings for his own home when the place was dismantled. Mrs. Cam liked gadgets.

Charity, looking very prim and efficient, led Cam along the corridor to a small room at the far end of the passage. Cam was struck by its neatness. A camp bed in one corner was made in fastidiously correct Army fashion. The books were all arranged according to size—obviously not a charwoman's idea—though Cam, who liked books and used them, felt this was carrying order a bit too far. The desk, unlike Robarts', was stripped for action, with the bare essentials arrayed compactly in the centre. Incongruously amidst this admirable efficiency a vase of daffodils, fresh and flaunting, glowed on the window-sill.

Charity, still on her dignity, left him on the plea of being needed by Dr. Robarts. Cam wondered idly how much she had heard through the door between the offices, and what her relations with her chief were. In the latter's one reference to her Cam had noticed a softening in the scientific expression. His musing was interrupted by the door flying open again to admit a sulky-visaged young man, black-haired and black-browed, with astonishingly vivid blue eyes, leaning heavily on a black walnut stick. He looked grimly at Cam for a second, knocking the door closed with his stick.

"Mr. Stone?" said the Inspector courteously.

"That's right. You're the police, I suppose. What's it about? Is is true what everyone's gabbling about Parry?"

"Are they?" said the Inspector with interest.

"Of course. We don't often have actual murders here, you know. It's true, I suppose?"

"I'm afraid so," Cam said, and the young man laughed roughly.

"Then you're the only one. Most of the staff here regard it as a relief from boredom. Poor old Parry!"

He sank down despondently by the desk.

"If you don't mind," Cam continued, "I must have a statement, Mr. Stone, on when you last saw Parry. My constable here will take it down. I understand you were with him last night."

Stone got up again and limped restlessly up and down throughout the conversation. Occasionally he stopped to straighten a book or a pen, and Cam was interested to note that the extraordinary order was not just the reflection of a secretary's zeal.

"It depends what you mean by 'with him', in the words of the venerable Joad. I don't usually spend my leisure time with messengers, though Parry was more interesting than most of our dotards. But I drove in the same car with him last night, if that's what you mean."

"You were working here late, I understand."

"Not very late. It was only eight-fifteen, and we work a damn sight longer than that often. But it was after the office staff had gone, anyway. I'd been down in the labs, and had just come up. Robarts saw a light in my room and offered me a lift down to the village. Parry was with him. They'd been having one of their chess games, I suppose."

"Dr. Robarts thought rather highly of Parry, I gather."

Stone nodded glumly.

"They weren't intimate, but a devout chess-player takes his opponents where he finds them. I don't know whether Robarts would even recognise Parry except across a chess-board. To him he was just a hand moving the pieces to awkward squares."

The last words were spoken more to himself than to Cam, but the Inspector leapt upon them.

"But you knew the man, Mr. Stone? You liked him?"

Stone shrugged.

"Yes, I liked him. But I didn't know him. You remember the spy, Chatsworth? That needed guts."

The Inspector looked his surprise. He remembered the spy Chatsworth—a research chemist who was arrested and executed at the time of the invasion for espionage. He did not see what Parry had to do with it.

"Oh, I thought Robarts would have mentioned it. Parry was the messenger who found the papers which did for Chatsworth. He reported to the DG. Most messengers wouldn't have had the sense—let alone the sense of responsibility!"

Stone had gone over to the window and was nervously stroking the petals of a daffodil with unexpectedly delicate tenderness. A flower-lover, too, thought Cam. He couldn't have had many in prison camp.

"You were saying," he continued, "that Dr. Robarts gave you a lift with Parry."

"Yes. Well, there wasn't much talk going down. Parry seemed to be rather shirty about something. About eight-twenty, I suppose, Robarts dropped us both at the 'Coach and Horn'. I went into the saloon and Parry into the public bar, and that was the end of that. I didn't see him again that night. You can only see a small section of the public bar from the saloon— even if you want to look."

"Ah, I'm not a stranger to either myself," said Cam cheerfully. "Now, just for the record, Mr. Stone, what did you do the rest of the evening?"

Stone grinned unpleasantly.

"So I'm on your little list, am I? Oh, don't apologise. Well, my story is short. I drank. I drank a good deal, and my best witness for that is Mr. Acton. I don't remember much of that evening, but I can assure you that until ten o'clock it was spent in the window nook of the saloon bar—or tottering upstairs occasionally, if you don't mind my coarseness. And Robarts took me home after closing time—carried me tenderly to my own doorstep and entrusted me to the much-tried charity of Mr. Witherspoon, my landlord and our local chemist. 'The rest is silence.' Unless—but I trust not—I snored."

Cam was regarding his boots.

"Dr. Robarts took you home, did he?" Stone looked up sharply and flushed.

"Yes. Didn't he mention it? Just like him. Misplaced gallantry. Thought he might be able to save my reputation, etcetera. He's a well-meaning blighter, really."

Cam would have liked to say that concealing evidence from the police did not come under the heading of well-meaning, but he respected the convention that one should not criticise a man to his subordinates.

"One more thing, Mr. Stone. Parry seems to have cast a lot of florid hints about that there was a dark secret in his life, that if the truth were known people would be surprised, etcetera, etcetera. You know the sort of talk. But do you think there was any basis of truth in this chatter?"

Stone did not seem to be as amused as Robarts had been, but he shook his head.

"No. I think Parry was a disappointed man, and he came to think that the things he might have done he actually had done. Of course the Chatsworth affair was his great moment, and it made him rather 'spy-minded'. But all that is a bit out of date nowadays, isn't it? Anyway, even if Parry had some secret, I didn't know him well enough to say what it was."

Cam detected a note of impatience in Stone's voice. There were still some things he wanted to ask, but he remembered that the man was not well, and decided to postpone them.

"That's all, then, sir. Thank you for your help." He pulled himself up, shadowing the whole room with his bulk. "Could you show me Mr. Ratcliffe's room? He's next on my little list, as you say."

"Oh?" said Stone with interest. "What's he done? Paralysed Parry with one of his witticisms and then slugged him?"

"He took him home," said Cam obligingly. "And now, sir . . ."

Ratcliffe's door was two away from Stone's. As they approached it Stone went first and opened the door, blocking it for a moment. But he did not block the sound of Charity's clear, sweet tones saying:

"Well, anyway, Bill, I think you'd be a fool not to mention them. You don't want to hang yourself, do you?"

Her words were interrupted by a man's voice saying hastily:

"Why, hello, Stone! Have you seen the hound of the Law yet? I hear he's hot on the trail."

"Here he is," said Stone politely, and as he turned to let the Inspector in Cam noticed a ghost of a smile crossing his face.

There was discomforted silence for a moment as Cam went in. Charity, sitting in the window-seat, blushed hotly, and looked anxiously from the Inspector to the broad young man lounging in his desk chair, with both legs swinging over one arm. He looked at Cam briefly with quizzical pleasure, his pencil poised delicately between his two forefingers. At length he swung round and got up.

"Inspector Holmes, I presume. Take a chair, sir. And a seat for your Constable Watson. This is quite an occasion. Not, I should explain, that it is my first contact with the law. (I suppose you *will* get my record from the Oxford constabulary, will you not? I should be hurt if you didn't.) But never before have I been concerned in a case of this kind. I feel quite honoured."

Cam seated himself solidly, while Stone slipped quietly away. Charity hesitated a moment, but finally, with a shrug at Ratcliffe, followed him. The suspense relaxed slightly. Ratcliffe offered Cam a cigarette, but he refused politely.

"Ah," the young man said, lighting his own, "I suppose that comes under the heading of bribery and corruption. I must be careful."

"Yes," said Cam cryptically. "You'll have heard all about the case, I suppose."

"It didn't take the news long to travel. I'm really very sorry, although I'm not hypocrite enough to pretend I ever liked Parry. But no doubt someone did, and anyway it's no way to die, and I've seen most ways."

There was a tinge of bitterness in his voice, and Cam realised that the boyish appearance—the freckles and tousled-hair façade—had something more adult behind it.

"I suppose I was the last person to see him alive—except the murderer?"

"So far as we know, sir. We have had Miss Penny's description of last night, but I'd be grateful if you'll tell me your own story."

"Right. To start at the beginning, I left the office about seven-thirty and went for a walk up Wassel Peak and down the other side, round by Wipton. That took almost two hours, because I didn't hurry. When I got back to the village the thought of a drink was rather attractive, so I went along to the 'Coach and Horn'. But it was rather noisy, and after I'd had one I decided to try the 'Dragon' instead. Well— Oh, I remember it was about twenty-five to ten when I left the 'Coach and Horn'. I looked at the clock to see if I would have time to get to the 'Dragon' before closing. I was walking down Clover Street when I heard a man and woman talking in that alley leading to a builder's yard. You know—it goes under the arch made by the first floors of two adjoining houses. I didn't take any notice at first. Then the woman started screaming. I was a bit hesitant, because it might have been a little matrimonial tiff; but I thought it would be better just to have a look-see, and went back to investigate. It was obviously quite a fight, so I pulled the man off and knocked him down. I saw then it was Parry, and I felt flaming angry. It's that sort of thing which makes us unpopular in the village. And in the present state of tension about de-requisitioning Wassel House a story like this might set light to the fire."

Cam nodded encouragingly, and the young man went on:

"The girl—or rather woman—ran off, and I pulled Parry up and lugged him home. He was almost dead drunk and a bit dazed from my blow, and talked all the way. But I managed to push, pull and carry him along (he was a little man, you know) until we got to Miss Penny's."

"What was he saying?"

Ratcliffe screwed up his face.

"He called me names, of course. It was drunken blather, really. He said he knew all about everyone, and everyone hated him (quite right, too). Then he said 'The Chief' would look after him—and about his powerful relations—and a few threats that someone had better look after him because Parry had the goods on him."

"Any idea who he meant?"

"Not a clue. Probably no one. You must know by now that Parry was our champion liar."

Cam nodded for him to go on.

"Where was I? At Miss Penny's. Well, she was in a great state, naturally. I swore to have him moved next day—and so I would—and put him to bed."

"You undressed him?"

"I took off his coat and loosened his tie."

"Did you do anything else while in the room?"

"Let's see." Ratcliffe shut his eyes and thought. "Yes, I shut the window and locked it, because it's not far from the ground, and I didn't want him trying to get out and falling. Yes, I know. He could have unlocked it, but not in the state he was in last night. And I put some coal on the fire because you usually feel cold after getting as tight as Parry was. That's all. I was only there five minutes, or less."

"Did you happen to look in the wardrobe or behind the door?"

"You mean someone may have been there? He can't have been behind the door, because I shut it as I went in. But the wardrobe—I don't know. I didn't have any *feeling* of someone there—the way one does sometimes, you know."

Cam nodded again.

"It was Christian of you to put some coal on his fire, Mr. Ratcliffe. Especially after he had been such a nuisance. Personally I should just have put him down and left him."

The young man looked slightly embarrassed.

"Oh well, you know how it is. One always feels a bit brotherly even about one's worst enemy when he's really tight. Do unto others, you know."

"How much coal did you put on?"

"Just a shovel."

"Any paper."

"No, the fire was alight already."

Cam questioned Ratcliffe more closely about the appearance of the room, and his description agreed generally with the Inspector's own recollection.

"Now the key, sir. You took it off Parry's own keyring, I suppose?"

Ratcliffe nodded.

"And you put it away for Miss Penny, I understand?"

"That's right. 'Third box from the left, Mr. Ratcliffe, please—not the second, because that's where I keep my bun-pennies for the hospital; and not in the first, because that's my lost-and-found department'."

Ratcliffe imitated Miss Penny's precise tones with such success that even solemn Constable Wootton giggled over his notebook.

"It was on the top shelf, I believe," continued Cam. "Did you climb up to put it there?"

"Yes. I don't fly. She has one of those little ladders flush with the wall which they have in shoe shops and libraries."

"Thank you, Mr. Ratcliffe." The Inspector cleared his throat. "Now, sir, we'll leave the shop, as I suppose you did. Can you tell me what you did after that?"

"Easily. It was about 10.10. I went back to my billet—it's with Mrs. Davis and her daughter at 'The Hollies', Bramble Street—and found them both listening to a wireless play. Mrs. Davis is an excellent cook, but of rather uncertain temperament. Last night, however, she was in top form—didn't even ask me why I was late—and invited me to share a glass of sherry (pre-war three and sixpenny from the local). It was all very pally until about eleven, when I pleaded fatigue and retired to bed."

For a few seconds the Inspector surveyed his boots with tremendous interest. Then he turned again to Ratcliffe with an expression of limpid and innocent enquiry.

"And now, sir, as a last question, perhaps you will tell me what Miss Brown was asking you to tell me as I came in."

"Ratcliffe leaned forward abruptly, all trace of nonchalance vanished. Obviously, thought the Inspector with satisfaction, he had trusted that little piece of conversation had gone unheard. The young man got to his feet and walked slowly to the window, where he stood with his back to Cam. At last he sighed, and, without turning, said:

"Well, I suppose you'll find out anyway. I swear it's got nothing to do with the crime; but Parry has been trying to blackmail me."

CHAPTER V

ANY surprise which Cam may have felt—must have felt—was masked by polite interest. Constable Wootton, who had looked up from his notebook with ill-concealed excitement when the word "blackmail" was spoken, thought with shamefaced reverence, "Now, *there's* a policeman!" Not unconscious of this admiration, Cam looked calmly at Ratcliffe's back.

"And was he successful, sir?"

"No." The syllable was rapped out sharply and uncompromisingly. "And he never would have been. He came to me last week and told me he knew something, showed his evidence and asked for money. I refused, and he threatened exposure. I threw him out. That was all there was to it."

"And what was his information, sir?"

"Is that necessary?" The young man turned round now, his face drawn and anxious. "Surely if I swear that it has nothing to do with the case you can leave it at that. No, I suppose not." His words had bounced off the armour of Cam's imperturbability, and, shrugging his shoulders, Ratcliffe came back to the desk. He sat there playing with a pencil. "Well, anyway, I hope there won't be any need to talk about this. Unless it gets into court, I presume it's confidential. Briefly, I have got into debt pretty steeply lately. Various expenses rather piled up. Parry found a private letter from my creditors on my desk, and he read it, like the little spy he was. If he told the Ministry about it my whole career in the Civil Service would be jeopardised. I am only a temporary now, but in a month or two I'll be taking the reconstruction exam, and if I pass I'll be established. But not if my financial record looks unreliable. And I'm rather keen on staying—in the Colonial Service, not this type of work. So although my difficulties are just temporary, Parry could have made himself damned awkward."

There was a pause. Cam wondered thoughtfully whether this ingenuous young man realised he had just outlined a first-class motive for murder. Murderers didn't usually weave their own ropes. On the other hand, he had been forced into this position by Charity's indiscretion.

Shaking his head to clear the cobwebs, he leaned forward.

"Returning to your meeting with Parry, Mr. Ratcliffe. Just how drunk was he? Do you think that after you left him he may have recovered enough to let someone into his room, for instance?"

Ratcliffe wrinkled his nose for a moment in thought. Then he shook his head.

"No, I don't think so. He got heavier and heavier as we walked along, and by the time we got to Miss Penny's he was definitely in a comatose state. He was right out by the time I dropped him on the bed. Anyway, he smelt like a brewery—or, wait a moment—like a distillery, now I come to think about it. The man must have been pretty flush to get drunk on whisky. Wish I could afford it!"

He laughed suddenly, and his face cleared miraculously. Very boyish, thought the Inspector glumly.

He got the address of Ratcliffe's creditors and was proceeding to probe more deeply the causes of the young man's indebtedness when an uproar broke out in the corridor. Female shrieks and male oaths shattered the official calm. It was impossible to define a single word, but obviously a crisis had struck the department. With an agility which amazed Ratcliffe, Cam sprang to his feet and flung open the door. Outside, at the other end of the corridor, the pretty blonde who had spoken to Charity on their first arrival was holding high court. Messengers were flying desperately up and down stairs, and typists stood in their doors with carbon paper clutched in their hands, asking each other shrilly what the fuss was about. The Inspector strode along with a masterful air and, as he expected, silence fell with his approach, and everyone stood waiting for him to take charge. Police training reached its peak of perfection in the deportment of Inspector Cam when a crowd had to be calmed and controlled.

"Now, now," he said, with a patronising calm which made everyone feel they were being very silly. "What's all this? Can I help?"

The little blonde, distraught and helpless, clutched at his arm.

"Oh, can you help? Please——! The DG——! Chatty and I were talking in my room and I heard a thump and went in, and there he was! Flat on the floor! I could have died. And then I thought of Parry. . . ."

The Inspector pushed past her abruptly, rather paler than usual. If something had happened to Sir Arnold——. Turning through the open door, he saw a portly figure flat on his back, with Charity bending over him chafing his wrists anxiously. Ludicrously the Inspector felt like laughing. He hadn't seen anyone chafing wrists since his Aunt Lucy fainted when the bank clerk jilted her and Mother had taken first-aid measures. Suppressing unofficial reminiscences, however, he knelt down in the place which Charity eagerly vacated. The Director-General's face was grey, his breathing—thank God he was breathing—came unsteadily, his lips were faintly blue, his pulse fluttered irregularly under the Inspector's strong fingers. Obliviously a heart attack, not an assault.

"Have they sent for a doctor?" he turned to ask Charity.

"Yes, and for the nurse downstairs. I sent the messengers. Is he all right?"

Charity looked tremulous and appealing. At any moment, thought the Inspector, she will be needing a manly shoulder. Now here came four likely ones.

Ratcliffe and Robarts had both entered the room and tentatively stopped a few feet away. Even when flat on his back, the Director-General impelled respect. Ratcliffe stood near Charity and put a friendly hand on her shoulder. Cam did not miss the angry glance, quickly averted, with which Robarts noted this. Aha, he thought maliciously, what a friendly little office this to be sure! And he wondered where Stone was. But probably he had returned to the labs.

Cam turned back to Sir Arnold, whom, in the delight of realising that this was definitely a medical and not a police case, he had temporarily forgotten. The great man was stirring slightly, and moved one of his hands to his head. A few seconds later he opened his eyes and looked round vaguely at the faces looming over him from such an unaccustomed angle. Eventually he seized on the Inspector's face, that being the nearest.

"Who are you? I—I think I've been ill—heart. You'll find some pills—in my right waistcoat pocket. Give me two."

With the same deft touch that he had shown in rifling the pockets of Parry earlier that morning. Cam found the box. Charity had got a glass of water by the time they were ready. Leaning heavily on Cam's arm, the Director-General propped himself up and took them in two gulps. He breathed more easily then, and as he became more conscious of his surroundings he looked round with distaste. As well as Charity, Ratcliffe, Robarts and the Inspector, the blonde girl—who Cam now realised was the Director-General's secretary—and a uniformed nurse, Constable Wootton and a couple of curious messengers were peering at him from above in a way which made it difficult for the prostrate man to over-awe them with a glance. Like spectators at a street accident, they stared at him with fascination. The DG was used to being stared at, but usually by reverent listeners to his words of authority. There was something pitying, even condescending, about these faces looking down on him. He collected himself for a damning dismissal.

"When you have quite finished, ladies and gentlemen, perhaps you will leave my room, unless you have some business with me. Miss White, do you usually allow persons to wander freely about my private room?"

The messengers evaporated magically, with a slight congestion at the door as they both tried to get out of it at once. The nurse, armoured in her professional uniform, set down her bag and proceeded to unpack a thermometer. Charity and Miss White disappeared into the latter's office. Ratcliffe, after balancing uneasily while he tried to decide whether an administrative officer was required to administer medical care, made up his mind, and slipped out at a look from the DG.

Constable Wootton followed him at a word from Cam and Robarts a moment later, with an uneasy backward glance and a murmur of sympathy to the stricken man.

The Inspector remained, and stood impassively while the DG threw looks at him which would have sent a more sensitive man scuttling.

"Well, who are you? The police fellow Robarts was talking about?"

He turned on the nurse.

"For God's sake put that away! If you think a thermometer is any use in a heart case you had better be sent back to finish your education. What's your name? Your presence is not required—now or ever!"

Withered and shaken, the hapless nurse bundled up the thermometer she had been trying to put unobtrusively in the great man's mouth and fled, leaving the two men alone together. The Inspector helped the Director-General to his feet—for all this time he had been reclining Roman fashion on one elbow on the floor—and gave him an arm over to the window-seat. He sat down with a sigh and mopped his forehead.

"Overwork," he muttered. "Sometimes get them."

Obviously the attack had shaken him. Cam wondered at the will-power of a man who could summon enough strength to flay his staff even when feeling next door to death. Cam found it difficult to rebuke his staff even in the best of health.

"Well," said Sir Arnold abruptly." Found out anything yet about the messenger fellow—what was his name?"

"James Parry, sir. Nothing definite yet, sir. It's a bit early."

The Director-General looked moodily at Cam. "He was my personal messenger. Used to carry messages up and down to London."

"So I understand, sir. What impression did you have of him?"

"No impression at all. I never bothered to think about him. He did his work well enough."

Inhuman fellow, thought Cam.

"There seems to have been something rather mysterious about the man," he ventured.

The Director-General rubbed his hand over his heart.

"What sort of something? Can't you be more explicit?"

"Well, frequent complaints about him reading private correspondence. Dark rumours, started by himself, that he was rather more than a messenger, that he had powerful friends, contacts. Most of it just his own bombast, I expect. If the war were still on I should have suspected espionage. As it is, I wonder if he was trying blackmail."

The Inspector did not mention Ratcliffe's confession. He was a kindly man, and he would need more proof before imperilling the young man's career.

But the Director-General turned with unexpected anger.

"Impossible! Do you think workers here aren't thoroughly investigated before they're admitted—and watched afterwards, too? As a matter of fact, Parry on one occasion—the Chatsworth incident—did yeoman service in trapping a spy. I should look for a less sensational explanation, Inspector, even though it may be your first murder."

Cam kept his temper, but only with an effort.

"I am bound, sir, to keep all possibilities in mind."

Sir Arnold calmed as quickly as he had flared up.

"Of course you must. And I can assure you you will get all the help you need from my staff. Well, Inspector, all this is very unfortunate, but one point is pre-eminent. We don't want more publicity about this department than is necessary. You realise that, I hope."

Cam nodded. Peace or no peace, the Government were not revealing to the world the location of all their valuable underground factories and research stations. Wassel House night be on peace-time research now—they hoped for ever. But they were taking no chances. And, in any case, the work on which the staff was engaged was secret, though secrecy was not as vital as that surrounding war-time research.

Sir Arnold took a turn up and down the room, one hand pressed to his heart, like an old-fashioned actor about to proclaim his affections. There was nothing histrionic about his manner of speech, however.

"Do you think Parry was killed by a member of my staff?" he asked quietly.

Cam shook his head.

"I don't know, sir. It's too early to say. All Parry's associations seemed to be with the Ministry rather than with the village."

The Director-General nodded.

"Still, as you observe, it's too early to say. What does the Chief Constable say?"

"I only just spoke to him on the phone to tell him what had happened, sir. He's not very well, you know—convalescing from 'flu—and can't come himself."

"Then you're in charge," said the DG, shooting Cam a keen look.

The Inspector nodded humbly.

"Well, Inspector, I'm sure you're very capable, and I wish you luck. But in view of the security considerations involved I want to make one point. If this case is cleared up in a few days I am certain the Press will pay it little attention, and no one will question the existence of the department. But if the case hangs about it's quite likely that some paper, with journalistic inconsequence, will blame the murder on the department and will raise the question *why* Wassel House is still requisitioned. Don't say it's illogical. I've seen it happen dozens of times. The only good publicity, Mr.——Cam?——is no publicity. Speed, therefore, is the essential of this case. And that is why I warn you, Inspector, that unless the affair is cleared up within a week I shall advise my Minister to ask the Home Secretary to remove the case into Scotland Yard's hands."

The Inspector's face grew obstinate.

"Yes, sir, I understand you. But you must realise that a case like this cannot always be solved so easily. I don't know yet. I may clear it up tomorrow, or there may be missing links to it which will take months to trace. I shall do all that is possible, but I cannot be expected to do more."

"Next week," said the DG, "I shall expect your final report."

Cam stiffened.

"Well, sir, it's a matter for the Home Secretary, isn't it?" He played this card triumphantly, because he knew that when it came down to bedrock the Ministry of Scientific Research had no jurisdiction over him. "It's up to him whether to call in the Yard. I'll mention your views to the Chief Constable, sir. But I think I can say that he'll probably want us to hold the case. There's a lot to be said for local knowledge in investigating crime in places like this, sir."

The DG turned aside for a moment and looked out of the window, through the limp strands of ivy hanging like ropes, to the green park beyond.

"Yes," he said finally. "I'm sure you're right. But we must hurry, Inspector. If your Chief agrees, we shall review the case in a week. I hope that by then our mutual problem will be solved."

He smiled at Cam with such charming courtesy that the Inspector, still bruised by his previous contemptuous accents, was too surprised for a moment to take the outstretched hand. He stammered out appreciation of the DG's trust, and in another minute was out in the corridor, vaguely conscious that he had been deftly disposed of, but still gratified by such kindness from the great man. As he stood rather vaguely wondering what tack to take next, Dr. MacDermot came bustling along the landing? He did not notice Cam until the other touched his elbow.

"Oh, hello there, Cam! I'm told Sir Arnold Conway is ill. They sent a car for me."

The Doctor was so obviously pleased at this opportunity to treat such a great figure that Cam laughed.

"Well, I don't think you'll he in there long, Doctor. But if you're still here about twelve I'll give you a lift down to the village. Just meet me outside at the car." He took hold of the smaller man's lapel and drew him closer. "Just a word in your ear about treatment, Doctor. No thermometers!"

The Doctor looked at him with the unconvinced smile of those who do not see a joke, though anxious to oblige, and went into Miss White's office, leaving the Inspector to his own voiceless mirth.

Cam's first work was again to visit Robarts and ask him sternly about concealing the fact that he had helped Stone home the previous night. Robarts admitted the fact without hesitation, but was not really impressed by the enormity of the crime of concealing evidence. An investigation, he observed severely, was no excuse for talking scandal, and to this the Inspector could find no adequate reply. He asked, however, with a meaning look, for the personal files of Robarts himself, as well as those of Ratcliffe, Stone, Charity Brown and Parry, to be sent down from London. Robarts agreed with indifference, and asked about the DG. Apparently he had been talking to him on the phone, and the DG had said something about not feeling well as he put the receiver down. The next Robarts knew was the outcry in the corridor. Cam said that Sir Arnold seemed quite recovered, and Robarts sighed with relief.

"Thank heaven! You know, he can be very unpleasant, or rather brusque, but he's about as indispensable as a man can be. He was largely responsible for making the politicians give scientific research its proper place as a weapon of war—prevented it being split up among all the different supply departments—and it looks as though he were going to persuade them that the Government has an interest in research, even in peace-time. He knows how to leave specialists to do their own work undisturbed—a rare characteristic, I can tell you."

"The spy Chatsworth was in the Ministry, wasn't he?" Cam asked suddenly. He noticed with interest that Robarts jumped at the mention of the name, and glanced nervously at the Inspector.

"Yes—yes, he was. Another department, naturally. Up North."

"Parry was responsible for his arrest, I hear."

Robarts' uneasiness increased.

"Yes, I believe so. He found some papers indicating shady business when he was up there on work for the DG."

Cam studied his boots. "So his curiosity was of some value on occasion—a case of curiosity bringing the cat a big, fat mouse, eh?"

"I suppose so," Robarts muttered, "but frankly I'd rather have spies about than *agent-provocateurs*."

"Then why didn't you pay more attention to Mr. Ratcliffe's complaints about Parry, Dr. Robarts?"

Robarts flinched at this sudden question, but answered firmly enough:

"Because I didn't think Parry meant any harm—it was misplaced intelligence, as I have said—and because even if he meant harm he couldn't do any. I didn't want to start trouble in the present state of the department, so I was willing to overlook the affair."

"I see," said Cam without conviction, and proceeded to other business.

During the next two tedious hours Cam questioned all the members of the Ministry who might have something to contribute about Parry's life and work.

There were three aged scientists—Smith, Wiggins and Custer—who had never apparently been aware of Parry's existence, although he passed frequently through their laboratories, and who heard of the end of that existence with calm indifference. They had not even Stone's vague dislike for the messenger. That anyone should think it worthwhile to question them about him filled all three with wonder. Cam felt that the police had gone down considerably in their scientific estimation when at last he finished their separate examinations. Their five assistants were all young men recently released from the Forces, and it was obvious to Cam that they were all much too busy worrying about finding local homes for their families to pay attention to other members of the staff.

The messengers, though far from indifferent, were equally unhelpful. Five of them confessed that they hardly knew Parry, and although they contributed many uncomplimentary anecdotes of his conceit and unpleasantness, it was clear that they had no close association with the man, either in the office or outside. Martins, the head porter, a solid, unimaginative fellow, but of obvious impregnable honesty, declared that Parry had once told him, after a minor disagreement, that he would have the porter dismissed unless he was more respectful. But Martins told the story to back up his own theory that Parry was mad and had committed suicide by beating his head on the wall, and he had no belief in its truth.

Two hours later Cam had sifted all Parry's probable contacts in the Ministry and he had come to the conclusion that his field of investigation was narrower than he had feared. Although Parry was generally and vaguely disliked, there seemed to be only a handful who had sufficiently close association with him to feel any active hatred. All of those, curiously enough, appeared to be on a far higher level, in the Civil Service phrase, than the messenger.

Cam's last task was to interview the clerk in charge of stationery. He spent a quarter of an hour with him, and went out to the car with a face beaming with self-satisfaction. To his surprise, the Doctor was waiting. He muttered grumpily that he had been talking over Ministry health problems with the staff nurse and that he was starving and that it was twenty past twelve. Clearly he did not share Cam's good humour. As they drove out he exploded.

"Insufferable fellow! I might have been a first-year medical student, the way he treated me. Next time, by God, he can bring his own doctor. And he insulted Nurse Jenkins, too—an excellent nurse. I don't know why they sent for me. Nothing I can do except suggest rest, and he just laughed at me. That's what comes of giving bureaucrats too much power. His people were shopkeepers, you know. In the North Country, too. And now he tries to pretend he's a gentleman! Well, he doesn't fool me!"

The Doctor, who had voted Liberal for the past twenty years, was a fiery Tory as regards social privileges and a furious regionalist in proclaiming the superiority of the West Country to all other parts of the country, but particularly to the North.

Cam smiled tolerantly and changed the subject.

"He's got odd ideas about criminal investigation, anyway," he said. "A week's what I'm given to clear the whole case up in. A week! Of course he hasn't really any say in the matter. It's the Home Secretary's job eventually—and the Chief Constable is the man I'm responsible to. But if they all put their heads together you can see me getting the boot. Still, perhaps I'll do it. Just to spite him!"

"Got any clues yet?" the Doctor asked with interest.

"Plenty," said the Inspector drily. "And even a suspect. But this is just between us, MacDermot."

"Naturally," the Doctor said, rather hurt that Cam should even mention the point.

As they drove slowly along Cam summarised for his friend the interviews of the morning. It was not orthodox, he knew, but for many years the two men had been accustomed to discuss their professional secrets together. As each was bound by his own professional honour to keep confidence, it was, as it were, a fair exchange, and it helped both of them to be able to discuss their cases with a friend of complementary intelligence. On this occasion Constable Wootton shared their confidences, but he was anxiously studying his shorthand notes in the rear seat to see if he could read them back, so they suffered no interruption.

As Cam reached the end of the story there was a pause while the Doctor thought it over. His face was clouded and he seemed depressed by what he had heard.

"About the time of death," Cam broke the silence. "Dr. Prescott should have been down by now, so we should have his opinion, too."

"Yes," said the Doctor absently.

"But anyway I think between nine-thirty and ten-thirty should cover it, don't you?"

"That sounds all right to me. But it's cutting it pretty fine, isn't it? I mean, Ratcliffe only left about nine-thirty. Whoever did it was taking considerable risks."

"Of course he was," the Inspector said emphatically. The Doctor looked at him sharply and almost spoke, but thought better of it. A few seconds later, however, he turned again to Cam, who, gripping the wheel with his usual concentration, watched the road before him with unswerving attention.

"Bill Ratcliffe," said Dr. MacDermot, "is a very decent type of young man."

"Ah?" said Cam.

"Apart from the fact that he's a friend of Charity's, I have always found him intelligent and reasonable. He has a hot, but not a violent temper." The Inspector vouchsafed no observation and the Doctor became impatient. "Well, man, what *do* you think of him?"

"He's very extravagant."

"Showy? Oh yes; the debt. But he admitted that. And he refused to be blackmailed."

"So he says."

"But you'll never get anywhere if you don't believe people sometimes," the Doctor said with the utmost simplicity. "And anyway, he wouldn't have admitted the blackmail if he had been guilty. After all, the blackmailer was dead, and who else was to know?"

"Perhaps there was some written evidence lying around. In any case, someone knew. Charity was telling him to own up when I went into the office this morning."

"I know, said MacDermot. "She was telling me about it after I saw the DG. And incidentally she said you gave her a most sinister look! She was quite upset, poor girl. But she didn't know about Ratcliffe's blackmail story until just before you arrived on the scene. Ratcliffe had asked her advice about telling you."

"I wonder why he suddenly started being so confidential," Cam mused.

The Doctor shrugged impatiently.

"Anyway, you're barking up the wrong tree. It sounds as though Ratcliffe had a good alibi from the time he left Miss Penny, so he couldn't have done it, even if he would."

"From the time he left Miss Penny," murmured Cam quietly to himself, as if lost in thought.

Dr. MacDermot looked at him anxiously and pondered for a few minutes. His expression became increasingly glum. He moved uneasily in his seat.

Relinquishing his pose of abstraction, though still watching the road ahead, Cam leaned towards the Doctor.

"Now, MacDermot, this is the way it is. So far I have found only three men at the Ministry who can be associated with Parry in any way: Robarts because of their chess games, Ratcliffe because of the blackmail story, and Stone because, of all things, he liked him—or tolerated him, anyway. There is no reason to suspect Robarts that I can see. Men sometimes become as insanely jealous over chess as they do over love, I'm told, but Robarts doesn't seem that type. In any case, if his story is to be believed he has a good alibi for the time of the murder. Against Ratcliffe, on the other hand, I already have a good working case. He had the motive, since Parry had in his hands the power to break his career. He had the opportunity, since he was the only person, except Parry and Miss Penny, who handled the key last night—at least, as far as we can tell yet. Miss Penny did her very best to act like the criminal this morning, but somehow I don't think she's the type. But not only did Ratcliffe have the opportunity to enter Parry's room, but we *know* he entered it, and, say what you will, he was, to the best of our knowledge, the last person to see Parry alive."

"But he couldn't have done it then!" MacDermot interrupted desperately: "Miss Penny was just at the foot of the stairs, wasn't she?"

"Parry was unconscious. It wouldn't make much noise to hit him over the head. Yes, the weapon—I know. Well, I haven't all the answers yet, but Ratcliffe was carrying a heavy walking-stick, wasn't he? Or at least I expect it was heavy, if he used it for hiking. I shall have to see it. And another thing—don't forget the burnt paper in the fire. Perhaps Parry had some documentary proof of the blackmail, and Ratcliffe found and destroyed it before he left the room. That would explain him taking time off to put some coal on the fire. Don't tell me that was just Christian kindness."

Dr. MacDermot shook his head.

"It's a pretty story, Cam; but you don't explain why Ratcliffe told you and Charity about the blackmail if he was so desperate to burn the evidence. When you come down to it, what you really like about the case is that Ratcliffe was the only one with an opportunity to get into the room. But you can't be sure of that yet."

"Of course not. I've got plenty of work to do before this is over. But it's a good theory to work on, anyway."

The Doctor was still deep in thought when they were passing Miss Penny's, and he looked up hastily.

"Oh, Cam, would you mind stopping here a moment? And would you mind if I asked Miss Penny a question? I know it's cheek, but it's just an idea of mine." The Inspector agreed genially.

"Always like to have your help, MacDermot." They drew up, and were admitted to the shop by Sergeant Rowley, perspiring from his morning exertions.

"They've all been and gone, sir," he replied to a question from Cam. "The papers are down at the station, and Dr. Prescott has taken him off to the mortuary."

"Right," said Cam, and they went in.

Miss Penny had to be summoned by the constable from her bed, whither she had retired in much distress on the arrival of a whole car-load of policemen, murmuring unnecessarily that such a thing had never happened to her before. She came down relieved to find two old acquaintances there.

"Oh, Inspector, Doctor, thank heaven you're here! You can have no idea what it has been like this morning. Nothing but questions and rush and policemen taking photographs of *my* bedroom instead of Mr. Parry's—and before I had time to make the bed, too—and policemen wanting *my* fingerprints—though I told them you were a friend of mine, Mr. Cam—and looking so fierce at me I could have died. Mr. Witherspoon brought me a mid-morning snack, or I certainly should have died. Such a thoughtful man! Doctor, can I have some more little sleeping pills? I shall never sleep tonight. And everyone says I ought to go away, but I couldn't leave the shop, you know. And then there's the funeral, you know. I must go to that. Poor man! Poor man!"

She brought out an already damp handkerchief. Apparently Mr. Parry was swiftly acquiring the mellow patina of the dead in her sentimental sight. The Doctor seized his opportunity to ask his question.

"Miss Penny. You told us about the one key that Mr. Ratcliffe put away for you and that came out of Parry's pocket. You're sure there was no other key?"

"Absolutely, Doctor. Mr. Parry was quite unpleasant when I suggested having a second one made when the first was lost, so I just didn't do anything about it."

The Doctor rubbed his chin and tried to avoid the sly look of triumph on Cam's face.

"No other keys, eh? Well, do you recall when the first was lost?"

"Yes, Doctor. Mr. Parry mislaid it soon after his arrival here. That was six months ago. He never said how he lost it, but he asked me for mine, and it was then he told me not to have another made."

"Damn my eyes!" blasted the Inspector, smiting his thigh with an impassioned fist. "And I am supposed to be a trained policeman!"

He rushed out, leaving a startled Miss Penny and a blandly self-satisfied Doctor. In a few minutes he was back with a mortified expression.

"They've been through the room with a fine comb, and there's no other key except those on Parry's key-ring—and neither of those is for the door." His expression cleared as he saw the Doctor's brave attempt to keep from crowing. "Well, MacDermot, you got me that time. Not that it disproves my case—and Parry *may* have lost the key, for any proof you have—but it opens up other possibilities. That key must be traced!"

With another look at the Doctor he unexpectedly burst into laughter, and MacDermot joined him in a moment, chortling with glee.

"All right, then, MacDermot," roared the big man, to Miss Penny's surprise. "You can play, too, if you want. And I promise not to arrest any of your friends without telling you first. But don't forget that I've only got a week. So you had better do some quick thinking—and so had I!"

CHAPTER VI

THE weather broke that night. After two days of oppressive heat the rain poured down upon Little Biggling with such concentrated persistence that one would have thought that Little Biggling alone was enduring the full strength of the downpour. It seemed impossible that there was enough water to spare for foreign parts. Starting at ten, it gathered momentum throughout the night, reaching its full force and determination at nine o'clock Friday morning, and continuing unabated until three in the afternoon, when it suddenly died away. At a quarter to four there was a very pleasant rainbow over Wassel Peak and the sun shone wanly through a veil of shower. Inspector Cam, who had spent the whole morning and early afternoon tramping round the village taking statements from witnesses to the case, and had only just arrived back at the station for tea, looked bitterly at the tardy sunshine, as he had at the pitiless rain. The discomfort of his day's work appeared even more trying in its light. Even now when the watery protection of his old grey mackintosh and shapeless hat had been removed he felt damp and uncomfortable about the collar and socks. What he really wanted to do was to go home, change and have a cosy chat with Mrs. Cam. What he had to do instead was try to bring order out of the miscellaneous information he had garnered that morning.

He looked gloomily round the room and, as usual, found no inspiration. The police-station had been designed by its builders not for the comfort and pleasure of its staff so much as for the discouragement of suspects brought within its walls. The square yellow walls of the Inspector's office, decorated with pre-war safety posters showing unhappy victims of road accidents in postures of agony, the stark Government-issue furniture, the bare brown linoleum and the filing-cabinet always offended Cam's highly cultivated sense of comfort. Now, at home, in his armchair, in front of the fire. . .

With a sigh he drew towards him a sheet of notepaper and wrote firmly in a large round script—

Billetors.	*Landlords.*
Mr. Witherspoon (Stone)	Mr. Acton ('Coach and Horn')
Mrs. Davis (Ratcliffe)	Mr. Sidebotham ('Blue Dragon')
Mrs. Cottenham (Robarts)	

There they were—his morning's work. And what had they added? Little but dull confirmation of everybody's evidence. Drawing elaborate patterns around their names, he ran over them in his mind.

Witherspoon, the chemist, first. Miss Penny's friend and confidant. A wizened little man who looked as if the acids of his trade had entered into his bloodstream. Yet, as Cam knew from past experience, a golden-hearted fellow—one of those shy little bachelors who, for lack of a wife's companionship, seemed forced to develop in themselves all the so-called feminine virtues of gentle tact, consideration, unselfishness. He was also an excellent cook, and many a good meal Cam had had at his flat over the shop, and much amusement Mrs. Cam (if she had ever entered his bachelor establishment) would have had in watching the meticulous way in which the chemist weighed out his materials, as if he were filling a prescription. He would have been delighted to help Mr. Cam, if only there were something he could do. Yes, he would certainly confirm what Mr. Stone, his billetee, had said. No, he didn't know what Mr. Stone had said yet, but he was sure it would be correct anyway. Oh yes, it was quite correct that Mr. Stone had been helped home by another gentleman—Dr. Robarts. He knew the latter through the shop, as he had filled a prescription not long ago. Poor Mr. Stone wasn't feeling at all well. Perhaps he *had* had a little too much to drink, but, poor young man, he had a sad history, you know—a fine war record. In prison camp for five years! No, he wasn't very cheerful, and Mr. Witherspoon had never been able to feel he really knew him, but he was an excellent young man undoubtedly. He was a gardener, for instance, and he had helped with the digging occasionally this spring. Only he preferred flowers to vegetables, while Mr. Witherspoon regarded all his garden from the point of view of the kitchen. And he kept his room immaculate. But what he needed was a wife. Mr. Witherspoon, a confirmed bachelor, was a great believer in marriage as a cure-all. Ten-five was when Mr. Stone had got back. That was right, because Mr. Witherspoon usually went to bed at ten, and he was beginning to wonder whether he should leave some supper for Mr. Stone. A great deal, Mr. Witherspoon felt, depended on feeding the young man up so that he recovered his health and his spirits. But Mr. Stone had not been hungry, and went to his room to lie down. Mr. Witherspoon had had a bath then, and when he came out half an hour later—for he was afraid he always liked a long soak—he had felt very grieved to find Mr. Stone still waiting for his bath. Surely there was no question of Mr. Stone—Oh, of course, routine questioning. The little chemist ushered Cam out of the shop, begging him to come soon to lunch or dinner—he had a new recipe for tomato soufflé on which he wanted the Inspector's opinion. Miss Penny had been most kind about it. Poor lady! he was afraid the accident must have been a terrible shock—living alone and unprotected as she was. And could the Inspector suggest how he could keep children off his vegetable beds— without prosecuting, of course? But it was rather trying now that the seeds were in.

The Inspector suggested a fence, and left the kind little man for Mrs. Davis. Here was a bird of another colour— and he tried to draw a rather predatory bird. He was well acquainted with Mrs. Davis. She was one of the regulars at the police-station. A month was rare in which she did not either complain that the police had failed in some part of their duty or accused her neighbours of some heinous crime. In a series of brilliant manœuvres she had married off five unpromising daughters, and she was now preparing the ground for her sixth and final campaign around the person of seventeen-year-old Rose. Cam had heard rumours that she had fought several unsuccessful skirmishes with her eligible billetee, Ratcliffe, during the last few months, and he was prepared for a certain amount of prejudice.

Mrs. Davis had undoubtedly been surprised to be visited by the police of their own accord, and she had even looked a bit uneasy when she opened the door. But she was full of helpful suggestions when Cam revealed he had come about the local murder. What, she asked truculently, could he expect when the authorities allowed—nay, encouraged—those Ministry people to stay in Little Biggling? Only last night she had said to Rosie that she mustn't *think* of going out with such creatures. A sweet girl like Rosie was so easily spoilt by contact with uncouth men. She was mentioning no names, but there *were* men who went about breaking girls' hearts as if they were biscuits! And trampling on the crumbs, if she might coin a phrase. Yes, it was quite true that Mr. Ratcliffe had come in about nine-forty on Wednesday night—exactly two hours after she had expected him for a delicious supper she had spent all afternoon over a hot stove preparing. Why? Was he suspected, then? He must leave at once! What were the police thinking of, leaving two helpless women to such a villain. . . . Oh, just routine, was it? Well, she couldn't say she *liked* Mr. Ratcliffe. He was a conceited young man, there was no doubt, and she'd heard stories about the sort of girls he went round with which the Inspector wouldn't hardly believe. The Navy, of course, did coarsen some men. But still, she hadn't thought he was a violent type.

Yes, Mr. Ratcliffe had gone to bed about eleven. He *said* he was tired. Well, yes, he did look tired, but there were plenty of young men she knew who would be glad to sit up all night with Rosie—and herself, of course. Not that they wished to push themselves where they weren't wanted; but it was very odd, didn't the Inspector think? Perhaps he *had* a guilty conscience and was shamed by the innocent purity of Rosie.

The Inspector assured her that to the best of his knowledge Mr. Ratcliffe was as innocent as Rosie herself and, having satisfied himself that Ratcliffe had indeed come home and had indeed slept (Mrs. Davis had heard him snoring when she went up at half-past eleven), he left her.

Next he turned his attention to Mrs. Cottenham. Mrs. Cottenham had, he understood, been married to a lieutenant in the Indian cavalry, who had died in World War I at the age of thirty-five without ever succeeding in making Mrs. Cottenham what she was obviously born to be—a Colonel's Lady. Regardless of this accident of fate, Mrs. Cottenham, returning to England to live on a small pension, had so surrounded herself with the accoutrements of Indian Army life, featuring the guns her husband had unsuccessfully used for tiger-shooting and the unengraved silver cups he would have won if he had been a better horseman, that there were few inhabitants of Little Biggling who would not willingly swear that she had been the queen of vice-regal society. Her lectures on India—she had spent three months there—to the Mothers' Union were much admired. She did not often go out, there being few residents except the Vicar's wife and the Doctor's wife whom she could visit without losing face. But she was kind to her social inferiors, even if not friendly, and on the whole she was liked by the villagers—who blasphemously gossiped that she was a little simple.

She greeted Cam, when he was shown into the parlour of her tiny house, as a Colonel's wife would receive his batman. However, after observing that he showed proper respect and could be trusted not to take advantage of her courtesy, she signalled for him to take a seat. Like the other billetors,

Mrs. Cottenham had confirmed her lodger's statement. Dr. Robarts, a very agreeable man, though lamentably ignorant of India, had come in about ten past ten o'clock. He had supper in the dining-room and was admitted into the parlour—only Mrs. Cottenham called it the drawing-room—at ten-thirty to say good night to her. They chatted for a few minutes about the food situation and Mrs. Cottenham's difficulties in obtaining offal, because she believed in making these Government officials happy in their unaccustomed surroundings, and then Dr. Robarts went to bed. There was a little difficulty when the Inspector tried to get some proof that Dr. Robarts had stayed in bed, as Mrs. Cottenham most emphatically did not spy upon her guests. But in the end he elicited the information that Dr. Robarts' bed had squeaked violently for the greater part of the night on the other side of the wall against which Mrs. Cottenham slept. Mrs. Cottenham could hardly mention it to the gentleman, as the subject was somewhat delicate, but she found his tossing and turning rather trying. After some encouragement she led Cam upstairs to examine the guilty bed. The joints were indeed very loose, and one of the small brass bars fell out when the Inspector tentatively shook the frame. He put it back carefully under Mrs. Cottenham's reproving eye and diverted her attention by further questioning about Dr. Robarts' nocturnal habits. He discovered simply that he was a very abstemious and quiet gentleman who seemed to work very long hours and had never given her any trouble, more than was inevitable, during the two years he had been with her.

So that was all the Billetor Contingent had to say, thought Cam ruefully. A bath, and a brass rod, were the only clues which he found interesting. He knew he should be gratified that his three chief witnesses to date had apparently spoken only the truth. But the spectre of next week's meeting with the Director-General hung over him, and he would have been relieved if, for some unexplained reason, one of the gentlemen concerned had been known to have left his billet surreptitiously. It would have given him something to take hold of.

Dr. Prescott from Gloucester had confirmed his own idea that the murder took place between nine-thirty and ten-thirty—the hour which began with Ratcliffe locking Parry's door and ended with everybody apparently safely at their respective billets. Cam sighed as he thought of the report lying upon his desk from the fingerprint experts—proving only that the murderer had the elementary sense to wear gloves at his work. Further examination of the room had been almost equally unprofitable. The floor of the wardrobe, where a stranger might have been hidden, was thick with undisturbed dust, and the same was true of the floor under the bed. Mysterious papers there were none, though Sergeant Rowley had observed cannily that there was a marked difference between the untidy room and the neat stacks of pamphlets, office circulars and other papers which were filed in the top drawer of Parry's chest of drawers. The search for a weapon had been equally fruitless. The fireguard rail had proved to be immovable. Obviously the murderer had carried his weapon away with him. But there was one point explained—why Parry had been moved off the bed. When the covers were removed Rowley discovered a long slit in the mattress—and the straw stuffing had been torn out roughly by someone exploring the hole. There was nothing to indicate the object of the search. But obviously the murderer had been interested in something concealed in the mattress—and had found it. There might, Cam thought, be some connection between that fact and the burnt paper in the fireplace.

Perhaps, he pondered, the brother will be able to provide some help. He was coming to Little Biggling on Sunday to escort the unfortunate Parry to his grave. The messenger's private life was a bit of a mystery really. His ostentatious secrecy gave the impression that much of his talk about powerful friends and influential connections was the typical bombast of an egocentric failure. Still, there might be something in it.

Cam sighed, and returned to his brief list. The landlords, they had been more helpful. What a lot of drinking had gone on that Wednesday night! Everyone popping in and out of pubs, like Jacks-in-the-boxes. It was convenient, because landlords were fortunately noticing sorts of people. Acton, for instance, rattled off the names of practically all his visitors on Wednesday night as if he had made a special list of them. Cam respected Acton as a careful, law-abiding publican—the type who would have all his customers out on the street five minutes after closing time—but he was a foreigner and a bit sly by Gloucestershire standards. Perhaps it was the fact that he was a Londoner which attracted to his pub most of the custom of the Ministry. Apart from an old-fashioned dislike of women at his bar, he welcomed the London talk and London manners of the newcomers.

He had certainly noticed Stone that night. Stone had been almost a part of the furniture, sitting and sulking in his window-seat. His only convivial gesture had been to provide drinks all round to the public bar. The saloon bar had not been included in the gesture. The young man had done this several times previously, Acton reported appreciatively. Apparently it had been a custom in his regiment. Yes, Stone had left the bar to go upstairs several times, but only for five minutes at most.

Parry had been there for only about half an hour. He had come at the same time as Stone, but into the public bar. He had plenty to drink, too—three double whiskies—and had made himself generally unpopular by flashing a well-filled pocket-book when he paid for the drinks. He had gone off early—about nine—saying he had important business to attend to. But, then, he always said that. It was one of the public bar's favourite jokes. Acton wouldn't say that he had got very drunk, but, then, whisky sometimes worked slowly, and perhaps going out into the open air he was overcome.

Robarts? Dr. Robarts came in about nine-forty five. Yes, that was the time, because he had noticed it was so near closing time and had joked with Dr. Robarts that there was no time for a chess game. Dr. Robarts played a lovely game of chess, and they had had several good ones together. Yes, he had also played with Parry once. A good player, but a rotten loser. Did the Inspector play chess? Because he might be interested in. . . The Inspector hastily broke into the threatened chess discussion and asked about Robarts and Stone leaving together. Yes, that was right. And very decent it was of Dr. Robarts, too, because Mr. Stone certainly wasn't too polite and hadn't acted at all grateful, although he obviously needed assistance. But he was pretty far gone then. Mr. Stone hadn't got a good head. Mr. Ratcliffe had also dropped in, but only for five minutes. He gulped a gin-and-it down, went upstairs a moment, and left. He seemed unusually quiet, being such a cheerful young fellow usually.

Albert Sidebotham, the keeper of the 'Blue Dragon,' only had news of one of the gentlemen in whom Cam was interested. He was a great, glowing ex-farmer, full of good spirits, but liable to occasional moodiness when anyone brought up the 'Coach and Horn's monopoly of Ministry business. He was pleased to repeat several times that Parry had never stepped within his doors, and that his customers were not the kind to get themselves murdered. Dr. Robarts was the only one of the Ministry people for whom he had any use. He could speak to a man civilly, without complaining that the beer wasn't drinkable, just because it didn't have as much water in it as the beer of some people he wouldn't like to name. Dr. Robarts had come about nine-ten and asked what the nine o'clock news had been, Sidebotham remembered. He hadn't been very conversational—but, then, he never was chatty—and after listening to the news talk wandered out again. That would be about nine-thirty.

Cam shuffled the notes he had taken. He would have to draw up a timetable soon—a piece of work he detested but the

Chief Constable enjoyed, and which must be attached to his report. In the meantime there was one interesting discrepancy between the reports. Sidebotham reported that Robarts left him at nine-thirty—just after the news talk. Cam had listened to the news talk that night, sitting with the Doctor. It had been a commentary on the problems of reparations—in the regular Wednesday survey of world affairs. He remembered that it had stopped a few minutes before the half-hour, and there had been incidental music to fill in the time until the next programme. But Acton was quite definite that Robarts came in at a quarter to ten. Could it therefore take a quarter of an hour to get from the 'Blue Dragon' to the 'Coach and Horn'? Ordinarily it was three minutes walk. There was no suggestion that Robarts had been under the influence of drink. Perhaps he had just gone for a stroll. But Robarts was not proving a very accurate witness.

Even more interesting, however, to the Inspector was the question of Parry's money. Acton had estimated there were at least ten pound-notes in Parry's pocket-book, possibly more. But the pocket-book, as Cam had found it, had contained only two pound-notes. It was very curious. How on earth could Parry have spent at least eight pounds that evening? Yet it did not look like an ordinary case of robbery, because why on earth should the thief leave two pounds behind him? It would be easier, as well as more in character, to grab the whole wad of notes. Acton reported that Parry had ostentatiously shown his money only a few seconds before leaving the bar, so it could not be one of the 'Coach and Horn''s customers who had filched it. Could he perhaps have paid it to that woman with whom Ratcliffe had found him fighting? She had not been traced. It was an idea. But from what Cam had heard of Parry, even when drunk he was careful with his money, and if he gave away one pound Cam would have been surprised.

Cam sighed. The more he considered the case the more complications it presented. Perhaps writing it down would help. He settled down to the task of drafting his report with the unhappy conviction that it would contain not a single conclusion to tie up his rich crop of theories.

★★★

Dr. MacDermot had not forgotten yesterday's offer of partnership in the solution of Parry's murder. Jocular or not, he intended to take it at its face value. It was not the prospect of beating the Inspector at his own game which attracted him, pleasant as it would be to pull his leg in the future. The Doctor was quite convinced that, modern legend to the contrary, the average police officer knew his job fifty times better than any amateur, and Cam was a better-than-average police officer. But Dr. MacDermot was worried about the Inspector's suspicions of Ratcliffe. Although he had implicit faith that, given time, Cam would get on to the right track, yet it might be possible that a perfectly good circumstantial case could be built up against the young man. And, being pressed for time by the Director-General, Cam might not give enough consideration to alternative solutions of the mystery. Cam was not a man who should be hurried, and it had appeared to the Doctor yesterday that his old friend was getting rather flustered. Of course, the Doctor admitted to himself, his own refusal to accept Cam's theories was based entirely on personal prejudice. He didn't believe—he didn't want to believe—that any friend of Charity's could be guilty of a crime like this. He did not entirely approve of Ratcliffe as an intimate friend of his niece—he was too casual, too flippant. But that was the modem way, and Charity seemed to like it. Certainly there was no harm in the boy. And as Cam seemed set upon him, the Doctor intended to look around for alternative suspects, more to his own taste.

For most of Friday he did not have much time to follow his new profession. Babies with the spring crop of croup, children with cut fingers and lacerated knees, expectant mothers with nervous qualms and all the other trivia of a general practice occupied his time and thoughts. At four-thirty he drove home from his round to discover an urgent call from a cottage two miles out of town where a woman was in need of attention for a broken arm. He snatched a cup of tea and a cake and drove grumpily off, eating a jam sandwich. The cottage lay nearer Wipton than Little Biggling and he thought that his Wipton associate might have been summoned. On the other, hand, it always flattered his self-esteem to have further proof that when cottagers in this part of the county spoke of "the Doctor" they always meant Dr. MacDermot.

It was a derelict little cottage, long overdue for rural slum clearance. The man who rented it, he vaguely remembered, was a hedger employed by the Rural District Council—a hulking great fellow, with a surly, lumpish expression which had attracted the Doctor's attention because it was so unlike the usual friendly candour of the Gloucestershire countryman. Going inside, into the sad little kitchen with its evidence of failure and indifference in the torn curtains, unswept floor, unwashed dishes, he found the patient—a slatternly type with her hair done up in curlers, sitting on a broken-backed chair, crooning miserably over her arm, and the husband, standing grimly against the wall, surveying her with sallow dislike. It did not need the Doctor's experience to guess that they had been fighting and that the arm was probably a casualty of the matrimonial tiff. He nodded curtly to the pair, and without a word got out his splint and bandages and proceeded to set the arm. Except for the occasional groans of the woman, there was silence until he had finished. He got up and started packing away his instruments.

"Well, how did it happen?" he broke the silence abruptly.

The man looked at him under dark eyebrows, his heavy, dull face brooding with resentment, but the woman, with a furious glance at her husband, answered angrily:

"You ask 'im what done it. It's 'im what done it. Rotten loafer! Callin' me names an' 'itting me like I was an animal! An' I ain't done nothing neither! No, I ain't, but sure as 'ell I will if you dunnat leave me be."

She turned violently in her seat as the man raised a threatening fist.

"Now, now!" interrupted the Doctor hastily. "Don't start again, you two!"

"I ain't starting nothing," shouted the man, his fury boiling over. "If a man can't do what 'e wants with 'is wife when she's bin lyin' around with 'igh and mighty gents like any bitch this ain't a free country no more, an' I'll ask you to keep your nose out of it, Mr. Doctor!"

"I ain't, I ain't, I ain't!" screamed the woman, almost hysterical. "Ain't I told you 'twas all that man comin' after me? Would I 'a' told you about it if I'd bin up to something; would I?"

"Quiet, both of you!" shouted the Doctor commandingly. "Now let's get this straight. Ramsden—that's your name, isn't it?—Ramsden, as far as wife-beating goes, this isn't a free country any longer. The magistrates take a very poor view of it. And if I hear any more about it I'll get the police on to you—or your wife can. If you must quarrel, keep it to words, and as you're pretty far from the next cottage, that can't do much harm. But any more blows and you'll be up before the magistrate in the twitch of a donkey's ear. And now I'm going back to my tea. Mrs. Ramsden, come and see me about your arm tomorrow morning about eleven and I'll take you over to the hospital to have it X-rayed. Try to keep the bandage clean."

He stalked out, satisfied with the pallor that the mention of a magistrate had induced in the man. Probably he was not unknown in the courts. The woman followed him out, clinging close behind as to a protector. As he opened the door of the car she looked at him beseechingly.

"Really, sir, it ain't true. About me, I mean. He do get 'imself worked up in such an 'orrible passion, sir. And like a fool I told 'im about one of those Min'stry chaps comin' after me Wednesday night. Oh, 'e fair tore me to pieces right there on the road, makin' believe I must 'a' led the feller on, an' then 'e went off, an' I didn't see 'im all night; an' then when 'e come back 'e just went for me all over again. I dunno' what to do with 'im, sir, that I don't."

"There, there," said the Doctor, mentally fixed on his tea, but pitying the poor woman. "If he does it again come to me and I'll see he gets well and truly frightened."

He stepped on the starter, and the woman was dragging back to her cottage when a sudden thought stopped him.

"Hi," he shouted out of the window. "Come here a moment, will you?" She came listlessly back. "About that man who attacked you. Did you know him?"

She looked at him resentfully.

"Ain't I been telling you I dunnat. . ."

"Well then, did he——? was he——? Well, did a young man come along and rescue you just in the nick of time?"

"Why, yes, sir! How did you know, now? 'e come along an' knocked the little beggar stone cold, 'e did. Laid 'im flat."

"And that was in the entrance to Jones' building yard, wasn't it?"

"That's right. Why, you might 'a' bin there!"

"Doctor's inside information, you know." He laughed cheerfully. "One more question. When did you mention this to your husband?"

"That night, sir. I met 'im going 'ome from the 'Blue Dragon', and 'twas because I wor still upset that I wor such a fool."

"Well, don't worry any more, Mrs. Ramsden. You know what to do next time. And don't forget tomorrow morning."

The Doctor drove off, leaving her standing by the gate looking blankly after him. As he rode along he smote his thigh jovially and laughed to himself. So Cam was going to find him a useful partner, picking up clues like this! It was really quite easy as long as you kept your eyes wide open. He thought of the black-visaged Ramsden, with his powerful arms and passionate temper. What more likely than that in the un-governed fury of the first moment of finding out the assault on his wife, he should have gone rushing back through the village in search of the attacker. Perhaps he was just in time to see Ratcliffe carrying Parry back to the draper's. He could wait, unseen in the darkness, until Ratcliffe had left and the coast was clear, and then make his entrance by some means and murder the helpless messenger. Beautiful, thought the Doctor, with bland pride! A few gaps, perhaps, to the theory, but really very workable, and Cam should be most interested. Tea was forgotten. He turned up the High Street when he entered the village, eager to tell his discovery and, perhaps, anxious in case Cam had anticipated it.

Cam, when the Doctor came excitedly into his office, was struggling manfully over the Chief Constable's timetable, and he greeted any interruption with relief. It was not until he saw the Doctor that he remembered suddenly yesterday's promise of co-operation, and he chuckled inwardly. It would be amusing to see how an amateur tackled a job like this.

"Well, Jack," he roared, waving him to the other chair. "How are you getting on with the case? Solved yet? I've been waiting here all impatience."

"Now, now," said the Doctor gaily. "You mustn't leave all the work to me, Bob. And if that's your report to Major Cottle, I hope you've told him that I've taken over, eh? Well, I flatter myself that I *have* got something quite useful for you today. A pretty little theory, with some hard facts behind it. How would you like that?" He coughed self-consciously. "Have you been doing anything about tracing that woman Parry was tampering with when Ratcliffe so gallantly—I repeat, gallantly—came to the rescue?"

"Of course," said Cam. "Rowley's been trying to trace her

all this morning, but Ratcliffe's description wasn't very clear—not at all clear."

"I have traced her," said the Doctor, with simple pride.

"Have you now?" exclaimed Cam, with gratifying astonishment.

"Well," said MacDermot, "I've found her, let us say. It was really quite an accident, except that I did put two and two together rather neatly, if I may say so."

He proceeded triumphantly to tell Cam the details of his discovery and of his theory. The Inspector was congratulatory about the first, scoffing about the second.

"How *did* Ramsden get into the room? It's all very well saying he got in—but I've got to have proof how. It's carrying coincidence a bit too far to pretend that he was the fellow who found Parry's key and that six months later it came in useful for opening the door of his wife's attacker! Not that I'm disregarding him, MacDermot. Jealousy is a rattling good motive. I'll go along and see the fellow tomorrow morning."

"At least you've got two suspects now," the Doctor said, getting to his feet. "And I'm quite willing to find more if you need them. But mark my words, you concentrate on Ramsden—a ruffian if ever I saw one—and leave decent young fellows like Ratcliffe out of the picture."

The Inspector looked at him absently.

"Oh, yes. There's a new feature, by the way, to this case. I've discovered that Parry was flaunting a good bit of money on Wednesday night in the pub. But, as you'll remember, we only found two pounds on him."

MacDermot thought for a second, and then rubbed his hands with satisfaction.

"Well, that pretty well supports my case, doesn't it? Of the two men, who do you think is most likely to have indulged in theft as well as murder?"

Cam shook his head slowly.

"But why leave the two pounds? A man like Ramsden, as

115

you describe him, would just grab the whole roll, not take the trouble to leave a little pocket-money behind. Perhaps we're on the wrong track to think it a simple case of theft. Perhaps there was a special reason why certain notes—not all, just some of them—were valuable to the murderer. For instance, if a man had paid over some money as blackmail, and wanted to hide the fact, he would certainly take the precaution to get them back in order to prevent their numbers being traced to him."

"Poppycock!" exclaimed MacDermot. "You know, you're just making this up as you go along. It's a fantastic theory. Why don't you pick on someone else, for a change? Robarts— he knew Parry better than anyone else, it seems to me. Or Stone—he's a moody fellow, isn't he? Or Charity—she's never pretended she didn't dislike the man. But no. Just because poor Ratcliffe acted the Good Samaritan and helped the fellow home." The Doctor was quite pink with indignation.

"But surely you must admit that Ratcliffe had a better opportunity than anyone—and also a motive," said the Inspector without rancour.

"Never mind," replied the Doctor crossly. "I don't like the way you have of weaving theories of the case about one or two circumstantial details, without—without relation to the wider psychological factors," he ended a trifle breathlessly.

"But what else are you doing about Ramsden?" said Cam in accents of amazement. "And as for psychological factors; tell me how you explain a man murdering the fellow who assaulted his wife and *then* going home and beating his wife? Surely when a man has just committed murder he has had his fill of violence for a few days. Unless he's a homicidal maniac, of course. No, no, Doctor. This weaving theories, as you call it, is all I can do just yet. I'm certainly going to get nowhere by waiting for the facts to fall into place by themselves. I can only try fitting them together, one way and another, until one day—they fit." He sighed wearily. "And I hope they fit before next Thursday."

The Doctor shook his head. In his profession you couldn't afford to play about with a diagnosis. But, still, Cam had his own methods—and he hadn't arrested Ratcliffe yet. So they shook hands on it, and as they parted each was saying to himself:

"Now, there's an intelligent sort of chap. But he doesn't seem to *understand* this case."

CHAPTER VII

FRIDAY evening was one of Cam's regular evenings with Dr. MacDermot. But with great events brewing, with the weight of an important case upon his shoulders, the Doctor had certainly not expected to entertain him this Friday, and when the two had parted in the afternoon he had made no suggestion about the time Cam should come.

It was with considerable surprise, therefore, that he answered the doorbell about eight o'clock that night to find the Inspector waiting on the doorstep.

"Come in, man, come in!" he cried with delight. "I never expected to see you. We're just having coffee. Come into the lounge."

"Ah," said Cam, removing his coat deliberately, "it would take more than a murder case to keep me away from Mrs. MacDermot's coffee, Jack. And as a matter of fact I want a rest from the case. It's going stale on me already. Let's keep off. . ."

He stopped abruptly as they entered the lounge, and his mouth fell open. Grouped around the fire, staring at him with equal surprise and a certain amount of alarm, were four of the people who had been exercising his mind during the last two days—Charity, Bill Ratcliffe, Betty White and Graham Stone. Charity was curled up on a large pouffé, looking like a rather companionable black kitten. She smiled tentatively at Cam, and he knew that although he was admitted it was only on sufferance. Betty White, sitting on the floor beside her, looked up with rapt curiosity at seeing an Inspector disguised as a human. Bill Ratcliffe lifted his head from a position, very much at home, flat on his back across the hearth, to call a greeting.

"Hello, there, Inspector. Which of us is for the rope? Or have you discovered we are all in it together?"

Cam shook his head, smiling.

"I'm not on business tonight, Mr. Ratcliffe, so you've got a few more hours freedom."

Stone, sitting rather stiffly in a long, low arm-chair which called in every line for its occupant to lie back and take things easy, laughed rustily.

"Were you saying you wanted to keep off the case as you came in, Inspector? You've certainly come to the wrong place. We haven't talked about anything else all evening. I'm so sick of the subject that if Parry were alive again I swear I'd kill him out of fury."

"Take a seat, Bob, and ignore these young people." Mrs. MacDermot beckoned Cam to a seat beside her with an impatient gesture at Charity and her guests. "Mr. Stone is quite right. (John, get another cup, please, dear.) They haven't talked about anything else. And they can't even talk sense about it. If you could hear their theories it would make you laugh!"

"Ah," said Ratcliffe darkly. "That's what he's after. He heard we were here and came to pick our brains. But no change, Inspector. You won't tell us about the case, and we won't tell you."

"I'm sure your theories about the case couldn't be any more fantastic than mine," the Inspector replied placidly. "But farther than that I won't go, Mr. Ratcliffe. It's no good trying to make me talk. I'm talked out after today."

"Investigating?" asked Miss White breathlessly, giving the word the full value of every syllable.

"Questioning the villagers," Stone replied for him. "He was after my billetor, Witherspoon. The old fellow tells me that he explained I was much too nice a man to do things like that!"

The young people laughed, and Ratcliffe added: "He was on to my Mrs. Davis, too. And from what I could gather she practically confessed that I did it. Anyway, the moment I came in she rushed her precious Rosie upstairs, came down swinging the bedroom key with a threatening look and then disappeared into the kitchen, which she locked behind her. It's a harrowing atmosphere. I bet they'll barricade their bedroom door tonight. But if it means she keeps little Rosie from under my feet I can bear the ostracism."

"I wonder who else he was after?" mused Charity, looking sternly at Cam.

But Mrs. MacDermot, with her strict sense of what was due to a guest, came to his rescue.

"Now, you four, stop talking as if poor Mr. Cam wasn't in the room. And stop talking about that awful murder. (Here's your coffee, Bob.) And if you can't think about anything else, play bridge or whist or something. Now tell me about your garden, Bob. My beet are showing no sign at all. Isn't that odd?"

For the next twenty minutes talk went on in a desultory fashion between the three elder members of the party about their gardens and crop prospects generally. The four members of the Ministry staff listened silently for the most part, and showed no desire to take up such active amusement as playing games.

Eventually a pause came in the conversation and they all sat there in comfortable silence. Cam looked round the group and noticed upon the faces of all the young people an expression of rather sombre anxiety, markedly contrasting with the comfortable placidity of the two MacDermots. Even Miss White, who did not strike him as a particularly sensitive person, appeared strained, though her expression, he noted, was largely a reflection of Bill Ratcliffe's, derived from frequent glances in that direction.

"By the way," he said suddenly to the company at large, "Is Sir Arnold still at the House? Or has he gone back now?"

The young people exchanged looks.

"He's gone," Miss White said definitely. "He's to be back next Thursday. I put you down for an appointment at three o'clock."

Cam nodded absently, and silence fell again. But the Doctor had pricked up his ears at the mention of Sir Arnold Conway. He grunted fiercely:

"That fellow! Did I tell you, dear"—he turned to his wife—"the way he treated me on Thursday? I've never been spoken to before like it! He . . ."

"Yes, you did mention it," said Mrs. MacDermot gently.

"He must be a very clever man though, dear. Do you remember how he trapped that spy Chatsworth during the war? That was clever, wasn't it?"

"He is a clever man," Charity agreed. "But he didn't trap Chatsworth. His name came out in the papers because he was DG, but if any man was responsible it was Parry. He found the papers and reported them."

"Did he now!" exclaimed Mrs. MacDermot absently, inspecting cups to see if she should make some more coffee. "Well, wasn't that clever!"

Bill Ratcliffe raised himself to a sitting posture, looking unusually solemn.

"I'm not sure about that business, you know. It's always struck me as pretty fishy. Parry wasn't the sort of fellow to go around reporting people when he could do better by *not* reporting them. The Inspector knows that." He shot Cam a mischievous look. "It wouldn't surprise me at all to learn that he had been trying to blackmail Chatsworth, and that only when he failed in that he reported him. I heard rumours that Chatsworth claimed Parry had been trying to blackmail him—but there was no proof, so, of course, no one believed him. Still, though I hold no brief for Chatsworth, there may have been something in it."

"What I don't like about that case." Charity joined in, "is that Parry got commended for doing something that other messengers would get fired for. I mean whatever his luck in this particular case, Parry had no right to be reading those papers. I think it's rotten luck, in a way, that he should have benefited from breaking the rules. I suppose that's why he kept up the practice."

Betty White shook her head.

"I don't know that he benefited so much really. I was in the London office then, and I heard the DG giving him the grandfather of all tickings off. I thought he was firing him, but perhaps he couldn't do that when, after all, it turned out for the best. But you notice that Parry didn't get any promotion."

"My God!" Stone burst in with fierce intensity, which made the whole group start. "Anyone would think you weren't pleased that Chatsworth was discovered! Do you realise what harm the man had done? He had betrayed at least two of our most valuable secrets about weapons for the invasion. I know it all seems a long time ago now, but it mattered then—it was life and death then. Thank God for Parry, I say. Whatever his faults, that one action in trapping Chatsworth redeemed him. I think it's pretty rotten, Ratcliffe, to say that a dead man's good deeds were probably crooked in some way. Even if you have got a grudge against the man, don't blame him for his virtues. I think he *did* have a way of reading private papers. But I think that was just because he had a spy complex, and was always on the alert for another triumph like his first. You may not like that characteristic now, but it once served a very useful purpose."

Ratcliffe muttered inaudible explanations in a rather shamefaced fashion, and Charity came to his rescue.

"Of course you're entirely right, Graham. The end justified the means in Chatsworth's case. But it's a funny thing, isn't it? People are so unexpected and illogical. Parry, whom I ought to admire for his loyalty, I instinctively distrusted and despised. Chatsworth, whom we all ought to hate, I suppose, was really quite a sweet fellow—awfully weak and not very bright, but well-meaning."

Betty White opened her blue eyes very wide, and Cam noticed Ratcliffe admiring them.

"Did you know Chatsworth, Chatty? Why, you never told me that!"

"I didn't really know him. I met him once when he came to see Robby. They were at Bonn together, you know, and quite friendly. Only Chatsworth came all over Nazi, and Robby didn't. But Robby was terribly upset when the news broke. He blamed Chatsworth, but said the trouble was he was a fool, not a rogue."

Stone swore rudely, and then flushed at a reproachful look from Mrs. MacDermot. The two girls did not seem to notice his language.

"I'm sorry, Mrs. MacDermot. But to me a traitor is a rogue, and that's the end of it. I suppose I've still got a war-time mentality. I knew Chatsworth, too—Robarts, he and I were all at Bonn, though Robarts left before I went up to do research—and I agree he was a fool. But after a certain point a man has no right to be a fool, and irresponsibility becomes roguery."

Cam, almost forgotten in the conversation, joined in, at a wistful glance from Mrs. MacDermot, to change the subject.

"There seem to have been quite a lot of you chemists at Bonn, Mr. Stone. Was it the best place in Europe?"

Stone shrugged.

"They said so. I don't suppose any better than Cambridge or London. It was the glamour of going abroad that got people, I think, and in some cases the glamour of National Socialism, if you can believe it! I was touched myself for a time, and look what happened to Chatsworth. I'd like to have given him five years in a prison camp, without a word from home during all that time to tell one how England was getting on, before he died."

The last words were spoken with such concentrated bitterness that the group fell silent for several minutes. Stone got up at last.

"I'm sorry, Mrs. MacDermot," he said with schoolboy courtesy, "but I must be up early tomorrow, so if you don't mind I'll leave now. I have enjoyed myself so much, thank you."

Betty White also had to leave—to darn some stockings, she said—and with a hasty peck at Charity and a wistful glance at Ratcliffe she went off with Stone. Their billets were next door to each other.

Mrs. MacDermot came back from seeing them off with the relaxed expression of a hostess who had got rid of a rather difficult guest.

"What an unhappy man poor Mr. Stone is! He doesn't ever seem to relax. Now, wouldn't it be nice if he and Miss White could make a pair. It would do him such a lot of good to have a nice bright wife, and I'm sure he would make a good husband once you got used to him."

Charity laughed at this wholesale disposal of her friends.

"I don't think Betty would be very enthusiastic," she suggested. "Graham is good-looking enough, but he sometimes seems very cold. He thinks we're all rather dim lotus-eaters, you can see. On the other hand," she mused thoughtfully, "he *is* rather pathetic occasionally—boyish in a wistful way."

Ratcliffe gave a melodramatic cry and turned to Cam dramatically.

"She has looked on another. Her eyes, to which I have started innumerable epic odes, have gazed elsewhere than upon my handsome person. Her thoughts . . ."

"Oh, shut up, Bill!" Charity stopped him in full flood, and Cam thought sympathetically that he detected a note of asperity in her voice. "Mr. Cam will be taking you seriously in a moment."

"Seriously!" Ratcliffe gasped, falling back in horror. "Seriously! Do you mean that you aren't ser . . . Oh, come, girl, you must be hysterical. After all," he said, lapsing into a more normal and cheerful tone, "who else is there but me? The village lads, with all their rustic playfulness; Stone, a worthy fellow, but surely not exciting to a girl of your spirit; Robarts—well, that's getting into the old-age pension class, though I do hear that ten shillings a week is quite a comfortable sum when . . ."

But Charity had sprung to her feet abruptly. "I'm afraid you're not very amusing tonight, Bill So if you don't mind, Mr. Cam, I'll go up and wash my hair."

She marched out of the room, back very straight, leaving an audience of amused elders. Ratcliffe looked helplessly around them.

"Now which do you think it was?" he said calmly. "The village lads, or Stone, or Robarts? One of them, I'll be bound. But she'll come around. She may be fickle, but she'll come back to starting point."

"Don't you be too sure," Mrs. MacDermot laughed, but with an undertone of reproof. "You're too cocksure, Bill. I wouldn't stand for it myself, and Charity's much more headstrong than I ever was."

Ratcliffe turned upon her the full force of his charming smile.

"I see in you, Mrs. MacDermot, the picture of the woman, gracious and charming, into which Charity, with a little guidance from myself, may some day grow. And I am willing to put up with her present immaturity in that glorious prospect. . . ."

"Immaturity!" burst out the Doctor, maddened by this reflection upon his favourite niece. "Why, you young pup, Charity is twice as mature as you as regards good sense. And if anyone's to teach anybody anything, you're the one who ought to be the student."

The young man, despite Mrs. MacDermot's reproachful clickings at her husband, looked quite crestfallen at this unexpected attack. In a few minutes he made his excuses and, as Cam, too, was beginning to feel sleepy, he suggested walking home with him. Without much enthusiasm Ratcliffe accepted the offer of company, and they put on their coats together.

The Doctor drew Cam aside rather apologetically.

"I'm afraid it hasn't been much of a rest, Bob. You'll have to come another night, when we haven't so many visitors."

"Rubbish!" replied Cam genially. "It's been very interesting indeed. Not quite the sort of evening I expected, but I enjoyed every minute. Thanks, Jack."

The two men walked slowly down Bramble Street together. Ratcliffe would have liked to go faster, but the Inspector set the pace.

"It's turning nice and fresh," he remarked conversationally.

"Yes, I think it will be warm tomorrow," Ratcliffe contributed.

"The crops needed the rain. They should do well now."

Ratcliffe sighed.

"I'm afraid I don't know anything about crops, Inspector, so shall we stick to the weather?"

The Inspector laughed shortly.

"It is a waste of time, isn't it?" he agreed. "Especially as I've been wanting to ask you something. We were interrupted last time I enquired. What did you spend your money on to get into such debt?"

He could feel the young man stiffen beside him.

"I much prefer talking about the weather," he said sadly. "Oh, odds and ends, you know, Mr. Cam. Races and gambling and parties and such like. You'd be surprised how soon a young officer can get through money when he's just released from the Forces."

Cam coughed politely.

"Not a bit, Mr. Ratcliffe. You're sure that's all?"

"What else could there be?" asked the young man, with limpid curiosity.

"It's usually women," the Inspector explained.

"No!" Ratcliffe was shocked.

"Well," he said eventually, "I'll tell you something because I have implicit faith in the police and I believe that what I don't tell you you'll find out. But I'd appreciate it if you would keep this hush-hush, too. There *was* a woman—but she's gone now. And I did spend a tidy penny on her. In fact, all my gratuity and a good bit more. But that's over and done. I don't see that it affects the case, unless you're just curious."

"Speaking as a friend of the MacDermots," Cam said severely, "I hope that it is really over and done. Charity is a very nice girl—too nice to play about with."

To his surprise, the young man suddenly sighed, though he could not see his face in the ill-lit street.

"There's nothing much in that, you know—Charity and me, I mean. She's not really interested. If she were I wouldn't have acted such a fool tonight—it's just nervousness, you know. She likes me all right, but it's all a matter of propinquity. No, if I don't look out I'll be marrying Rosie Davis on the rebound."

Cam wished him better luck in heartfelt tones, and as they reached "The Hollies" he turned up Clover Street. He had come a long way round, but it was worth it. He had suddenly realised that Ratcliffe, so far from being the normal cheerful young man of juvenile lead type, was in fact a rather moody, nervy young man. The uncertainty of his life at present, worry about his debts, threats of blackmail, disappointment about Charity, perplexity about his career—these were all very big problems for a young man adjusting himself to a new life. Sauntering down Clover Street, Cam wondered whether a rather temperamental man, pressed by so many troubles, might be tempted to take a short cut out with one or two of them. Especially if a highly unpleasant character was trying to profit out of them.

He should have got the name and address of that girl, he suddenly remembered. They must check up on how much Ratcliffe had spent on her. Swinging on his heel, he started back towards "The Hollies" at a rapid pace. He ought to be able to catch the young man before he got to bed, and then he could put his men on to the girl tomorrow morning. The urgency of the case still oppressed him, and to him every moment without some action upon it seemed wasted. He laughed silently to himself. It had been too bad using the

MacDermots as decoys. But he couldn't very well confess that he had noticed the four Ministry workers through the bright lounge window as he passed on his way home, and that he had dropped in just on the off chance that he might hear some interesting views expressed. It had been rather clever, he congratulated himself, the way he had pretended he came in for a rest. If he had been asking questions, the whole bunch would have buttoned up like an oyster.

Raising his head suddenly as he came down the hill of Clover Street, Cam's satisfaction evaporated as quickly as it had come. For an instant of horror, though he was not an imaginative man, he stopped in his tracks. It was as though some dark spirit were brooding over him with threatening hatred. There were no street lamps down the hill, and the only light he could see was from a bright upstairs window in a house at the foot of the hill. The window was about on a level with Cam. Framed in it, featureless and black, was the figure of a man, hands uplifted in fury, staring along the street with still and sinister intensity. Although he could not see the face, Cam was convinced that eyes were watching him and that the hands were uplifted against him. For a moment he stood paralysed. The unexpectedness of the sight, the lonely, dark street and the vividness of the framed figure against the bright light overwhelmed his good sense for a moment.

Then he gave himself a little shake. What a fool he was! That house was "The Hollies," that room was Ratcliffe's bedroom, that figure was Ratcliffe thinking—as he had reason to think—before going to bed. Those hands were not uplifted against anyone; they were simply resting on the top of the window-frame. Cam shook his head. At this rate he would have a nervous breakdown before the end of the case. But he was nevertheless relieved when Ratcliffe abruptly withdrew into the room. It had been an eerie sight.

Cam just reached the gate of the house as Ratcliffe returned to the window to draw down his blind.

"Hello there!" the Inspector called in a stage whisper like a young gale.

Ratcliffe hesitated, and looked out. Cam waved violently, and the young man, shading his eyes against the light behind him, at last made out the Inspector's bulky figure. He threw open the window.

"What is this?" he asked. "Burglary or a run-away marriage?"

"Just an after-thought," Cam explained, speaking in a low voice. "I forgot to ask you the name and address of the young woman you mentioned. We shall need that, you know!"

The Inspector could not see Ratcliffe's expression, set as it was against the light, but he could detect in the young man's voice a steely ring which he had never heard before.

"Not on your life!" he said slowly and distinctly. "You needn't have bothered, Inspector. The lady concerned is now married—happily, I hear—and I'll be damned if I set the police on to her."

"Come now," Cam said reasonably. "We wouldn't be clumsy about it, you know. There's no reason why the husband should find out. But we'll have to question her. And if you don't tell us we shall have to find out elsewhere. You said yourself that we were pretty smart at finding out other people's business."

"No matter," Ratcliffe said firmly. "If you find out, let it be on your own head. But you'll have a pretty hard job. And anyway, I won't have anything to do with it. Good night, Inspector," he cut off further protests. "I'm afraid it's past my bedtime. Sleep well."

He shut the window and drew down the blind with emphatic firmness. Cam, feeling rather peeved, turned back again up the hill. That was a bad ending to a day. The young fool was asking for trouble if he began hiding information at this late point in the game. Was it only misplaced gallantry, Cam wondered, which caused him to stick out about the lady's name when he had been so accommodating about the rest of his secrets? It should be quite easy to trace her, as presumably there were some cheques made out to her name. He would get the Yard to approach Ratcliffe's London bankers.

He reached the top of Clover Street rather breathless and turned into the Market Place. It suddenly occurred to him that it was about this time on Wednesday night—ten-fifteen—that all the trouble had started. It might be a good idea to see what the scene looked like.

He strolled across the Market Place in time to meet odd groups of 'Coach and Horn' customers continuing their discussions outside the bar. Acton certainly turned them out on time, he remarked approvingly. If he had had the energy he would have gone down the hill again to see how Sidebotham was doing. He was probably saying his first "Time" about now, if Cam knew anything about his methods.

Passing the men with a nod and greeting to those he knew, the Inspector entered Cat Alley. There was nothing to see here. The light in Parry's room was out, of course, and the door was locked. He spoke to Constable Wootton, who was on guard duty, and wished him a dry night. The sight of the constable who must face a whole night of sleepless watchfulness reminded Cam of the attractions of his own bed and, feeling he had not learnt much, he turned out again to the Market and round the corner of the shop.

Looking up, he noticed that Miss Penny's window was a blaze of light. It was odd, he thought, the way six years of black-out seemed to have erased from people's minds understanding of the purpose of blinds—even modest people like Miss Penny. It occurred to him that she was keeping late hours.

With a feeling of rather school-boyish guilt he crossed the road, hoping that the men in front of the 'Coach' would not notice the manœuvre. Then, striding quickly homewards, he cast another look at the window. He caught a glimpse of Miss Penny which startled him. She was standing at a table, piled with materials. Her hair was almost as untidy as on the morning after the murder, and her expression seemed to Cam, in the quick glance he gave, to have something of wild excitement in it. But that, he thought, was probably the reflection of the firelight. In any case, the sight filled him with gloom, and he walked on home thinking seriously that he ought to do something about Miss Penny. Everyone said that she was in a terrible state of nerves and that unless she got away there was no telling what she might do. After all, it couldn't be very pleasant for an elderly spinster lady to have murder committed in her house—and then to live alone while the case was being investigated. Tomorrow, Cam thought sternly, he would go to see her and try to persuade her to stay with friends until the case was finished. In the state she was in now she wouldn't be a very helpful witness at the inquest, anyway.

The houses of two more persons in whom Cam had a certain interest lay on the homeward route—Graham Stone's billet and Miss White's. He looked at the houses as he passed. There was no light from the chemist's. If Stone arose early to get to work, he presumably went to bed early. At the house next door, however, there was one lamplit window upstairs. The blind was drawn, but Cam guessed it must be Betty White's bedroom. The old people with whom she lived would regard it as sinful to stay up later than nine-thirty. Was she darning stockings, he wondered, or was she thinking about Bill Ratcliffe? That was an interesting situation. If Ratcliffe married anyone on the rebound, he thought, it would be Betty White, not Rosie Davis. And a nice little wife the secretary would make, too, he thought approvingly. Not bad to look at either.

His own home was two doors farther on, and as he turned in he saw that the lounge light was on. Jane would be waiting for him.

They had a cup of tea and biscuits, sitting together on the little sofa like a young married couple. Jane's grey hair, Cam noticed for the first time, went very nicely with the blue curtains. He wondered if that was why she had chosen the light shade of blue when he wanted the dark. Subduing the desire to follow up this theory with a thorough investigation—for Jane had frequently complained that he carried his police methods of questioning into domestic conversation—he asked whether there was any message.

"One," Jane said. "The Chief Constable is better today, and he would like you to call on him in Wootton-under-Edge tomorrow afternoon if you have time. But he doesn't want you to neglect the case, and will understand if you can't make it."

Cam nodded glumly.

"I think I can do it. But I wish I had more to tell him—more facts, not mere theories. I've got plenty of those."

"Little Man, you've had a busy day," Jane said cheerfully. "Come on to bed, dear. And by tomorrow afternoon all your theories will have grown into nice healthy facts. Isn't that right?"

"I suppose so," Cam said doubtfully, following her upstairs. "But there are an awful lot of weeds in this particular case, and all I hope is that they don't choke the real plant to death."

CHAPTER VIII

LITTLE BIGGLING had heard the news of murder in its midst with excited interest. But it was a pity that the victim was so little known to the villagers. Lack of exact and scandalous information about his mysterious past tediously confined conversation to guesses which seemed wild even to their originators and to the actual details of the murder. On the latter event, however, there was very little information to be had. The Inspector, it was resentfully reported, was keeping very close, except for long chats with the Doctor, who was equally non-committal. Although the murder was still the only subject of conversation at the Ministry, by Saturday the question was beginning to languish in the village for lack of sustaining gossip. The Press had given little attention to the case, owing to the superior attractions of a chain of murders in London by a jewel-thieving gang. What comment there was concentrated on the fact that Parry was a MSR employee, and Little Biggling itself received scant mention. Hurt by this indifference, Little Biggling proceeded to ignore the case and to claim that the murder was just another manifestation of London bad manners.

But then, like paraffin on the flames, came tremendous news—much more sensational than the actual murder—that Miss Penny had disappeared. Miss Penny! Everybody knew Miss Penny, and everything about her, too. A rich vein of gossip was opened up. There was her father, now. Back in 1920 he died, and he was such a drinker! Oh, a devil of a fellow, who beat his wife to death, some said, and then lived on his daughter until he died of DTs. And there were all Miss Penny's idiosyncrasies—her passion for neatness, the old-fashioned clothes she wore, her teetotalism, the young farmer she had once fallen in love with and sent two yards of white dimity as a birthday present. After fifty years in the village there were few secrets about Miss Penny, and the disappearance opened a vast field of reminiscence and speculation. Poor Miss Penny! After fifty years of teetotalism, to have her name bandied freely about the local bars; after fifty years of spinsterhood to have elaborate and ribald explanations of her disappearance discussed by every housewife in the village. This was real news to Little Biggling, and they made the most of it.

The news, then not much more than a suspicion, reached the police-station about noon on Saturday. Cam was in his office about to begin questioning the surly Ramsden when Mr. Witherspoon begged to see him on most urgent business.

The little man bustled in, carrying in his hands a large casserole dish, steaming deliciously with hot stew. Cam sniffed at it with mingled surprise and hope—for his dinner hour was fast approaching.

"This—this is for Miss Penny," stammered Mr. Witherspoon, looking quite distracted.

"Is it now?" said Cam resignedly. "And very nice, too. But she isn't here, you know."

"It's most extraordinary," said the chemist. "But I think she's disappeared."

He paused a moment to put the casserole at his feet, as it was beginning to burn his hands through his handkerchief. It steamed there contentedly, driving everyone else in the office distracted with hunger.

"Disappeared?" said Cam helpfully.

"Yes. You see, she hasn't been out of her house since the—the unfortunate death of her lodger. And I thought that she might like something tasty to cheer her up. Well, I saw her yesterday, and she was very unhappy, and I offered to bring some stew, and she said how nice. So about half-past eleven, because I know she lunches early, I had this ready, and just ran around to her shop with it. The shop is still closed, you know, but her street door was open, and I called upstairs, 'Miss Penny!'—just to let her know I was there, you see. But there was no answer, even though I called several times. So I thought she must be asleep, and that I would put it in her oven to keep warm until she woke up. I went upstairs, and as I was going into the kitchen I couldn't help seeing—the door was wide open—that her bedroom was all topsy-turvy and dresses thrown all over and open suitcases and everything. And then I suddenly remembered that the milk was still on the doorstep, and the bread, too. Yet she wasn't anywhere in the flat. So then I thought I'd better come round and see you, Mr. Cam."

Mr. Witherspoon ended his story with a gasp and a gulp, as though he had quite run out of breath. Cam scratched his head with a pencil and thought for a moment. He remembered uneasily Miss Penny's wild appearance last night, but there was no point in exciting the chemist.

"It's certainly odd, Mr. Witherspoon, but we mustn't get unduly alarmed. She may have gone around to see a friend or—or something like that." Cam's powers of imagination failed him. "Anyway, Rowley, you go around with Mr. Witherspoon and see what you can find out. See if any of the neighbours have seen Miss Penny today. When I've finished here I'll join you."

The two men went out. Before he left, Mr. Witherspoon took up and cradled his stew again.

"In case we find her," he said shyly, and the Inspector sighed and agreed.

After they had left he sat silent for a minute or two. Suppose something had happened to Miss Penny. That would be a nice complication. She had certainly acted rather curiously throughout the case, he pondered—with her hysterics and fear of questioning and excited talk, never leading to action, about finding a solicitor. He had attributed a great deal of it to her passion for detective stories, but perhaps that had been careless. There might be deeper roots to her obsession.

Ramsden, sitting uncomfortably on the edge of a designedly uncomfortable chair, interrupted the Inspector's musings.

"Well, if yer wants me about something, can yer get on with it? I've got to be on wi' my 'edges."

Cam examined the man for a moment, and Ramsden looked away uneasily. Either an old lag, thought the Inspector, or frightened about something.

"Well, Ramsden, I hear that you had some trouble with your wife on Wednesday."

The hedger flushed brick red under his coarse, dark skin.

"It's that nosey-parkin' old Doctor, is it? Well, that's none o' your bus'ness. My wife ain't complained, 'as she? And 'til she does you can't touch me. If that's all, I'll be on my way."

Cam stopped him with a gesture.

"That's not all. The trouble you had with your wife was about a man whom she said had attacked her. That man was found dead—murdered—at the draper's shop."

It was impossible to tell whether it was fear or simple surprise which fixed Ramsden's expression for a moment. His mouth fell stupidly open.

"By Gawd!" he exclaimed. "So that was 'im, was it?" Suddenly he noticed Cam watching him, and he leaped angrily up from his seat. "Well, what about it, eh? What's that got to do wi' *me*?" A purple vein was pumping desperately in his forehead, and his fists clenched and unclenched spasmodically.

"Sit down, Ramsden," said Cam quietly, and waited until the other man sank down. "It's got this to do with you. When your wife told you about her experience you left her. You didn't return that night. Where were you during those hours?"

Drops of perspiration stood out on Ramsden's forehead, and the pulsing vein still rose and fell, but he answered in a quieter tone:

"I went off walkin'. I didn't believe 'er—p'r'aps I still don't—and I were afeared o' puttin' my 'ands on 'er too rough. So I went off into the hills and slept out in an 'ay-stack. 'Tain't the first time I've done it to get away from 'er loose ways. Ah, but when I got 'ome the anger was still 'ot i' me, an' she still w'ining, so I 'it 'er."

"Did you see anyone during your walk?"

"Dave Locker, up near Whipple Farm barns; Bob Conover on the road between Iron Acton and Wootton-under-Edge; some other souls I dunnat know."

"Iron Acton, eh? That was a tidy walk. What time did you see Conover, then?"

"Twas about twelve-thirty. Conover been deliverin' a calf."

"And it's about seven miles as the crow flies. That's good walking. Did you go cross country?" The man nodded and Cam changed his approach. "Did you know this man Parry?"

"Knowed 'im by sight—seen 'im in the 'Coach', braggin' 'bout 'is friends and 'is money. Good riddance o' bad rubbish, I say."

"Ever spoken to him?"

"Once told 'im to shut up."

"Did he reply?"

"Not 'e. Shut up like a clam."

"When was that?"

"Two weeks ago about."

"What makes you think your wife knew this man?" asked Cam abruptly.

"If the man was Parry, I dunnat. Even 'er wouldn't be such a fool—silly old man like that. But usually she'll be a'ter any man who'll 'ave 'er."

Cam shuffled his notes busily, while Constable Peak in the corner finished off the shorthand report. Ramsden glowered gloomily out of the window.

"Well, I think that's all for the present," said Cam. "I'll be checking up on you later. So don't try going far. You can go now."

The hedger got to his feet and stumped out without a word. Cam felt, with annoyance, that not only was he, understandably, relieved to be dismissed, but that the questioning had not been as gruelling as he had expected. He had been afraid of being asked something which had not come up. Cam thought for a few moments, and then summoned Constable Peak, who had taken his shorthand into the outer office. He instructed him to look into every detail he could find of Ramsden's reputation in the village and to check whether the man had a police record—either under his own or an assumed name. He must also interview the men whom Ramsden had claimed to have met during Wednesday night. But most important, he must keep a check on the hedger's cash outlay in the next few days and watch for any unusual expenditure. If Ramsden had stolen the money he was the type to spend it.

The only advantage of being an Inspector rather than a constable, thought Cam, as he left the office, is that although you are responsible for keeping up the painstaking and incredibly detailed work of the police-station, you can at least palm off most of the actual drudgery on to your subordinates. At present his men were doing such miscellaneous work as investigating the financial straits of Mr. Ratcliffe, tracing the whereabouts of the missing key to Parry's bedroom, checking the numbers of the pound notes in his pocket-book, questioning all those who were known to have been in touch with Parry, including all Wednesday night's customers at the 'Coach and Horn', trying vainly to trace any close acquaintance. But on none of these investigations had there been any success so far—and it was now Saturday. Three days gone in apparently fruitless effort.

As Cam gloomily approached the draper's shop he saw a group of Market tradespeople engaged in vociferous argument around the door, while their helpless customers formed a second spectator ring around them. There were Mr. Cummings, the butcher, and Mr. Freemantle, the greengrocer, Mrs. Woolley from the tobacconist and young Miss Collins from the fishmonger and old Miss Cooper from the "Gifte Shoppe"—all paying as much attention to each other as so many chattering sparrows. Cam broke through the curtain wall of spectators and looked at them sternly.

"Now, now," he said, with a vague feeling that he was beginning to repeat himself.

But this group, perhaps because it knew Cam so well, was not amenable to his restoration-of-the-peace technique. As one, its members turned upon him and continued their separate harangues at him instead of at each other.

"About six o'clock I heard it——"

"Poor little soul! Frightened out of her wits, she was——"

"Yesterday evening I said to Mr. Woolley——"

"Not a mite of fish has she 'ad all week——"

"The river——"

"In *my* experience——"

"Now, *now*," shouted Cam, longing to use a stronger term. "Not all at once, please. I can't hear a word you say. Mr. Cummings, you're next door. What do you say?"

The butcher looked triumphantly at his rivals, and composed his hands over his aproned paunch in a manner that would have done credit to a bishop.

"As I was trying to tell these ladies and gentlemen, Mr. Cam, about four-thirty this morning Mrs. Cummings (who is now prostrate, Mr. Cam, with the shock of this terrible experience) was wakened by a clatter next door. I am a sound sleeper myself, but Mrs. Cummings wakened me in order that I could hear it, too. I will not pretend that I was not rather put out, Mr. Cam, by being wakened at four-thirty a.m., and, as I thought the noise was only Miss Penny moving furniture, I simply told Mrs. Cummings to go to sleep and forget about it—a thing which, Mr. Cam, to my dying day I can never repent enough. But Miss Penny is an early riser—was, perhaps I should say—and as our two staircases adjoin, we often hear early morning sounds. I have often said—"

"What sort of noise was it?"

"A thump, Mr. Cam—several thumps. They went down the

stairs, one by one. It makes my blood run cold to remember it. Like a body being dragged down by its feet. Thump—thump—thump!"

Mr. Cummings imitated the thumps in spectral tones, and a shudder of appreciative horror ran through the crowd. Cam looked at them with disapproval and, earning many weeks of resentment, ushered his group of witnesses into the draper's shop, to which he had the key. There, when the door was shut, he turned upon Cummings again.

"Do you really mean the thumping sounded like a body?"

"N-no," said the butcher sadly. "Not really, because it was a sharper sound, if you know what I mean. But, as Mrs. Cummings says, he might have put the body in a suitcase. It might easily have been a suitcase."

"'He'?" said the Inspector angrily. "Who?"

"The man who did it, of course. The same man who killed her lodger returning to the scene of his crimes."

The rest of the tradespeople nodded sombrely and Cam looked at them with disgust. A simple little crime seemed to send quite sensible people off their rockers. He looked round impatiently, suddenly remembering his sergeant.

"Where's Rowley?" he asked. "Anyone seen him?"

"Oh yes," sniffed old Miss Cooper. "Gone cycling off about ten minutes ago. As if there weren't enough to do here, without going on pleasure trips."

Very odd, thought Cam, but he turned on the "Gifte Shoppe" proprietor with some asperity.

"And have you anything to contribute, Miss Cooper?"

"I certainly have," she said. "I well remember a similar case just after the last war, when a farmer's wife eloped with the cowhand. Old Marple's wife, that was. They went off like this—"

"Interesting," said the Inspector wearily, "but I'm afraid we haven't time for reminiscence now."

He questioned the others, and only two of them had much

to contribute. Mr. Freemantle, the greengrocer, reported that Miss Penny had seemed quite distracted with fear the last few days, and when his wife had seen her yesterday she had been muttering about the police being Relentless Bloodhounds. At this everyone looked at Cam reproachfully. Elsie Cooper added the information that as Miss Penny hadn't come for her fish as usual that Friday she had come round to ask if she wanted it. She didn't get much sense out of the old lady, who kept repeating that she wouldn't be needing any more fish, thank you, no more fish for her, and had shaken her head sadly as she contemplated her fishless future. Miss Cooper said, thus earning the frowns of her elders, that she couldn't help giggling then, but she felt real bad about it now, because she hadn't thought the old woman was going to throw herself into the river. This started the argument whether murder or suicide was the solution of the problem, and soon the Inspector was forgotten.

He paced the shop gloomily for a few minutes. Suddenly the shop door burst open and Sergeant Rowley appeared, face glowing with exertion and pride. He returned Cam's critical stare with the blandness born of righteousness.

"I've been down to the station, sir." Cam's expression cleared at once. "And she got on the four-forty milk train—the express to London that just stops here to collect the milk. Old Jones, the porter, he saw her, and tried to talk to her, but she shied into the Ladies' room, and didn't come out until the train was in. She had a big bag with her. She booked right through to London."

"Excellent!" said Cam. "Now go back to the station and phone London at once. Give them a full description of her. Did Jones tell you what she was wearing? That's right. And tell them to find her and return her as a matter of urgency. She's wanted for the Coroner's Court. Off with you!"

But just before he left Cam got from him the key to the lodger's room.

"Now," he said to the assembled tradespeople, who were

silently digesting the latest information. "Thank you for your help, but I suppose you'll be wanting to get back to your customers. I'm glad *I'm* not queueing today!"

With tardy zeal the shopkeepers rushed back to placate impatient customers with the latest details of the Little Biggling Murder Case.

Cam was just locking the door after them when a car drove up, and Charity, followed by the driver, Robarts, got out.

"Hello, Mr. Cam!" said Charity. "What's happened to Miss Penny? We just stopped at the chemist's, and he told us she had disappeared. (He had a casserole for her sitting on the counter!) Is it true?"

The Inspector nodded, and as they seemed anxious for more news, stood aside from the door so that they could enter.

"Yes," he said. "She's hopped it. Gone to London."

"How absolutely extraordinary!" exclaimed Robarts in amazement. "But surely a little woman like that couldn't have—have—well, created all this mess?"

Cam looked at him briefly.

"The fact that she runs away doesn't prove she killed Parry. She's been in a great state ever since he died. Thinks the police suspect her because she lives in the same house."

Charity looked at Robarts reproachfully.

"Of course she hasn't done it. A dear little woman like that. I'd as soon suspect my—my aunt!" Cam made a mental note to tell Dr. MacDermot that his niece was casting suspicion upon his wife. "I came to see her yesterday morning before work. Somehow it seemed to me it's the Ministry's fault all this happened—I mean Parry wouldn't have been here unless he was a messenger, would he?—and someone from the Ministry ought to visit her. Anyway, she was in an awful state. Did you say she went to London?"

The Inspector nodded.

"She was saying yesterday that she had some relatives near

London—she didn't say where—and that she thought she would go to them after the inquest for a rest."

"Well," said the Inspector, "we shall know soon enough, because if anyone thinks they can get lost in London nowadays they're very much mistaken. Especially with the rigmarole of ration books and identity cards to help the police. I should think they'll have found her by tomorrow."

As the pair went out Cam detained Robarts for a moment.

"Dr. Robarts, do you remember I was asking you about your movements on Wednesday night?"

"Yes?"

"Well, I've been checking, of course,—just routine you know—and there's one discrepancy I'd be grateful if you'd clear up. Sidebotham at the 'Blue Dragon' says you left him about nine-thirty, and Acton at the 'Coach and Horn' says you got to *his* place about a quarter to ten. Now, it's a three-minute walk between the two. Can you tell me what you were doing in the intervening quarter hour?"

Despite the offhand manner in which Cam asked this, Robarts shot him a nervous look, but he answered him calmly enough:

"Certainly. You remember it was a very hot and humid night. The 'Blue Dragon' had been like an oven, and I took a turn down to the river before going on to the 'Coach'."

"Did you see anyone on your walk?"

"No one I knew," said Robarts. "I don't know many people here, anyway. By the way, the personal files have arrived, and are being sent down to your office."

"Thank you," said Cam politely. "You are not a regular customer at the pubs, I understand, Dr. Robarts. But you seem to have spent a good deal of time in them Wednesday night." He looked questioningly at the scientist.

The latter looked restlessly at the door.

"Yes, I know. As a matter of fact I went to the 'Coach' primarily to see if Stone was there and in what condition. You see, I had mentioned his drinking earlier in the day, and wanted to see if my sermon had any effect. It hadn't!" he laughed.

"One other thing," Cam asked. "I understand you knew the spy Chatsworth rather well."

Robarts set his teeth.

"Yes," he replied shortly.

"You were at the University with him?"

"Yes."

"Do you think that his claim that Parry tried to blackmail him before he reported him may have been true?"

Robarts studied the ground for a few seconds.

"No," he said at last. "Chatsworth was a better fellow than you might think, but he was a born liar. It was significant of his general weakness."

"Thank you," said Cam cordially, and he ushered the scientist to the door. "Lovely day for a drive," he said.

The rain yesterday had cleared the air, and given the struggling green shoots and buds on the trees which towered from back gardens in the village a new lease on life. It was not very warm, but the air was springy and clear, and the sky an unstained blue.

Robarts nodded happily. Now that the questioning was over, Cam suddenly thought that he had never seen the man look so young and carefree. The responsibility of murder in his department was certainly not weighing heavily upon his shoulders.

"Lovely! Miss Brown suggested that we visit the cathedral in Gloucester and hear Evensong. I was going to come back early and work, but perhaps that would be a waste of fine weather."

Cam agreed heartily, and watched the pair drive off, feeling that he himself could do with a nice long run. He wondered about the relationship between Charity and Robarts. They were certainly formal in the use of surnames, yet he was sure that the latter was more than half in love with Charity. But as for her—well, Ratcliffe had more attractive qualities, though she certainly hadn't appreciated them last night.

He turned from this scene of spring and young love into the dark shop and upstairs to the lodger's room. Nothing had been changed since he saw it on Thursday, except for the removal of the body. One shaft of sunlight slanted through the dusty window and fell dramatically upon the place on the hearth where the body had been found. Cam stood looking at the fireplace for a moment. The ashes were still there, though rather disordered by police investigators. They had proved that the paper which Cam had discovered had been placed on the fire after it was well alight. So there was no chance that Parry had been using it to light the fire. Cam's interview with the stationery clerk at Wassel House had also revealed that the paper which had been burnt, judging only from the charred scrap he had found, was of a type used in the laboratories for recording the results of scientific experiments. Cam's heart had leaped at this news, which would narrow the field of enquiry to two or three men. But the stationery clerk dashed his hopes by reporting that although used only by the scientists, the paper would be available to anyone who cared to have some. That is, both Dr. Robarts and Mr. Stone kept some in their offices upstairs in unlocked cupboards, and any clerk who was attracted by the quality and colour of the paper could help herself when no one was looking. Still, Cam thought, it might prove useful corroboratory evidence if he ever found a suspect of whom the Doctor didn't disapprove.

He went over to the window and looked out. Cat Alley was so narrow at this point that if the window were open he could almost touch the opposite building—the side of the 'Coach and Horn,' that would be. A sudden thought struck him, and he opened the bedroom window and looked out. Opposite there was one of Pitt's Pictures—a bricked-in window dating from the days of window taxes. Three feet farther along the opposite wall, away from the Market entrance of Cat Alley, there was a real window, but a window barred from top to bottom, by some careful keeper of the 'Coach and Horn' who realised that surreptitious entry from the little alley at night would not be difficult. Cam looked at the sill of the window out of which he was leaning. The paint was peeling with age. Towards the sides the blistered and the curling fronds of paint were unbroken. In the centre they were squashed flat. But that might only prove someone had been leaning out of the window—possibly Parry himself on one of the recent hot evenings. There were no long scratches to show that anyone had climbed through. The wood beneath the broken paint did not look as if it had been very recently exposed.

He tried the window lock. It moved smoothly, and had obviously been in frequent use. That was easy to understand. If Parry had been so careful about locking his door, he would not forget an easily accessible window like this. Cam leaned out again. It was about seven feet from the ground, but the drain-pipe near it and the sill of the shop window beneath made it an easy climb for a man of average athletic ability.

Cam did not leave the window for a moment. It was warm in the shaft of sunlight. Down the alley towards the Market he could catch a glimpse of Saturday afternoon shoppers crowding the street. Cat Alley, however, was quite deserted. Suddenly he heard steps coming up the Alley towards the Market. As they came round the curve he saw it was Mr. Witherspoon, carrying his large market basket and bustling like a preoccupied old woman. Cam's childish sense of humour prompted him to keep silence until the chemist was just beneath him, and then to say in deep tones, "Hello, Mr. Witherspoon." But he felt rather a fool when the little man jumped forward two feet, turned towards him a face of inexpressible horror and ran down the alley as if the devil were after him. He had never realised Mr. Witherspoon was so nervous. But it would be rather unnerving to have a voice speak to you from a room which was supposed to have been empty since a murder took place there. And Mr. Witherspoon had been taking Miss Penny's troubles very much to heart.

Before he drew in his head Cam gave one more look at the opposite windows. On the sill of the expressionless Pitt's Picture he noticed an old brick. It seemed a curious place to leave one, but quite possibly it had lain there since the window was first bricked in. It was, in fact, of the same type and colour as the bricks used for that purpose. With the pleasant feeling of contact with a workman of the eighteenth century, he leaned over and picked up the brick. To his surprise, there lay under it a tiny scrap of paper. He put down the brick and picked up the scrap. It was the most uncommunicative piece of paper he had ever seen, so small as to look quite lost in the palm of his hand. But he stood looking at it for several minutes, glancing occasionally at the window from which it came. For the paper was certainly no relic of the eighteenth century. It was quite fresh, and might have been rolled yesterday. How on earth, he thought with faint indignation at the improbability of it, did it get under the brick? Who would move a brick on a window-sill? Who would be such a fool? Then he laughed. Except himself! Perhaps Parry had been moved by the same curiosity as himself on some occasion and had lifted the brick. And perhaps a stray scrap of paper had blown on to the sill before he put it down again. All things, he thought with satisfaction, are capable of a rational explanation. This was no exception. But he fished out an empty match-box from his pocket and put the scrap of paper into it. Cam's training had been very thorough.

As he closed and locked the window, however, a far more important idea drove all thought of the paper out of his head. He struck his leg with an exclamation. Something had certainly been wrong with Ratcliffe's story, and now he saw it. Didn't the young man say the window had been unlocked when he brought Parry back, and that he had locked it before leaving? But why should the window be unlocked? Parry had not been back all day, and he would certainly have left it closed and bolted. Either Ratcliffe was lying or someone had been in that room during the day.

At this point in his considerations a loud noise on the stairs and a muffled oath announced that he was no longer alone. Someone was coming upstairs.

CHAPTER IX

CAM waited silently by the window as the footsteps came up. Although he had scoffed at the butcher's idea of the killer returning to the scene of his crime, he felt a faint thrill of expectant horror. But as the door swung open, a stranger stood in the entrance—short, stooped and with an expression upon his face of perpetual anxiety. The two men regarded each other with mutual surprise. Cam, as he had trained himself to do when he did not know what to say, waited for the other to speak.

The stranger, shifting a suitcase he carried from one hand to another, at last said:

"I—are you the next lodger? Is Miss Penny here?"

"I am the Inspector of Police," said Cam portentously. "Can I help you?"

The little man's face cleared.

"Oh yes. I'm Robert Parry—James' brother, you know. And I just arrived."

He spoke precisely, but rather too carefully, as though he were continually on the alert for a treacherous aspirate.

Cam nodded rather suspiciously.

"And you thought you'd like to see your brother's lodgings?"

"That's right," Robert Parry said, his face becoming suitably grave. "I thought I'd like to see the last resting-place, as it were, and as I saw the name of Miss Penny over the shop door as I passed on my way from the station, I thought I'd drop in. Poor fellow! Poor fellow!"

He looked around with a macabre interest, and Cam understood, despite the sanctimonious tones, that no great loss was felt here. Parry turned back to him from the suit hanging upon the wardrobe which he had been fingering with proprietary interest.

"It's bad enough poor James dying, Inspector. But murdered, that's a terrible blow to a brother." Mr. Parry bowed his head, to examine a pair of shoes. "The papers," he added with some asperity, "have little to say on the case, Inspector. Where was it done, may I ask?"

"There," said Cam rather brutally, pointing to the bed, "and we found the body there." He pointed out the bloodstain.

The little man shook his head and repeated, "Poor James! Poor fellow!" But Cam thought he detected a faint glitter in his eye—this would be something to tell the folks at home!

"And have you traced the villain? Do you know who did it?"

"Not yet, Mr. Parry. But we're working hard on it. As you're here, perhaps you would like to look round your brother's personal effects and tell me if you see anything unusual about them—anything missing, anything new. My main trouble with this case has been that there's no one who knows Parry personally. He kept himself very much apart."

The little man nodded as he started eagerly round the room.

"Yes, James was very tight, very tight. I can't say I know much about his life myself. We were only half-brothers, you know. Our father was a retail grocer by trade. His first wife, who had herself been married before, died giving birth to James, and then he married again—my mother, James' mother had been married to a mechanic before she married our father. But *my* mother had been a maid, and James always thought our part of the family was a bit of a social come-down." Parry's lip twisted unpleasantly. "Even as a kid he used to keep himself to himself. But he came up to see us last Christmas—sort of family reunion—so I take this very hard, very hard."

Throughout these remarks, delivered offhandedly and between long pauses, Robert Parry was rummaging through the wardrobe, fingering the materials, such as they were. Cam remembered that this man would probably be the next-of-kin, and would inherit the meagre goods that were James Parry's worldly remains. Unless there were a will—and none had been found.

"Nothing new here," said Parry, with a disappointed air as he finished in the wardrobe, and he looked round the room vaguely. "I suppose the furniture is the landlady's?"

"That's right," Cam said.

Parry's face twisted again.

"For all his fine talk, he doesn't seem to have done so well for himself, does he? Rich relatives—!" He caught Cam's curious glance and recollected himself. "I don't really know his personal things very well. He only brought a small suit-case last Christmas."

There was another pause, and then he went over to the chess set standing by the bedside.

"This, though. This must be new. He played chess a lot, but he boasted when he was up at Christmas that he never needed a set of his own—he always borrowed other people's. He was queer that way—liked to feel he could live at other people's expense. Apparently it didn't work this time!"

Cam was interested in this. He examined the chess set more closely. Although he did not play himself, he recognised the design as one mass-produced cheaply for those who could not afford hand-carved pieces. No prancing horses, or kings enthroned in splendour with attendant bishops in full regalia here—instead plain wooden pieces and pawns, the pawns with little knobs for heads, the knights roughly fashioned in expressionless horses' heads, the bishops with only more elaborate knobs than the pawns, and the queens and kings distinguished by different-shaped crowns. The pieces were in two parts, and unscrewed in the middle. He tried unscrewing a rook, but it had jammed. Then, with a last look at its position in the room—on a small table beside the bedhead—he jumbled the players into their box, which stood beside them, and put it under his arm.

"What was Parry's mother's name, by the way?" he asked suddenly.

"I don't remember her maiden name. Could find out,

though. Her first husband was called Conway. James used to use that name sometimes until he joined the Ministry." The two men both laughed. Conway was the DG's name, too. "That was it! As James was going to be Sir Arnold's messenger, he didn't want any difficulties to arise. At least, that was what he said. Knowing James, I should think he was paid something to change his name and avoid confusion."

Mr. Parry examined the room further, with disappointing results both to himself and to Cam.

"Well, well," Cam said at last. "You'll be wanting to have a wash and meal. We've booked a room at the 'Coach and Horn' next door, so if you'll come with me I'll get you settled. Then I'd like to see you again about six fifteen, if that's convenient."

"Always at your service" said Parry, again the bereaved brother. "This horrible crime must be solved at all costs."

They went downstairs, Cam locking the door behind him, and next door to the 'Coach and Horn'. Cam was amused by the deference Acton showed to the Brother of the Deceased and the sorrowing indifference to material comforts with which Parry reciprocated his attentions. Both knew their parts in the play to perfection. Cam was anxious to follow up his investigations next door by seeing the windows of the building which were opposite Parry's, so he followed them upstairs and wandered about in the hall while Acton took Mr. Parry to his room. At last, guessing which room appeared to be in the right position, he opened a door. Conveniently, it turned out to be the bathroom—one of those capacious old-fashioned bathrooms in which every part of the furnishing is twice as large as normal and which gives the impression that our forefathers were much larger men than ourselves.

He went in, locking the door behind him. The bottom half of the window, veiled with a crisp white curtain, was slightly ajar. He pushed the curtain aside and opened it wide. Yes, there was Parry's grimy window, about three feet farther down the

152

opposite wall. He tried the bars on the bathroom window. There were four, stretching from top to bottom, and securely screwed to the window-frame at both ends. One of them shook slightly and seemed a little loose in its screws, but this might merely be the result of wear and tear. He examined the screws. There was not a scratch upon them to show that they had been shifted. Another theory he had been formulating, therefore—that someone could have climbed from pub window to Parry's window, using the bricked-in window sill as a stepping-stone—expired sadly.

Picking up the chess box again, Cam unlocked the door and went out of the room. As he stepped out Acton came along the corridor and waited to go downstairs with him. He seemed a little worried.

"I've been thinking about the case, Mr. Cam," he confided, and Cam nodded pleasantly. "As a matter of fact, I've remembered something very slight, which I thought I ought to tell you about. It's quite trivial, really. Only that—you know I said Parry was here from eight-thirty to nine? Well, he was, but he did leave the bar for a little more than five minutes during that time—just to go outside, you know—but still I thought I ought to mention it."

"Outside?" said Cam blankly.

"Yes, to the Public Bar Gents."

"Oh, I thought they went upstairs," Cam said in surprise.

Acton looked at him with some hauteur.

"Certainly not. That's for Saloon and Private. Public goes outside."

Cam had never really appreciated before the extent of separation between the sheep and the goats. He nodded humbly, conscious of having erred in a matter of breeding.

"Well, thank you for mentioning it, Mr. Acton. Yes, it's little things like that which help us a great deal. At what time, now, did Parry go out?"

"Oh, about a quarter to nine, and he was out until almost

five to nine. I noticed because he had already had two double whiskies, and I thought he had skipped out without paying. So I watched carefully for him to come back, you may be sure!"

"He really might have gone anywhere during those seven or eight minutes."

"He came back through that door."

Acton pointed to a small door beside the public bar through which they were now passing.

Cam opened it and looked out into the 'Coach and Horn''s back yard. To the left was a brick out-house, opposite a small door leading, he judged, into Cat Alley.

He grunted and came back thoughtfully.

"He paid you all right?"

"Rather! And how he flashed his pocket-book! If I had known he was so flush I wouldn't have worried."

"Did he pay you with a note, then?"

Acton laughed.

"No! After showing everyone just how rich he was, he counted out his bill in loose change—and then grumbled because he said I overcharged him!"

They returned to the bar, where Cam accepted a glass of the landlord's private stout.

"New developments, eh?" said Acton conversationally. "I hear little Miss Penny has run away. Now, there's a likely culprit!" They both laughed, Cam perhaps less whole-heartedly. "And what's this about you questioning that scoundrel Ramsden? Is it true his wife was the one Parry was playing about with that night?"

Cam nodded.

"Is he a regular customer?" he asked.

"Fairly. But he mostly goes to the 'Blue Dragon.' If I had to choose two unpleasant characters they'd be Parry and Ramsden. One of them always bragging and boasting, the other always sulking and threatening. A nasty pair!" He took a drink. "Vicar saw Ramsden on Wednesday night, you know."

"The Vicar!"

Cam would have liked to remain nonchalant, but he could not hide his interest.

"That's right. I was telling him this morning, when I was seeing him about next Sunday's service, that Ramsden had been questioned, and he remarked that he'd only seen him last Wednesday night."

Acton was one of the churchwardens, much to the annoyance of the Little Biggling Temperance Society, of which Miss Penny was secretary.

Cam nodded.

"Well, I'll go and see him. There's one witness, for a change, who can be trusted."

They laughed and chatted for a few minutes about the Vicar and his ways, and then Cam left.

He passed the vicarage on his way to lunch, so he thought he would clear this point up. The Vicar was in his study, writing a powerful sermon, he announced with relish, on the unbiblical text: "Onward, Christian Soldiers."

Cam shuddered slightly.

The Vicar, freshly enthusiastic about the military virtues after three years with an active wing of the R.A.F., had come to Little Biggling with crusading zeal, determined, as his first civilian job, to evangelise the village. When he had finished there and recovered his war-worn health he would proceed to a city, and preferably a slum parish. Eventually, Cam hoped, he would be a bishop, as he was the type of man who would maintain his enthusiasm and vigour unabated throughout life.

But Cam pitied him. He was having his work cut out evangelising Little Biggling. He would find the slum parish a rest from sin after this. For varieties of wickedness there are few places to beat an isolated village. Cam didn't mind. Sin was his trade, he frankly admitted, and village sin had an individual, fey quality which made it rather endearing—not like the sordid brutality of the city. But a clergyman, no doubt, took a different attitude. The Vicar was making great headway with the children, who delighted in his lively sermons, spiced with anecdotes of R.A.F. life. Their elders, however, though they liked the Vicar and flocked to hear him, showed no signs of moral regeneration. If the Vicar's faith in human nature could stand out against Little Biggling, he would go far, Cam thought. He came straight to the point.

"I'm checking up on the hedger Ramsden's movements on Wednesday night, Vicar. Acton tells me you saw him."

"That's right, Inspector. Does this mean he was mixed up in that affair at the draper's? I hope not."

"I don't know yet. It depends on the results of my investigations."

"Of course. Well, I was at the Scout meeting until twenty-two-ten hours. Those kids ought to be in bed by nineteen hours, but they won't go, you know. I'm going to take it up at the next Mothers' Union meeting. Get your wife to come, will you? I know she'll agree. Anyway, they might as well be at a Scout meeting as running the streets, so I let the meeting stay on late. As a matter of fact I was trying to interest them in becoming Air Scouts. Scoutmaster Freemantle isn't very keen, as he doesn't know the engine from the fuselage of a plane. But the boys think it's wizard, and they're the ones who matter.—Well, yes. I saw Ramsden as I was turning from High Street into Jubilee Street, and I sang out because I missed his wife at the Guild meeting. He didn't hear me, and thumbed a ride on a lorry before I could cross the street to collar him. That's all, I'm afraid."

"You're sure about the time?" Cam asked urgently.

"Well, yes, except it may have been a few minutes later, because I stopped to chat with the Scoutmaster after the end of the meeting. About twenty-two-twenty, let's say."

Cam took his departure. It was about one-thirty, and past his lunch hour, but he sauntered slowly home, eyes fixed raptly upon the pavement. He did not hear the Doctor hail him from across the street, and it was not until the little man, puffing hard, had run across to him and caught his arm that he stopped.

"Well!" the Doctor exclaimed. "You certainly must tell me what the latest is! Pretty absorbing, I should think. Anyway, you're coming home to lunch with us. Yes, you are," he brushed aside the other's protests. "Your wife is busy at the hall trying to finish off those pyjamas they've been working on all week. She couldn't tear herself away from the pyjamas, and Mary offered to get your lunch with mine. So when I came back I was sent out again to find you—and here I am practically starving, and all my reward is to be cut dead!"

Cam apologised, and willingly turned to go with the Doctor. Mrs. MacDermot was a famous plain cook. To explain his absorption he told MacDermot the Vicar's news about Ramsden and compared it with his interview with the hedger that morning.

The Doctor nodded wisely.

"Something crooked there. I suppose he left the lorry somewhere near Wipton and then met those two labourers he cites as witnesses. If he isn't mixed up with the case I don't see why he should have pretended he walked all the way. It certainly looks odd. Especially. . ."

He stopped, and Cam looked at him enquiringly.

"Well, I took Mrs. Ramsden to hospital in Stroud this morning, you know. She talked all the way about her hard life and her husband's brutality. Personally I shouldn't be at all surprised if he didn't have every cause for his suspicions. But that's not the point. As regards the night of the murder, she didn't know anything. But she did say that her husband had sworn to kill any of the men she knew if he could get his hands on one. Seemed to take a sinister sort of pride in the fact! You know that sort of woman. She also hinted vaguely, and then rather repented the fact, I think, that Ramsden had some dealings with the police before he came to this district."

"We're checking his record," Cam said. "I suspected as much after the interview this morning. He had an experienced way of answering questions. If I've time I think I'll follow up at once, and see him this afternoon about the Vicar's evidence. Give him an idea that the police aren't deceived for long by clumsy lies. But I've got an appointment with Major Cottle at three-thirty in Wootton-under-Edge."

"Find out where he is after lunch," suggested the Doctor. "He may be working in that direction."

Mrs. MacDermot had excelled herself, and Cam felt fully prepared to solve the case by the time lunch was over. He expressed only regret that Charity was not there.

"A good girl," MacDermot admitted with avuncular pride. "She's taken this case very much to heart. She doesn't like your suspicions of Ratcliffe, you know."

"I saw her going off with Dr. Robarts," said Cam, puffing with appreciation at a Woodbine. "She seemed quite happy."

"She likes him very much," confided the Doctor. "As a matter of fact, I'm not sure that she doesn't like him more than she realises—or he realises. She's always telling us what a clever fellow he is, and how nice to everyone, and how miserable he must be at Mrs. Cottenham's. Though I hear the lady's very good to him and tells him tales of her life in India long into the night."

"I think he likes Charity, too," said Cam—"he looks at her that way."

"I've noticed," said the Doctor. "But he's a deep fellow. Perhaps it's because he's so clever; but I find him difficult to understand. He was in Germany for six years before the war, you know," He added, as though it explained any oddness.

"As long as that?"

"Yes. He's a chemist, you know, and was studying at Bonn. But you remember Charity saying he was a friend of that traitor Chatsworth. I must say I agreed with Stone last night. A traitor's a rogue in any language."

Cam did not pursue the subject, and there was comfortable silence while they finished their smoke. Then the Inspector borrowed the phone and called the Council Offices to find out where Ramsden would be working this afternoon. It appeared that he would be near Wipton, whither the Doctor was going to lecture to a Women's Institute, so he suggested driving Cam over. The Inspector could get a bus on to Wootton-under-Edge. It would save him collecting his own car from the police-station. Cam agreed, and by two-thirty they were off.

The Doctor was as careful a driver as the Inspector himself, and until they were safely past the maelstrom of traffic in the High Street—consisting of three bicycles, half a dozen pedestrians and two cars—he did not venture to speak.

"Any more news of the Ratcliffe theory?" he then asked.

"I got the report on his debts this morning. They amount to five hundred, which is quite a pile for a man earning eight hundred a year. I'd like to know how he spent it. It's all accumulated since he was demobbed, and when you think it includes his gratuity, it's pretty good going. He took out several large sums in cash. No cheques to anyone in particular. But as to evidence directly connecting him with the murder, nothing at all. Except that I'm not convinced he was telling the truth about that window in the bedroom being unlocked. If Parry was such a careful devil about locking the door, I can't believe he would leave that window open all day. But I cannot see why he should bother to lie about it. Why mention the window at all?"

"If he were the murderer," said the Doctor, unwillingly determined to look on all sides of the problem in recognition of his responsibilities as unofficial confidant, "he would probably pretend the window was open in order to make you think that someone was in the room before he and Parry got there."

"But in that case he should not have locked the window

after him. Then it would have looked as if someone could have come in *after* he left—a much more likely proposition. But the window was locked. And apart from Miss Penny, who knew where the key was hidden, it beats me how anyone except Ratcliffe could have got into the room."

The Doctor looked at him in surprise.

"Why, there's the other key. You haven't forgotten that?"

"As far as I'm concerned there isn't another key," said Cam gloomily. "We certainly haven't been able to trace even a mention of it. Perhaps Parry did lose it—dropped it in the river or something."

At that moment they saw in the distance the figure of the hedger, astride a ditch, with his razor-sharp sickle slashing at the thick growth of weeds beneath the grey stone wall that separated field from road. At the sight of that sickle the Doctor announced to his friend that he intended to stay with him until the end of the interview. Cam was not unwilling to have a witness.

They drew up beside Ramsden, who turned with a sulky stare, obviously expecting a motorist to ask the direction. (And I bet he'd give the wrong one just for the devil in him, thought the Doctor.) When he saw Cam he turned grey under his dusty mask and looked instinctively out of the corner of his eyes for an escape route. Cam got out of the car and talked to him, leaning on the door.

"Hello, Ramsden. Come down here, will you?"

The dark hedger—Cam suddenly realised that he must have a touch of gypsy in him—stepped down from the high bank on the other side of the ditch and headed through the long grass towards them. He still carried his sickle in a defensive attitude.

"Well, my man," Cam said severely, "I hope this time you'll trouble yourself to tell the truth, and spare me the annoyance of coming all this way to dig it out of you."

The hedger sneered unpleasantly.

"Who's bin tellin' you diff'rent?"

"A more reliable gentleman than yourself—the Vicar. I understand from him that you were at the crossroads of Bramble and High Street at a quarter past ten on Wednesday night—not well on your way walking to Iron Acton—and that you thumbed a ride on a passing lorry. Is that right?"

The man shrugged his shoulders indifferently.

"Well, I suppose you'll believe Vicar, not me, so w'at's th' use o' denyin' it?"

"Then tell me what you were doing between nine-fifteen, when you left your wife, and a quarter past ten."

"If yourn so clever, p'r'aps you can find that out, too. Dunno why I should 'elp an' get called liar for my pains."

Cam looked at him impatiently.

"Try the truth for a change, Ramsden. You don't want to talk because you're afraid of getting involved in the case. I'm telling you you couldn't be more deeply involved than you already are. I'm quite prepared to put out a warrant for your arrest simply on the basis of your presence in the neighbourhood of Parry's lodgings at the time of the murder, your jealousy over your wife and your lies when you were interrogated. So, unless you're anxious to call for bail, suppose you tell me why I *shouldn't* think you were Parry's visitor that night."

Ramsden did not answer for a few moments. His hand, which had gripped his sickle desperately during Cam's warning, gradually relaxed, and his expression of defiance changed to one of depression and despair.

"You wouldn't believe me," he muttered gloomily, and swung savagely at a bunch of dandelions. Their heads fell at Cam's feet and Dr. MacDermot almost jumped from the car. Cam remained impassive.

"You might try, anyway. You haven't said anything yet worth believing."

After a few more aimless strokes of the sickle Ramsden

grunted.

"All right. Well, 'ere's the truth, take it or leave it. I went back 'long 'Igh Street. As I reached t'corner of Clover Street two fellers come along, one of 'em soused to the gills. T'other sober an' carryin' 'im along. I knew t'drunk un'd be my woman's friend—or w'atever she said 'e was—an' the sober un would be the feller what knocked 'im cold. Anyway, I thought I'd foller, just to see w'at 'appens, see? There ain't no 'arm in watchin', is there? An'way, they goes into t'draper's shop, so I nipped into Cat Alley an' 'ides be'ind the 'Coach' 's back-yard door. I waits there 'alf an hour or longer, an' don't see nothin' except t'sober un an' t'draper gabbling in the shop. An' I saw t'sober un comin' to a window upstairs an' closin' it. . . ."

"You're sure of that?" asked Cam with interest.

"Ain't it the truth?" Ramsden replied sullenly.

"Are you sure he didn't first open and then shut the window again?"

"'E shut it—that's all."

"All right. Go on."

"Then after I'd bin waitin' all that time t'sober un comes out an' goes off down Bramble Street. So I was goin' to nip in an' say w'at I 'ad to say to Mr. Busy Body. . ."

"So your long wait wasn't pure curiosity?" Cam interrupted again.

The hedger gave him a surly look.

"I wanted t' speak to 'im. I didn't mean 'im any 'arm. That's all right, ain't it?"

"How did you expect to get into his room? It was locked."

"'Ow was I to know that? I wasn't thinkin' much, anyway. I waited five or six minutes for the old woman to get to bed. Then, just as I was gettin' ready to go up, there was footsteps again cornin' up the alley, an' I 'ad to duck back again into the yard. This somebody, 'e comes quickly up the alley an' stopped outside the shop. Then 'e turns and goes in the side door an upstairs. So I waited again. And this 'un takes about

162

five minutes upstairs, so when he comes down again and goes off I'm pretty sick of the whole thing. So, 'stead o' goin' up, I goes off an' takes an 'itch-'ike up Iron Acton way. An' that's the truth."

"This second man who went up—did you see him?"

"No, I couldn't see through the yard door, could I? I only 'eard 'im coinin' up. And as 'e left afterwards I saw 'is back."

"Then you did see him. What was it like and what was he wearing?"

"O, I dunno. Just a back like any other back. Well, it weren't big an' it weren't small, an' 'e was youngish, I'd say, or p'r'aps 'e just looked young. I dunno—I'm not a blinkin' copper. 'E 'ad a brown coat on, an' 'e looked like a gent. So it couldn't 'ave bin 'im what done it. Only poor chaps like me does murders!"

Ramsden laughed unpleasantly, but Cam ignored him.

"Which direction did he go after leaving the shop?"

"Through Market Place—'e crossed over."

Cam thought for a moment or two. Then he moved towards the car.

"All right, Ramsden. I think there's more truth in that story than in your previous efforts. But I'm going to check every word of it, so if you think of anything else you'd like to say, come and tell me quickly."

He jumped into the car, and the Doctor drove off, leaving Ramsden silently watching them and wreaking havoc among the neighbouring dandelion heads.

"Of course it may be just a pack of lies," said the Doctor, after a pause. "He's the likeliest-looking murderer I've seen yet."

"A bit circumstantial for a fellow like that. That fact about the window, for instance. The only bit I'm not sure about is whether he did actually go off after visitor number two left Parry. And of course he wasn't just lingering for more than half an hour in a dark alley just to have a talk with Parry!"

"Yes," said the Doctor with satisfaction. "That bit about the window was pretty conclusive. Somebody had been in that room since Parry left it in the morning."

"But they didn't stay there. The examination of the room proved that no one could have hidden there. People don't lie under beds or stand in wardrobes without leaving some trace."

"Well, perhaps this fellow who has the second key had been there for some reason—perhaps earlier in the evening, hoping to find Parry in."

"What second key?" asked Cam dryly. "I don't believe in that until I see it."

"I say!" exclaimed the Doctor. "Perhaps you needn't bother about it, after all. Do you realise that Ramsden admitted he saw Miss Penny and Ratcliffe through the shop window. It hasn't any blinds, has it? Well, then, he'd have seen them hide the key, wouldn't he? And what's to stop him taking it? He could get through the open window."

Cam nodded cautiously.

"But he's not a fool. Would he have admitted watching them if he had taken in that part of the scene? I would still like to know who Parry's second visitor was that night."

"A brown coat seems to be his only characteristic."

The two men looked at each other and laughed. Both were wearing brown coats.

Cam nodded thoughtfully, and suddenly turned in his seat and started rummaging in the back seat of the car, producing eventually the box of chessmen from Parry's room. He took a few of the pieces out of the box and showed them to MacDermot.

"Do you recognise these?"

"No. I don't play, anyway. Whose are they?"

"Don't ask me. I just wondered if you knew." He played idly with them, unscrewing their heads and replacing them. "Did you know, did I tell you, that Robarts once visited Parry in order to get back some chess men he had borrowed? Parry always borrowed his chess men, according to his brother. I wonder why. . . . Whoa!"

The doctor veered dangerously at this exclamation at his elbow and put his brakes on sharply. He looked reprovingly at the Inspector, who was fumbling wildly somewhere about his feet.

"What the devil. . .?" he asked politely.

The Inspector came up again, flushed and eager, with a tiny pellet of white paper in his hand. He unscrewed it delicately, read it and showed it to the Doctor with an expression of bland triumph. Across the torn and wrinkled scrap was written:

> Jose Maranda,
> c/o Dorset Hotel,
> London, W.I.

"Who is it?" MacDermot asked, bewildered. "Where did you get it? What, in short, about it?"

"What it means I haven't the faintest idea," answered the Inspector, no whit abashed. "But it dropped out of here."

And he held up the decapitated form of a white bishop. The screw which attached the head to the body had been slightly shortened, and in the cavity this made the white paper pellet had been inserted.

"Now," said Cam happily, "the case is getting really complex."

CHAPTER X

MAJOR COTTLE lived in a handsome Elizabethan house about a mile outside Bocester, the attractive county and market town. Like many heads of county constabulary, his early career had been entirely military rather than constabular. It is apparently considered by those in authority that long experience in governing the tribesmen of the North-West Frontier and the more backward peoples of Africa is the best preparation for controlling the rougher instincts of the English countryman. In Major Cottle's case the system was proved successful. He was a gentle-seeming man, small and rather bent, but beneath a smooth and almost noble forehead gleamed a pair of uncommonly shrewd and humorous eyes. Major Cottle was not to be trifled with, his police officers had soon discovered. But he was also a man who willingly, and without compromise, delegated responsibility once he had decided that the delegates were reliable. He regarded his post as semi-retirement, months of un-strenuous routine varied by occasional flashes of real excitement. In the day-today procedure of police work he interfered hardly at all, though he kept his eye upon the whole organisation, and was apt to stop constables on their beats to praise or rebuke them personally for actions which they thought were buried in the breasts of their Inspectors.

In Cam the Chief Constable had implicit trust. If it would not have led to jealousy amongst the other Inspectors he would have liked to have known him better. As it was, he was only regretful that Cam carried out his duties so smoothly and efficiently that there was rarely cause for the two to meet. He was, unlike the Inspector, looking forward to the day when he would have the excuse to promote Cam to the post of Superintendent and to enjoy closer contact with his work.

He greeted Cam, arriving promptly at three-thirty, from a long deck chair laid in the orchard.

"Hello there, Inspector. Nuisance to interrupt you just at the height of the case, I'm afraid. Take a chair."

Cam sat down obediently with his legs four square, feeling rather like a young constable. He liked the Major, and admired his work, but he had seen too little of him to feel at home.

"No trouble at all, sir. I was going to report to you as it was, but somehow I haven't had a moment, except for the written report you'll have received."

"Yes. I passed a copy to London. Even if we don't want to call them in—and I see no reason to—they may have a few suggestions to make." The Chief Constable paused. "Superintendent Jones is not at all well, Cam. I'm afraid you'll have to remain in charge. It will mean a lot of extra work, I suppose."

Cam shrugged his shoulders.

"It's interesting, sir. And Sergeant Rowley takes over the routine work when I'm busy. He's shaping very well."

"Good. I read your report about meeting Sir Arnold Conway. He seems very insistent about speed. I thought a week rather hard going!"

The Major smiled sympathetically and Cam nodded.

"I can't pretend, sir, that I see the end of the case yet. And it's three days gone now. What do you think about calling in the Yard?"

Cottle pursed his mouth.

"No," he said thoughtfully. "Not unless I'm forced. When you tell me the case is hopeless I'll give in, but I'd like to show London that there are just as many brains down here as on the Embankment. And I think you can do it, Cam. Your report reaches no conclusions, I admit, but it shows a lot of hard work. I'm willing to bet that you finish in a week."

Cam laughed shortly, flushing at the other man's praise. But he wondered briefly whether it was possible for a man who had never handled a case himself to know the difficulties involved. Still, Major Cottle had done everything else, and his praise was worth having.

"I still stick to that decision," the Major was going on, "despite some rather grave news which reached me this morning." His voice had become more serious, and he looked sharply at Cam. "Do you know, Inspector, much about the research they are doing in Wassel House?"

Cam shook his head.

"Only that it has something to do with textiles—some new material. It always seemed odd work for a Government department."

Major Cottle grunted.

"During the war Wassel House research station made an important discovery about a new material—a synthetic product not unlike nylon, but with certain improvements. In particular, even when tightly woven it is soft as finely spun wool, and it is absorbent, thus making it very suitable for underwear, I'm told, particularly for ladies. But it can be adapted for anything— furnishing material, table-cloths, blankets, even carpets. Well, that may not sound vital to you—though don't forget this is all in confidence—but on a great many firms in this country, and on the economy of the country as a whole, it has wide repercussions. I needn't tell you that the textile industry is one of the spearheads of our export drive. The traditional materials are going well ahead. But with a material like this—new, practical and extremely attractive—our exporters feel they could sweep the world's markets. Look what nylon has done. Well, this material can be produced more cheaply and would make it almost old-fashioned."

He paused for a moment to see if Cam was taking in the importance of the discovery. The Inspector shifted in his chair.

"Yes, I can see the point, sir. If people ever want it as much as my wife wants a pair of nylon stockings, this country should be in clover. But why not let a private company work on it?"

"Ah," said the Major. "Now there you've hit the point. In the first place, this was a Government discovery, and the Government naturally feels that the invention should not be used for private profit. So the idea is that, when the scheme is perfected, certain existing manufacturers of cotton and woollen materials should be allowed to build factories to produce the new material. The firms will be selected according to their relative efficiency and their manufacturing record. They will get the secret free as long as they produce the material according to specifications. Any developments and discoveries they make to improve it will be their own. New companies are also to be set up in development areas, which will make the stuff.—'Britex' they call it, I think. Wool-and cotton-manufacturing towns are to be given certain facilities to produce it, in order that they shall not feel the Government is under-cutting them, and eventually many of them may turn over entirely to the new product. The idea is that Britain will flood an ill-clothed world with this cheap and attractive material and that, perhaps, Britex will become to this country what coal was in the last century—our great export commodity. Factories are already being constructed for the drive, although their purpose is still secret, of course. I believe some of their builders think they are making atom-bomb factories! Well, Cam, until the invention is perfected—there are still a few snags—the Government isn't going to give the idea to any individual manufacturer. If it once gets into private hands there's no knowing where it may go. You can understand that there are plenty of foreign textile manufacturers who would give their souls to get the secret. And plenty of them have offered much more money than their souls are worth. But we are going to keep the idea to ourselves until we are in a position to make a real showing in the world market. And that's why Wassel House Research Station has been kept on so long, and that's why the Government is extremely anxious to keep the secret of its work."

The Major paused. It was clear that he was now coming to the point of his lecture, and Cam made no remark.

"This morning, Cam, I heard some bad news about Britex. A letter from Sir Arnold Conway was brought by special courier to tell me that certain South American technical papers have recently published reports of Britex. They have not referred to it by that name, but it is clear that there has been a leakage. There was, fortunately, no indication that they have the basic secret of its manufacture, but they certainly have the general idea. The Minister of Scientific Research has reported to the Cabinet, and has been warned to redouble all security precautions about the invention. All scientists concerned are to be watched. The experiments are to be brought to as speedy a conclusion as possible. Work on the factories is to be speeded up. That's all right. But what we want is to find out the source of the leakage. Sir Arnold Conway says he has discussed the matter with his Minister and that he considers that the murder of Parry may have some connection with the publication of the secret. I must admit that the same idea struck me as soon as I heard about the publication. It may, of course, just be the juxtaposition of two rather sinister events in a small establishment. But if that is a coincidence, it is an unusual coincidence, and I have therefore told you all this, Cam, in order that you may bear this new angle in mind during your investigations."

Cam considered the problem thoughtfully, while Major Cottle leant back in his chair. Then he carefully took out of his pocket the white bishop, which he had opened half an hour before. Major Cottle regarded it with interest.

"You said there was a chess set in Parry's room. Is that part of it?"

"The white bishop, sir," explained Cam unnecessarily. "And I think it has some bearing on what you have just said."

He carefully unscrewed it and rolled on to the table at the Major's elbow the paper pellet which the piece contained.

The Major unfolded it with interest and read the address upon it.

"What does it mean?" he asked at last. "You found it there, I gather. Who put it there, and why?"

Cam was disappointed.

"I don't know, sir, but I rather hoped you'd know the name."

"Aha!" said the Major. "You think this foreign gentleman may be after Britex. I see. Well, you maybe right, Cam. But I don't really know anything more than I have told you. The name wouldn't mean anything to me. The DG would know it, if anyone did."

"Has he told Dr. Robarts about the leakage?" Cam asked suddenly.

"No, I understand not." The Major shuffled among his papers. "He mentions that in the letter. Here it is. Hm, hm, yes. 'I gather from Inspector Cam's report, of which you kindly sent me a copy, that among the suspects in the case is Dr. Robarts. Dr. Robarts was largely responsible for the invention of Britex, and in the ordinary course of events he would be among the first whom I should inform of the unauthorised publication of important details. In view, however, of the possible relationship between this publication and the murder of James Parry, I suggest that it should be left to the discretion of Inspector Cam, so long as he continues to be in charge of the case, when and how to inform Dr. Robarts of the leakage. This is most unorthodox, but I feel that the situation calls for extraordinary measures, and I have the greatest confidence that the Inspector will not abuse the power which I thus put in his hands.' Very handsome, don't you think, Cam?"

Cam looked suitably embarrassed. Coming from Sir Arnold Conway, that last sentence was like an accolade. He changed the subject rapidly.

"Have you any ideas, sir, on *how* the two cases could fit together? I must admit that, having seen that foreign name, I agree with Sir Arnold that there *is* some connection."

The Major gave the matter some thought.

"Well," he said eventually, "between us two, Ratcliffe looks to me like the one you want. He had the opportunity, of course, as you pointed out in your report. He had the motive of blackmail. And you know there may be something deeper to that blackmail than he admits. Every Civil Servant knows that if he gets into debt his officers will find out sooner or later. After all, the income-tax authorities are in the Civil Service, and there isn't much they don't know about one's private finances! It always seemed to me an unlikely reason for blackmail. If that were all it was, Ratcliffe would have done far better to go straight to his Establishments Branch, make a clean breast of it and ask if he could have an advance of salary. But if the cause of blackmail was something more serious—espionage, for instance—of course Ratcliffe had to pay up. If Parry found out that he was stealing the Britex secrets and selling them in order to recoup his financial losses—*then* he would have a real basis for blackmail, and Ratcliffe would have good cause for murder."

"Ratcliffe, of course, denies paying blackmail, though I must say his bank balance shows large lump sums paid out regularly. More important, if he sold those secrets, it's odd that he didn't get any richer. He couldn't have paid over all the money in blackmail."

"Stranger things have happened, and blackmailers are notoriously insatiable."

"But what," Cam asked reasonably, "about Parry's character? I thought he was the man who trapped a German spy. Why should he suddenly start conniving at espionage?"

"Pah!" exclaimed the Major, with military emphasis. "I don't believe a word of that story, Cam. If you ask me, it was just a case of blackmailer turning King's Evidence because he wasn't paid enough to keep his mouth shut. Parry doesn't sound to me like an 'honour-and-duty' boy."

"Ratcliffe said the same thing the other night," murmured Cam thoughtfully.

"Well, he probably knew from experience!"

"The only thing about the Ratcliffe theory that really worries me is that he didn't have ready access to the Britex secrets. He didn't go into the labs, and he certainly didn't have the combination of the safes down there. From that point of view Stone or Robarts himself would be likelier suspects."

The Major shook his head.

"I don't see Robarts. Inventors usually feel very protective and possessive about their secrets. He would be the last to give them away, I should think. But Stone strikes me as a rather sinister figure, from your report. And rather bitter, too. Did he have any opportunity for the murder?"

Cam shrugged.

"I think he did. Mr. Witherspoon was in a bath for half an hour after Stone came back to the house on Wednesday night. During that time Stone, if he wasn't as drunk as he is said to have been, could have got out of the house and back to the draper's."

"But no proof, no key, no motive, eh?"

"Well, if he *was* the one, his motive may have been that he was selling the secrets of Britex. Parry may have been blackmailing him—not Ratcliffe, as you suggest. Or perhaps Parry and he were working it together and quarrelled over something. Stone was much more tolerant about Parry, you know, than most of the staff."

"Except Robarts, I understand. Parry and he were playing chess that night, weren't they?"

Cam agreed, and both men looked gravely upon the little white bishop, standing sedate and expressionless among the papers.

"Any more news, then, Cam?" the Major asked eventually.

Cam thought.

"Good heavens, yes! I almost forgot, sir. Miss Penny, the draper, has disappeared. You know, the woman. . ."

"Of course I know Miss Penny," Cottle interrupted. "Disappeared? When and why?"

"Run away, I think. She's been in a great state about the case. I thought it was just nerves and reading too many thrillers, but this is carrying things a bit too far. I'm going to give her a stiff questioning," Cam announced firmly, "when she gets back. She took a ticket to London. I got the Metropolitan police on to her."

The Major shook his head.

"I certainly hope it wasn't her. My wife gets all the grandchildren's clothes through her! Well, Cam, any more suspects, as we seem to be vilifying everyone?"

"Just the hedger, sir. A tough customer—with every motive, opportunity and manifestation of guilt. I've just come from questioning him, and he was definitely hanging round the draper's at the time of the murder. But of course he denies going in. Somehow I would be rather disappointed if it were he. It doesn't seem to fit in with the rest of the case. His motive was pure accident. If he hadn't met his wife going home he might never have got mixed up in it at all—unless they're both lying and there's more behind it," Cam ended on a gloomy note, and the Major laughed.

"You mustn't let human depravity depress you, Cam. That's fatal in a police officer. You never know. Perhaps some of your witnesses are speaking the truth. Stranger things have happened. By the way, you may like to use my phone to ask London if they can trace Mr. Maranda—just to keep an eye on him."

Cam got this done, phoning from the library. As he came out into the hall, the Major, still a bit unsteady on his feet after severe influenza, was waiting, and shook hands.

"By the way, Cam, Sir Arnold said he wanted to come down to discuss the case in the light of the news from South America. I suggested your office, at two o'clock tomorrow, as a convenient centre. He doesn't want all Wassel House to know about it, and I'm going to be in Little Biggling in any case. That suits you, I hope?"

Cam agreed, and they parted, the Inspector feeling a trifle overwhelmed by the prospect of two such distinguished guests on top of his more serious problems. He must remember to have his room specially dusted tomorrow, and the window washed. There is, he thought bitterly, no end to it.

Cam walked along into Wootton-under-Edge, glad to have a chance to stretch his legs and enjoy the spring sunshine. He was planning to catch a bus at four-thirty which would bring him into Little Biggling. But as he reached the village and turned along the High Street he saw the tail of his bus disappearing down the hill. He cursed fluently, though briefly. This would make him late for his interview with Parry. And all his constables' reports would be piling up on his desk. And the spring cleaning for his guests tomorrow had to be ordered.

The sound of a brass band interrupted his gloomy reflections, and, as he had an hour to wait for the next bus, Cam slowly drifted towards the sound. He remembered now that Wootton-under-Edge was having its Easter fair this week, and of all things in the world the Inspector loved a fair. It was not because, as his wife claimed, a country fair was usually the scene of concentrated law-breaking—everything from pocket-picking to arson—but the simple, childish delights of tin music, too much lemonade, the cattle show and coconut shies which delighted Cam. Though he felt that his age and dignity now precluded active participation, he could stand for hours watching the children, astride fiery but static steeds, gravely riding on the merry-go-round.

The fair had already lasted two days, but most of the Wootton-under-Edgians had apparently planned to come on their free Saturday afternoon, so it was crowded with family parties. The youth of the surrounding countryside had gathered in strength, and wandered round in silent couples or talkative groups, according to their age and tastes. Children, racing around with wide-eyed joy, were trying to see how many exquisite delights they could taste with the minimum expenditure of money. Cam, in a fatherly mood, dowered with sixpence occasional little groups which, with furrowed foreheads, were trying to split their remaining penny between six different sideshows. Heaven, he considered, was cheaply purchased at this rate. He tried some of the sideshows himself, watched by the admiring train of children whose patron he had been, and who attached themselves to him, partly out of gratitude, partly in the hope of favours to come.

There were several raffles—for a wedding cake, for a wicked-looking rabbit with a powerful kick, for two bottles of plums, for a train ticket to London. Cam inspected all the prizes gravely and paid his shillings, promptly losing the tickets. He passed on to the hoopla and succeeded in winning a large woolly dog, a tablet of herbal soap, an Oxo cube and an engagement book. The woolly dog he gave away to the smallest and ugliest child. The others he pocketed for the delight of Mrs. Cam.

Cam's favourite sideshow, however, was always the coconut shy. He liked it best in the old days when there was a head poking through a back wall at which he could aim with furious zeal. As he was a very bad shot, Cam had never been known to hit the head. If he had, perhaps his enthusiasm would have evaporated. But in recent and more sensitive days the coconut shy, aiming at the concussion of a human head, had been replaced by the coconut shy which aims at knocking prizes off pedestals. Cam thought this a rather decadent development. He wondered whether the average customer was now unwilling to contemplate assault upon a fellow-creature's skull or whether, more likely, barkers now had difficulty in finding men willing to act as targets. Anyway, for human heads or prizes, he enjoyed the feeling of throwing a hard object with abandoned energy at another object which, with any luck, might break.

He asked the way to the coconut shy, and was immediately led there by his retinue. In sight of it, however, he stopped abruptly. Two customers were already there, with the wooden balls piled in front of them, and a small heap of prizes at their feet to show the success they had been enjoying. Cam was amazed. Hadn't Robarts said that he and Charity were going to Gloucester Cathedral? It was a far cry from Evensong to the coconut shy.

He strolled across to the stall, and Charity, turning to look around her, noticed him. She waved her hand cheerfully, but with a slightly withdrawn expression which might have indicated disappointment at a happy *tête-à-tête* being interrupted. But Cam showed no perception, no delicacy.

"Hello there, Charity, Dr. Robarts. How are you? I thought you were in Gloucester?"

Robarts turned quickly, and his welcome was even less warm than Charity's.

"Oh, Mr. Cam. No, we decided that as there was a fair on it would be a shame to miss it. We are going to the Cathedral another time. It's a fixture—this isn't. Are you—er—on duty?"

Cam grinned genially.

"Just relaxing, Dr. Robarts, just relaxing. Nice spring day, an hour to wait for a bus, a fair in a nearby field, so I came along to see the sights. You go right along with your turn. I'll watch."

Robarts turned back to the stall and, watched admiringly by Charity, he picked up the three balls and sent them, hot on each other's heels, hurtling among the pedestals and the prizes. His aim was perfect. With the first shot he got a pink doll, with his second a brown dog, with his third a yellow box. The stall-holder picked out the prizes gloomily and presented them without enthusiasm.

"It's pretty 'ard," he said, speaking to the Inspector as a sympathetic onlooker, "when a chap spends all 'is dough tryin' to fix up a decent stall and other chaps come along an' pinch all 'is prizes. I ain't complainin', I ain't startin' no trouble, but it's pretty 'ard, I say."

Charity looked at him with quick sympathy.

"Of course it is," she exclaimed. "Look, Robert, let's give back some of these. I don't know what we'll do with them, anyway. You don't mind, do you?"

Unexpectedly, Robarts spoke sharply.

"No, we shall not," he said. "This man has set up his stall at which people who do certain things are rewarded with prizes. He has no right to grumble when someone is too successful. He ought to make the shy more difficult. As a matter of fact, I do want the dolls, and have no intention of surrendering them to moral blackmail."

Charity looked helplessly from the obdurate Robarts to the sulky stallholder and then to the interested Cam.

"Well," she said, speaking more to Cam than to Robarts, "of course you're right, Robby; but you can see the man's point."

Cam cleared the atmosphere, which was becoming rather strained.

"It's my turn next," he said cheerfully to the stall-holder, "and if you don't get back on me all you lost on him I'll give you my boots."

In a series of flashing displays Cam proceeded to spend half-a-crown on desperate attempts to hit at least one of the pedestals; his energy and cheerfulness never diminished, but his aim was unchangeably erratic. It seemed impossible that anyone could be such a bad shot, yet it was obvious from the gleam in Cam's eye just before each attempt that every time he was convinced that this shot was going to be a success. Charity was weeping with laughter by the time he turned away, while Robarts seemed torn between amusement and amazement that anyone could fail to hit such obvious targets.

The three of them strolled around the fair-grounds together for a while, Charity and Cam discussing the fairs of their respective childhoods, and Robarts rather pensively silent. Can it be, Cam thought innocently, that he doesn't enjoy my presence? Even Charity seemed a shade impatient with him.

"Well," she said eventually, "Robby and I are driving back to have high tea at the Biggling Inn. So I'm afraid we must say goodbye, Mr. Cam."

The Biggling Inn, a famous river-side pub, was on the other side of Little Biggling. Cam smoothed his chin.

"I say," he said diffidently, "you couldn't give me a lift to Little Biggling, could you? You see, it's ten minutes till my bus, and it would save me a lot of time. But if I'm in the way. . ."

Charity and Robarts gave each other a despairing look.

"Are you sure," the latter said grimly, "that we won't be tearing you from the fair? You haven't seen half of it yet. And we know how you like fairs."

Cam shook his head sadly.

"Duty before pleasure, Dr. Robarts. I must get back as soon as possible."

"It's nice when you can combine both," said the scientist, with a shade of temper, and led the other two towards the car park.

There was just room in the dicky of Robarts' car for the Inspector. He thought himself that Charity could have fitted in with less trouble, but there was no suggestion that she should leave her seat beside the driver. So Cam wedged himself uncomfortably between piles of wire netting, chicken-feed and sacks. As he was doing so the bus passed in a cloud of dust.

"Its all for Aunt Mary," Charity explained, watching him maliciously as he adjusted his bulk. "I'm afraid you might have been more comfortable in the bus, Mr. Cam."

"Not at all," he said cheerfully. "And it's nice to have your company, my dear. What does Mrs. MacDermot want with all this wire? She has a good run already, I thought."

"Oh, that's for Mr. Witherspoon," Charity explained as the car started off. "He says you advised him to put a fence round his precious vegetables. I prefer flowers, myself."

"What sort?" asked Robarts, looking at her sideways.

"Old-fashioned ones—roses, Canterbury bells, primroses—olde worlde cottage-garden stuff, I'm afraid."

"That's right," he said approvingly, but rather cryptically, and they exchanged a friendly look of understanding.

There was silence while Cam surveyed the backs of their heads. Then Charity, perhaps conscious of this examination, turned impatiently.

"What are you doing this far out, anyway, Mr. Cam? Taking a holiday from the case?"

"I've been working, I'm afraid," he said. "Seeing Major Cottle, and then earlier your uncle drove me out to speak to a hedger who's mixed up in the case. He claims to have seen a visitor to Parry's lodgings after Ratcliffe left for home."

Charity turned in her seat and looked interested in this unexpected piece of intelligence. Robarts, intent on his driving, did not move; but Cam wondered if his whitening knuckles upon the steering-wheel were the indication only of his tight control of the car.

"Do you know who it was?" asked Charity.

"Not yet, but it shouldn't take long to find out," answered the Inspector, with bluff confidence.

"Well, I'm glad of anything which steers your attention away from Bill Ratcliffe. Now, don't deny that you did suspect him, because I guessed you did when Uncle refused to talk about him. Uncle's silences are just as informative as his occasional indiscretions, you know." She laughed charmingly, and then turned to Robarts with innocent candour. "Isn't it fantastic, Robert? Poor Bill! He's been looking quite harassed these last few days. You've probably noticed—and that's why. He's told me all about it, almost weeping on my shoulder, poor boy."

"Really, Charity?" said Robarts, and, despite the exchange of Christian names, Cam could not have been mistaken in detecting a certain coldness in his manner.

But, for an apparently intelligent and sensitive girl, Charity seemed remarkably obtuse this afternoon.

"Yes," she went on merrily. "The last person on earth who could do such a thing! Bill! He's so—so nice, so lovable!"

She seemed to grope for the right word and, having found it, with innocent triumph gave a sidelong look at Robarts, seeking for agreement. As he only grunted and was entirely concentrated on his driving, she turned to Cam for appreciation.

"I suppose it *was* that—that niceness of Bill's which changed your mind, Mr. Cam? You do see what I mean?"

"I see exactly what you mean," said Cam, not without amusement, "but you're going a bit fast for me. I'll go so far as to say I haven't any more proof that Mr. Ratcliffe did murder Parry, but neither have I any proof that he didn't. He still had more opportunity than anyone else—lovable or not."

Charity's face dropped, and she looked rather crossly at Robarts, who had simply said "Ha!" with sudden vigour.

"Well, you can't prosecute him because he might have done it. Not in England. I might have done it if I'd had the chance. I certainly didn't like Parry. How do you know what I did after you left that night? Or if not me, why not Robert here, or Graham Stone? He's fierce enough! Or the Director-General—why was he at Little Biggling that night—or. . ."

"Don't talk nonsense, Charity," Robarts interrupted, so fiercely that both Cam and Charity looked at him with amazement. "This is too serious a case to joke about."

Charity hushed with unusual docility, and for a few minutes the three were silent. The tranquillity was broken by Cam starting to fumble desperately behind and about him, among the wire-netting and chicken feed.

"Where on earth. . ." he gasped. "Surely I've not lost. . ."

Charity, leaning over the back of her seat, became quite worried, and looked anxiously with him for she knew not what. The next moment, however, as Robarts, too, was beginning to slow down and look behind him, Cam found and produced the chess box that he had taken from Parry's room that morning. He wiped his forehead and smiled broadly at Charity.

"Well! I thought I must have left it somewhere. I should have been in the soup!"

She looked at the box narrowly.

"What is it? Surely—no, of course it can't be. Robert, do look! Isn't that the image of your chess box?"

The car swerved wildly under the nose of an on-coming lorry and back to safety beside the ditch, while Cam shut his eyes and prayed. Robarts himself was pale when he opened them.

"Sorry," he said simply. "I didn't see it." He turned in his seat. "What were you saying, Charity? My chess box?"

"This one," Cam said, offering the box.

Robarts touched it gingerly.

"Yes, that's mine," he said, and looked gravely at Cam.

The Inspector was relieved that he made no attempt to ask where it had been found, or show surprise. At least they might hope to go straight ahead from here.

Charity was manifesting extreme bewilderment.

"Where on earth did you find it? What an odd thing! Isn't it, Robert?"

She turned, amazed, to him. He made no reply, but looked at her with dumb eloquence. Without any further explanation she seemed to know that the box had a serious connection with the case, and she sank back in her corner, her face averted from the two men. They completed the drive in gloomy silence.

At the police-station, as Cam got out, Charity looked at him with such cold dislike that he felt a pang of self-reproach. It must seem malevolent the way he went after every man the girl liked. No wonder she hated him.

Robarts, on the other hand, seemed to be quite calm, and even to have recovered his good humour. He looked at Cam over Charity's head and spoke quite casually.

"By the way, Cam, I'd like to see you today, if it's convenient. Would it be all right after this high tea of ours?"

"Certainly," said the Inspector with equal civility. "Would seven suit you?"

Robarts agreed, and drove off with Charity towards the doctor's house. Charity would be saying unpleasant things about him, he could swear. Well, the children liked him, anyway, he thought sadly. But sixpence wouldn't help Robarts. It was a sour job always to be spoiling people's afternoons.

CHAPTER XI

THERE was a message waiting for Cam from Scotland Yard. The errant Miss Penny had been traced in Putney, and would be sent back with escort to Little Biggling the next day. She had become hysterical when questioned, and was not medically fit to travel today. The tracing had been childishly easy, as Miss Penny had, without any attempt at disguise, gone straight to cousins in Putney, whom the police found within twelve hours. It had apparently not occurred to her that the police operated outside Little Biggling—that mere escape from the village would not end her trouble. Cam shook his head over this. It did not seem possible that anyone capable of such stupidity could have committed a crime which he was still unable to solve. On the other hand, he thought, there is nothing so disarming as an appearance of naïve ignorance, and a cunning criminal could adopt no better disguise.

After reading the telegram, he put through a call to Mrs. Davis. Mr. Ratcliffe was not there. He had gone to play golf at Stinchcombe. Damning the expense, the Inspector phoned Stinchcombe Hill Golf Course and got hold of Ratcliffe just as he was coming in from his round. He sounded understandably worried as he answered the phone.

"Sorry, Mr. Ratcliffe, to bother you like this, but I wanted you to repeat again, as accurately as you can, the words Parry used when you were helping him home."

With some hesitation, Ratcliffe repeated them, and the Inspector made him go over them several times until the young man swore they were as accurate as he could remember. Cam thanked him and hung up, reflecting that there was another afternoon he had succeeded in ruining.

With a mug of tea warming his hands, he brooded over the case for some twenty minutes. Before him on the desk lay the two mysterious scraps of paper—the one discovered under the brick, the other in the white bishop. How long, he wondered, would it take the London police to get on to Mr. Jose Maranda. There was no knowing, of course, when the address had been hidden in the bishop. One thing puzzled him. It was not a complicated address. Why should anyone go to the trouble of writing it down when it could be so easily learnt by heart? The obvious explanation was that it was a message to someone. Had Parry put it there? Or was he the recipient? In either case it looked as though the messenger was not only a blackmailer, but an active spy. Why should he write it down? Cam returned to the puzzle. But, even odder, why in manuscript?

Once the interviews with Robert Parry and Robarts were over his next job would be to compare the writing with that of his suspects. That might give him a lead. Obviously someone had scribbled this address down with the intention that it be immediately destroyed by the recipient of the message. By what fantastic carelessness had this not been done?

Cam put the address away. Without knowing more about Jose Maranda he could not hope to solve the riddle.

The other piece of paper he examined with the aid of forceps and a magnifying glass. A more characterless piece of paper he had never seen—white but slightly soiled, a right-angled triangle in shape, not more than half an inch long and an eighth of an inch wide. It seemed absurd to pin any importance to such an insignificant scrap—thousands of better pieces were lying in the gutters of Little Biggling. He held it up to the light with forceps and noticed that a strong watermark ran through it in wavy lines. That was more helpful. There could not be many types of paper so carefully watermarked that a tiny piece like this could show definite lines. Even the best-type note-paper—he snapped his fingers and hastily fumbled in his pocket, producing his pocket-book. Taking a pound note out of it, he held it up to the light. There was no doubt about it. Though the main colouring of the note was buff and blue, there were white strips at each end, and through the whole of the note ran the close design of watermarks which the Bank of England finds necessary for the discomfiting of forgers. With deep satisfaction Cam put his pound note away and looked proudly at the scrap of paper. It was consoling to have given it a name. But on second thoughts he did not see how it helped him in the case. It was curious, but not helpful, that a corner of a pound note should be found under a brick in a bricked-up window.

He turned his mind to the question of the window in Parry's room. It had occurred to him, as soon as he had heard of Parry going out of the bar for almost ten minutes, that perhaps the messenger had slipped out of the back-yard gate and up to his room for a moment or two. It would not take two minutes to get there. But why should he go?

Cam pondered further, and he remembered something else. Acton had spoken as though it was after Parry's absence outside that he had started flourishing his money about. Certainly it was after he returned that he paid for the drinks. Might there not be some connection between the absence and the money? Perhaps Parry had gone up to his room to collect his money. But he wasn't the sort of man to leave money lying about his room, locked or not. Or had he met someone who gave him the money? But in the twilight near the 'Coach and Horn' (for he could not have gone far in those few minutes) it was not likely that Parry had risked meeting his victim or vice versa.

"Ha!" exclaimed Cam suddenly to the furniture. Very nice indeed! Of course Parry wouldn't leave his money in his bedroom. But he was the type of man who would delight in secret hiding-places. And certainly he had imagination, or he wouldn't have been the great liar that everyone declared he was. Wouldn't he have been struck then, just as Cam had been, by the mystery of the brick lying in the Pitt's Picture opposite him? And what an excellent hiding-place that would make,

Cam thought appreciatively. Even his own men in searching the room had never considered looking, not only outside the window, but in—or on—an entirely different house! On the evidence of the torn pound note he felt quite prepared to swear that Parry had used the brick as a cache for his money.

How did it affect Ratcliffe? he pondered. The young man had certainly been at the window. Could he have been after the remaining money? Ramsden declared he had only shut the window. Against the bright window the hedger could hardly have mistaken the young man's movements. But he was not a reliable witness.

Still Cam was not satisfied. Having solved to his satisfaction one aspect of the case—the purpose of the brick—he felt that again it was leading to a dead end. Into his dissatisfaction Sergeant Rowley, hesitant about disturbing his chief in a moment of thought, came delicately to announce the arrival of Mr. Robert Parry. Cam welcomed the interruption and the opportunity to get his teeth into something practical like an interrogation.

It did not need much perception on Cam's part to see that his brother's unexpected decease was by no means a calamity to Robert Parry. His sorrowful expression was never securely fixed, and before long he discarded it altogether in favour of one of lively interest and pleasure. Obviously the unfortunate James had long been a thorn in his flesh, and Robert was congratulating himself that out of so many years of tribulation he was reaping at least an hour of notoriety and interest.

Cam immediately steered him to the subject in which he was interested by asking if his brother had ever mentioned any of the people at the Ministry or his work there. Parry looked at him with amazement.

"Mentioned them? Talked about it! Did he ever talk about anything else? A terror he was when he once started gabbing, and to hear him talk you'd have thought he ran the blooming place. He always said the work was 'hush-hush,' but I never noticed him hushing! He would tell a whole bar about the work he was on—'he' was on, you know, as if he were in charge of it all! But he always said the Ministry wouldn't fire *him,* that he had friends in high places who would help him in trouble—you know the line. Oh, to hear him talk you'd think he had the whole Government in his pocket."

"He talked a lot about these so-called friends, did he? Did he mention anyone by name?"

"No, he was too cagey for that. There was one person he often used to mention who was 'just like a brother,' but I didn't pay much attention to his talk myself. And he used to say that he and this friend here were going to be rich soon—so would I lend him a fiver to get along with! Never paid me back neither. Even though he was my half-brother I always thought he was a wrong 'un. He used to talk about all his money, you see, and I didn't see how he could get much money as a Government messenger. Rotten pay they get, I hear. I don't mind telling you now that I used to think he was mixed up in some dirty work—fencing or something. But I guess it was just his talk, because he certainly hasn't left much money!"

There was mingled relief and disappointment in his voice.

"Do you know whether Parry had anything to do with his mother's family?" Cam asked rather unexpectedly.

"No, I don't know. They were Hull people, I think. But I don't think James ever had anything to do with them."

"What about her first husband's family?"

"Oh, no, nothing at all, I'm sure. They weren't his relations, you know."

Cam asked a few more questions about James Parry's past, but it was clear that from the age of sixteen, when he left home, the two brothers had maintained only the slightest contact.

It was seven fifteen by now, and Cam, who was intensely eager to see Robarts, got rid of the bereaved brother. It had been necessary to postpone the inquest until Monday, owing to the unexpected disappearance of Miss Penny, but he hoped that Mr. Parry would find means to entertain himself over the weekend. As they said goodbye Cam had no doubts on that score. All he hoped was that Parry would not turn up drunk at the inquest as a result of too generous treating in exchange for the story of his own and his brother's lives.

Robarts was drumming his heels in the waiting-room as Cam shook hands with Parry. Cam kept him waiting for a few more minutes while he read a message just received from London. It was brief and disappointing. Jose Maranda, well-known Colombian rancher, visiting Britain to inspect British tweed manufacture, had left Southampton last week by the *Ile de France,* on his return home. Dead end, muttered Cam savagely, and turned back grimly to Robarts.

At a sign from the Inspector he followed him into the private office. They sat down without a word, and each took out a cigarette. Then Cam leaned back, and they looked at each other.

"Well," said Robarts finally, "I suppose I've been a fool—at least, not to have mentioned the box. And I suppose, too, I could drag this all out by continuing to deny going to Parry's lodgings. But I don't really think it's worth it, do you?"

Cam nodded, rather startled by the other's self-possession.

"I think it will pay you to tell the truth, Dr. Robarts. I can't hide the fact that I've formed a most unfavourable impression of your association with the case so far, and further prevarications won't improve things."

Robarts flushed.

"I suppose it does look as though I had something to hide. That's my fault. But the absurd thing is that the only reason I didn't tell the exact truth when you first questioned me was that I didn't want to have anything to do with the case. You see. . ."—he hesitated, glancing at Cam—"I've been, in a sense, in the hands of the police before, and I was, I suppose, obsessed by the fear of these interminable questionings all over again. And as a result here I am!"

He laughed wryly, twisting his long fingers until the knuckles cracked.

"When was that?" asked Cam.

"I thought you'd have guessed. During the war, when they were considering inviting me to take over the department—but before they had told me about it—I was 'grilled' (I think the word is) about my life in Germany. I lived there six years, you know, studying and teaching. I came out of it all right—witness my presence here—but it was a nasty experience."

Cam made a note to obtain a transcript of this interview, then turned to Robarts again.

"And now, Dr. Robarts, will you tell me what you did on Wednesday night?"

Robarts told his story slowly and carefully, searching, it seemed, for every word in order not to err in a syllable. Up to the time he left Stone at Mr. Witherspoon's there was no change in his previous statement.

"As I left Witherspoon's I suddenly remembered that Parry had gone off with my chess set that night. I have been lending it to him pretty frequently, as he liked to work out gambits with the pieces, not on paper as I do, and he probably had taken it from the car automatically as he got out at the 'Coach and Horn'. We had been using it that evening, you see. Well, it didn't really matter, and I wish to God I'd just left it, but I had been hearing all day about Parry's faults—and I'd had a taste of one that evening when I spoke to him about reading correspondence—and I suddenly felt that I wouldn't let him get away with it. I mean, continually borrowing someone's chess set is almost as bad as borrowing a man's fountain-pen. My set isn't anything to boast about, but I'm rather attached to it—at least I was, not any more. Anyway, I didn't see any reason why Parry should think he could take it without asking, so I decided to drop in at his lodgings and get it back. The quickest way was by Cat Alley from the chemist's, so I went that way. Nobody was about when I got to Parry's place, and I went in through the Cat Alley door and up his stairs. I knocked several times and there was no answer. I hadn't got the key, so. . ."

"Whoa!" cried Cam. "What key are you speaking of?"

"Parry once lent me a key to his door when I had to retrieve my chess set urgently. But I returned it next day, and that was about two months ago."

"Do you mean his own key or another?"

"Well, he had two on his ring when I borrowed one. He said they were both to his flat."

"Do you know if he still had that second key?"

"Yes, I think so. Last week when I wanted to get my set out of his room—it really was a nuisance, you know, letting him have it all the time—I suggested borrowing the key, but he said he had lent it to someone else."

"Parry was very secretive about his room usually. It seems odd he should have lent his key around so freely."

Robarts laughed.

"Well, I don't suppose even my worst enemy would suspect me of being likely to pry into other people's bureau drawers! Not that Parry was very willing to lend the key—I had to be quite firm. As for the other fellow, I don't know. Perhaps it was a friend of his."

Cam grunted and indicated that Robarts should continue.

"Well, as I say, not having the key, I couldn't do anything except leave, feeling rather disgruntled. And from there I went straight home. It's not much to have been so secretive about, but—well, that investigation four years ago really put the fear of God into me, and I didn't want to have anything to do with the case."

"Why didn't you report that Parry had taken your chess set?"

"That was just stupidity," Robarts explained simply. "I didn't want my name mixed up in it."

"Did you see anyone after you left the lodgings?"

"No. I've remembered since, thinking about the case, that there were footsteps coming up the alley behind me as I left. But I didn't see anyone."

Cam played lightly with the magnifying glass on his desk.

"You haven't yet explained satisfactorily, Dr. Robarts, your stroll between visiting the 'Blue Dragon' and the 'Coach.' Do you still claim it was merely for the purpose of taking a breath of air?"

Robarts showed more embarrassment than he had yet demonstrated.

"Yes, that was all right," he muttered. "I walked up Bramble Street and then round by the Market to the 'Coach'."

"That would take only five minutes," Cam pointed out mildly. "You took fifteen."

Robarts looked acutely unhappy, but he answered determinedly.

"I stood on the corner of Bramble Street and the Market for ten minutes or so. If you must know, I was wondering if Miss Brown would be coming out for a walk. Yes, I'm quite aware it sounds insane. And if you want to laugh, don't spare my feelings."

Cam permitted himself a faint smile of sympathy. It did sound eccentric behaviour for a man of this type, but Robart's evident agony at having to admit it made it difficult to disbelieve him.

There was silence in the little room while Robarts recovered from his embarrassment and Cam scribbled in a notebook. Then the Inspector looked up and regarded Robarts sternly.

"Is that all you have to say?" he asked severely.

The other man nodded.

"Then what have you got to do with this?"

With an abrupt gesture Cam threw on the desk in front of Robarts the paper pellet which he had discovered in the white bishop. The other looked in bewilderment at it and back to Cam. He picked it up and, slowly unrolling it, smoothed it out upon the desk. His face, which had been puzzled, turned slowly pale with horror.

"My God!" he exclaimed in a frozen voice, and his hands trembled on the paper. He looked at Cam in stark amazement. "Where in God's name did you get this? Does he come into this?"

He stopped aghast.

Cam regarded him silently. His response was certainly very satisfactory, but the Inspector was not sure how to go on. Evidently Robarts thought he knew who Jose Maranda was. Would it be wise to let him know that he had not the faintest idea? He decided to risk a finesse.

"Sir Arnold does not know yet," he said coldly.

"But he must be told at once," said Robarts, springing to his feet. "This makes the whole case much more serious."

"Tell me first," said Cam, feeling desperate, "exactly what you know of Jose Maranda. And sit down, Dr. Robarts. What harm has been done has been done some time."

"Done!" said Robarts blankly.

Cam answered slowly, emphasising each word:

"Important details of Britex were published last week in certain South American technical magazines."

There was no doubt about Robarts' reaction. Dismay lay in every line of his face.

"Oh Lord!" he said quietly, but there was a note of agony in his voice. "All that work for nothing!"

He hid his face in his hands.

Cam watched him with cold analysis. The man certainly seemed shocked. But that might work either way. He would like to see his face again.

"You know Jose Maranda?" he asked.

Robarts' face was strained but calm when he lifted it to reply. He spoke with a tone of dead calm.

"I knew of him, of course. We were all warned, when he arrived in Britain three months ago, that his real purpose was to act as agent for a wealthy South American combine which plans to set up textile factories, particularly woollen fabrics, on a big scale throughout the sub-continent. So far, so good; but apparently the combine was also keen on getting the secret of Britex so that it could break into world markets with something new and exciting. A few days after we received the warning I had a letter from the gentleman himself, saying he had heard I was working on woollen fibres and would appreciate an interview to discuss the South American problem. I, of course, replied that I was not in a position to give interviews—owing to Civil Service procedure—but that our Director-General would be delighted to see him. From that time I've heard nothing."

"Have you seen this scrap of paper before?"

"Never."

"It was found," Cam said slowly and carefully, "in a cavity specially prepared in the white bishop of your chess set."

It took a few moments for this to sink in, and then Robarts seemed to be seeking for some means of explaining his innocence. But finally he simply shook his head, and with a gesture of his hand said baldly:

"Well, I can only say I don't understand what's going on. And that the DG must be summoned at once. If I'm suspected—and I don't honestly see how you could help but suspect me"—he smiled wanly at Cam with disarming candour—"I can't very well take any part in the investigations."

The Inspector nodded. Robarts seemed to be sincerely horrified by the situation and ready to take due responsibility. But, after all, what else could he do when faced abruptly with the discovery?

"Who has access to this material on Britex? Surely the whole staff doesn't handle it."

"No," Robarts said miserably. "Stone and I are the only ones with ready access. The basic material is kept in a safe in Laboratory 2. We two know the combination. No one else does, except the DG. But. . ."

He paused uncomfortably.

"Well?"

"I suppose I ought to tell you. It can't relate to the case. Last Tuesday Parry—to think he was alive so recently!—found some pages on Ratcliffe's desk. They were important formulae connected with Britex. Ratcliffe denied knowledge of how they got there, and Stone knew nothing about them. Anyway, I put them away."

Cam scribbled thoughtfully.

"Have you ever noticed that the bishop came apart like this?"

Robarts shook his head unhappily.

"Of course I knew they all came apart, but I had never noticed the white bishop especially. And I certainly never felt any desire to bisect them myself."

"Would it surprise you to know that Parry was accustomed to speak of you as someone over whom he had considerable influence and who was, to be blunt, in his power?"

"It certainly would." Robarts flushed angrily. "Except for our games, Parry and I had nothing in common. I think anyone, or at least most people, in the department would confirm that whatever my faults, I cannot be accused of favouritism. If Parry was pretending that he could influence me one way or another, I'm afraid that confirms the opinion some members of my staff had of him."

"Miss Brown and Mr. Ratcliffe, that would be," Cam simplified.

"Yes. Good——"

A sudden thought seemed to strike Robarts and turn him a shade paler than he already was. He cast a quick glance at the scrap of paper lying beneath the white bishop which Cam had used as a paper-weight. Then he sank back in his chair.

Cam frowned.

"Well, Dr. Robarts?" he said severely. "You've thought of something. Speak up, please."

For a moment Robarts seemed to be going to refuse. Then he squared his chin.

"Let me see that paper," he said firmly.

Cam handed it over silently, and the scientist examined it with concentrated interest. He brought out from his pocket another scrap of paper and compared the two. With a sigh he tossed both of them to Cam and gruffly spoke.

"Those two writings are alike." he said. "And they are both Ratcliffe's."

CHAPTER XII

A T seven o'clock on Sunday morning the Inspector was hard at work at his desk. Though not a regular church-goer himself, he was an ardent believer in the seventh day of rest, and these sabbatical labours offended orthodoxy. Not only was there the prospect today of Major Cottle and the Director-General's visit, but Miss Penny would be returning under guard, and must be duly questioned.

It was for Miss Penny that Cam was waiting now. She had been coming by the night train from London, and should have reached Little Biggling about six-forty. Cam had decided, partly on grounds of kindness, partly to strike while she was still presumably in a vulnerable mood, not to keep her waiting for the interview which must follow her return. He had come down to the station early to study the statement she had made when first questioned. Having finished that he had gone on to study the personal files of Ministry witnesses which Robarts had ordered to be sent to him. He learnt from these that Robarts was considered a brilliant, Ratcliffe a capable, Stone an exceedingly promising and Charity a satisfactory worker. Parry's file was very thin, merely consisting of the Director-General's scribbled note suggesting his employment, a carbon copy of the letter of appointment and his letter of acceptance. Robarts' and Stone's files both contained secret reports on their records in Germany, but in both cases the investigators had decided that the men concerned had shown no Nazi proclivities. He also discovered, to his interest and surprise, that Robarts, not Parry, had been mainly responsible for the arrest and conviction of the spy Chatsworth. Certain information had come into his hands which he had handed over to the DG. No wonder, Cam thought sympathetically, that the execution upset him. It can't be very pleasant to send your friends to death, even when they deserve it. A minute in the file recorded Robarts' part in the affair and his request for strict secrecy. As there was no mention of Parry's part in the case in his file, Cam guessed that the rumour that the messenger was responsible for the arrest was presumably another instance of the man's imagination.

Cam next compared the paper bearing the address of Jose Maranda with all the examples of handwriting which these files contained. There was no doubt about it. Ratcliffe's large and flowing hand was the only comparable manuscript. The Inspector was surprised to find himself sighing. The trouble is, he thought, that one doesn't mind a nice young man being a gambler, a spendthrift, a fool; but it's a disappointment when he turns out to be a traitor.

Extracting examples of handwriting from all the files concerned, Cam put them in a large OHMS envelope, together with the scrap of paper from the white bishop in a smaller envelope of its own. He summoned Constable Peak from the outer room.

"Hop on your motor-bicycle, Peak, and take this over to Stroud. I want Mr. Lacey to tell me whether the handwriting contained in this small envelope in here is the same as any of the other examples I enclose. And I want an answer by this afternoon. Drag him out of church, if necessary. You'll have to go to his house, anyway."

Five minutes after Peak had left, while Cam was still pondering over the mysteries of human nature, shuffling outside in the corridor heralded the appearance of a weary-faced but grinning Sergeant Rowley, who, overdue for relief after night duty, had still lingered at the station to see the return of the erring village draper.

"Miss Penny, sir," he announced in sombre tones, and stood aside from the door.

With all the appearance of guilt of a feminine Eugene Aram, Miss Penny entered, her hands clasped before her as though with imaginary gyves upon her wrists. Close on her heels came a vast and muscular London CID man who might more fittingly have been chosen as guard for a professional wrestler. Miss Penny gave the Inspector one frightened look and dropped her eyes fearfully to the floor. The CID man, at a gesture from Cam, placed a chair for her and took her arm to lead her to it. But at his touch she jumped away with startled horror and looked at the Inspector in desperate appeal. The same appeal was reflected in the CID man's gesture of despair to the Inspector, and Cam choked inwardly as he thought of the trip from London with this large and probably genial detective trying to make the elderly lady feel comfortable by elephantine offers of kindness, which she probably mistook for threats of coercion.

"Sit down, Miss Penny," he said gently, and turning to the detective. "Thank you. We shan't need you any more, I'm sure. Have some breakfast here, and Rowley will tell you about trains to London."

The CID man saluted, and with a final despairing glance at Miss Penny left. As the door closed behind him she seemed to take her first breath since arrival, and managed to raise her eyes to the Inspector's. He looked severely back, and she murmured feebly:

"Oh dear, dear me. I *am* in trouble, Mr. Cam."

"You've brought it on yourself," he replied sternly. "It was very silly, Miss Penny, to go rushing off like that, and has been most inconvenient for me. The inquest, even, had to be postponed. Although I know it's not very nice coming back under guard, I couldn't afford to take chances after the way you'd treated me."

This appeal to her personal sympathy reduced Miss Penny to feeble tears. Her days of hysterics seemed, mercifully, thought Cam, to have worn themselves out.

"I'm just a stupid woman," she wept. "No good to anyone— not even myself. But oh, Mr. Cam, if you knew how frightened I was about all these investigations. And my conscience, my conscience! And my dear, dear mother. . .! Dear me, I'm surprised I'm not dead from misery."

She breathed a little sigh and cast a stricken look at the Inspector.

"Well now, Miss Penny, suppose you tell me why you ran away. It's no good hiding anything now, you know."

From Cam's firm but kindly expression the draper gradually seemed to draw enough strength to answer the dreadful question and confess her secret.

"Murder," Miss Penny whispered softly.

"Murder!" Cam echoed, in a stentorian voice which confirmed all Miss Penny's worst fears. Surely the case was not going to be solved just like this—a simple confession. He leaned forward in an agony of anticipation.

Miss Penny seemed to guess whither his thoughts were leading.

"Oh, not *this* murder, Mr. Cam, not *this* one," she said, bridling protestingly.

Cam sank back in his chair with a groan. The case was getting too much for him. Let them call in the Yard. He looked at Miss Penny with a rancorous eye.

"Yes, Mr. Cam, I know, I know! It's terrible! B-but I did it!"

Miss Penny burst again into tears, giving Cam time to recover from his feelings of disbelief and amazement. There was something very unconvincing about all this, he thought dourly. Yet Miss Penny seemed upset enough. He gestured for her to continue.

Beginning each sentence with a sigh and concluding it with a sniff she went on:

"It was my father, Mr. Cam. Perhaps you remember him? Not a very nice man, I'm afraid. Poor Mother! She had such a lot to put up with. And when she'd gone I didn't seem to have anyone—no one at all, Mr. Cam. People said he'd killed her, you know; but that wasn't true. Except that he broke her heart. B-but that doesn't count, does it? I'm sure he didn't mean to do it; but he just didn't think, you see, Mr. Cam. Men *are* like that, aren't they, Mr. Cam? I mean when liquor gets hold of them. Not that you've ever given Mrs. Cam a moment's trouble, I'm sure. Anyway, when Mother died there was just Father and me. And though I *tried,* Mr. Cam—I truly did—I just couldn't love him as I ought, and I was *so* miserable."

Miss Penny had to stop for a few minutes, while Cam grimly examined his boots and remembered what a thoroughly depraved fellow old Fred Penny had been.

"Then Father was very ill, Mr. Cam. He had fits and things. But though it sounds horrible, I was happier then than before because, although I still couldn't love him, I was sorry for him and I could act more like a daughter than before—looking after him, you know, and making him comfortable. I liked that. I didn't feel so wicked, either. But poor Father had a lot of pain. He used to wake in the middle of the night and scream with agony. I was terrified, Mr. Cam. And nothing I could do would help. So Dr. MacDermot gave me some pills to help. They must have been good, because just one would send him off to sleep. Oh dear!"

Miss Penny broke down again. When she resumed her confession, she was speaking hardly above a whisper.

"I kept the pills shut up in the bathroom, Mr. Cam, because I knew how awfully strong they were, and Father often used to threaten to *kill* himself because he said I was such an ungrateful daughter. But one terrible evening we had a quarrel. Father started complaining about Mother. He said what a bad wife she had been to him and how she—she had gone about with other men. Oh, it *wasn't* true, Mr. Cam! It was a terrible, terrible untruth! And oh, I became furious, Mr. Cam. And I flew out of the room before I would do or say something to be sorry about. I went out for a long walk, and didn't come back for hours. But just as I was leaving the house I remembered the pills were beside the bed. And I was so angry, Mr. Cam, so angry that I said to myself, 'Well, he can have them if he wants', because he was so wicked about Mother. When I came back, Mr, Cam, he was dead, and the pills were almost all gone! I wasn't angry any more—but it was too late."

Miss Penny put her face in her hands and sobbed. Cam did not think it infringed on his official dignity to lean over and pat her shoulder gently.

"There, there, Miss Penny! I don't know anyone who wouldn't have made just the same mistake. It was a hard position to be in."

A few minutes later he asked softly:

"But where does Parry come into all this, Miss Penny?"

She lifted her miserable face.

"When Mr. Parry came he was so sympathetic and nice that I was quite happy to have someone to confide in. Of course, I didn't ever come right out and tell him about the pills, because I'd never told anyone. But somehow he questioned me this way and that way, until he guessed what had happened. And *then*, Mr. Cam, he turned out to be quite a different sort of man from what I had thought. Because he said that unless I paid him five shillings a week he would come and tell you all about it, and that I—I would go to gaol or even be hung!"

She stopped a moment to see the Inspector's reaction.

All he said was "Five shillings!" so Miss Penny went on tremulously:

"My life was miserable, Mr. Cam. That man was always about. And I had to pay my five shillings promptly or he would threaten me terribly. But that wasn't the end. Because he said that he had confided my secret to a friend of his, and that if anything happened to him the friend would tell the police! He seemed to think that I might do something to *him,* Mr. Cam! His friend once came to see him, Mr. Cam, and he told me afterwards that he—the friend, you see—had sworn to be avenged if a hair of Mr. Parry's head was hurt. It made my flesh creep, Mr. Cam. I never saw the friend. But I heard him. And then on the night of the murder I heard him again. When I found Mr. Parry dead, and the Doctor said he had been murdered—then I *knew*, Mr. Cam, that before long you would be told about Father. So I *had* to run away, Mr. Cam, and heaven knows what will become of me now!" Miss Penny concluded, looking miserably at the Inspector, awaiting his verdict.

Throughout this grim story he had looked gravely at his boots. It hardly seemed possible that an intelligent adult could have believed that such a story told in a court of law would result in a conviction. But as he raised his eyes and saw that expression of simple and terrified good faith, he realised that this was no intelligent adult, but a rather elderly child. Lord, he thought devoutly, what virgin territory for a confidence trickster like Parry!

He soothed Miss Penny's agony of apprehension by smiling kindly at her. The Unprotected Female in person, he thought. There ought to be an organisation to provide husbands for women like this in order to save them from themselves.

Constable Wootton, just come on duty, was whistling "Another Little Drink Wouldn't Do Us any Harm" in the corridor, and the tune was punctuated by Miss Penny's sniffs. What a beginning to a Sunday! Cam thought, and with an impatient gesture shouted for Wootton. The constable put his head round the door, still struggling into his uniform tunic.

"Get us a pot of tea, please, Wootton. Neither Miss Penny nor I have had breakfast, and I think we both need it."

Miss Penny looked up with watery gratitude. Kindness, the Inspector thought, pays dividends, apart from the fact it's more comfortable. Until the tea arrived and had time to warm their vital organs he chatted cheerfully, though without much response from Miss Penny, about village affairs during the two days since she had left. She was much touched by the story of Mr. Witherspoon's casserole.

"He is so kind," she said tearfully. "So kind; and I'm sure it was an excellent casserole."

"With your needlework and his cooking you'd make a fine pair," said Cam, feeling god-like in his disposal of human destiny.

Miss Penny giggled shyly, and a faint touch of colour came back to her pale cheeks.

"You are *naughty*," she exclaimed, with a trace of her old coyness.

The Inspector returned at last to his questioning on the Parry case. He wanted her to repeat to him what had happened on the night of the murder in the light of her new confession. To some extent the evidence was disappointing. Miss Penny still stuck to her story that she had taken a sleeping-pill ten minutes after Mr. Ratcliffe left. But soon after she had gone upstairs she had heard footsteps going up Parry's staircase and a few minutes later coming down again. The visitor would have been upstairs about five minutes. Cam guessed that this would be Robarts. Five minutes seemed a long time to stand outside a locked door. No, Miss Penny had heard no knocking, but she was clearing up in her kitchen at the time, and perhaps the noise of the dishes would drown any other sound. She heard the footsteps going down while she was locking her flat door, and two minutes later she was in bed.

Pressed by the Inspector, Miss Penny admitted that she had heard other but less definable noises just before she fell asleep. They came from Parry's room, which was on the opposite side of the partition between the two flats. The sound was a series of thumps on the floor at irregular intervals. It was this sound which she had heard before and which, she understood from Parry, were associated with his threatening friend.

"Footsteps, were they?" Cam asked.

"No, not footsteps," she replied. "I couldn't hear those."

"What about this friend?" Cam asked. "Did you ever see him? Did he ever hint who he was?" He reassured her quickly as she looked nervously around. "Don't worry, Miss Penny.

Now you've told your story you're safe as houses. The police won't let you come to any harm."

It struck him as an odd remark from a police officer, after hearing a confession of indirect murder. But it reassured Miss Penny. She answered bravely:

"The other time he came I saw the back of a man disappearing up Mr. Parry's stairs, as I happened to be working late in the shop. And later, upstairs, I heard the thumps, too. But Mr. Parry never said who the man was, and indeed, indeed, Mr. Cam, I didn't want to know, because I would have been even more frightened to know."

Cam looked at her hopelessly.

"Well, what did this man's back look like? Was he well-dressed or not? What sort of coat was it—fitting or box? About what height was he?"

"Dear, dear, Mr. Cam. I'm not very helpful, I'm afraid. You see, he was in the shadow, and I only caught a glimpse. But it was a loose coat, I think. And he was middling tall. But whether he was a gentleman or not I couldn't say. Still, I don't suppose he could be if he was Parry's friend."

"Did you ever mention your troubles to anyone?"

"Oh no, I couldn't do that. I suppose I did hint to Mr. Witherspoon, because he is such an old friend, that I was very unhappy and that Mr. Parry was not the sort of lodger I should have asked for; but I never mentioned Father. I didn't dare."

Cam studied her for a moment or two.

"Did you know where Parry hid his money?" he asked abruptly.

Miss Penny flushed indignantly, and looked at the Inspector with pained surprise.

"Certainly not, Mr. Cam. Why on earth should you think I knew that? It would be of no interest to *me*! Anyone would think I were a thief."

Cam forbore to mention that she had already accused herself of a worse crime than simple theft, but he dealt with her carefully and after a few more questions about Parry's visitor which revealed nothing helpful, he decided that he was merely depressing his visitor by continuing the subject. She ought to have a sleep before further questioning. But where?

"Now, Miss Penny, I suppose you don't want to go back to your shop right away. It has unpleasant associations, hasn't it?"

Miss Penny nodded sadly.

"But where can I go, Mr. Cam? I'd like to be where people wouldn't bother me with questions, if you don't mind."

He rubbed his nose thoughtfully.

"Well, I'd like to say come home with me, but we've got four Ministry typists billeted on us, you know, and there's not a spare inch on the floor. I know!" He hit his thigh resoundingly. "Mr. Witherspoon has two spare rooms and only the billettee—Mr. Stone. He'll be glad to put you up."

Miss Penny cackled protestingly.

"Oh, but, Mr. Cam, I couldn't. Mr. Witherspoon! What would people think! Surely. . ."

Cam overruled her protests gravely.

"Ah, but Mr. Stone will be there for chaperone, Miss Penny. So I don't think anyone will give it a second thought."

Further expostulations that poor Mr. Witherspoon might not find it convenient he put aside by phoning the chemist, who showed the utmost delight at being Miss Penny's host for a few days, and immediately began planning a week's menus. Cam explained that Miss Penny had not yet had breakfast, and the little man announced that his own was just on the table and he would esteem it an honour and a privilege if Miss Penny would come round and share it with him.

In order to put the stamp of official approval upon the *ménage,* Cam accompanied Miss Penny to her temporary home and agreed to have breakfast with the pair, as Mr. Stone had gone to the laboratories and was unavailable for chaperone duties. Mr. Witherspoon had concocted a dish of bottled tomatoes and sausage meat, baked in the oven with a dash of sauce and garnished with a rasher of bacon, which was declared delicious by both his guests. It was, in fact, a pleasant meal, and Miss Penny relaxed visibly under the warming influence of Mr. Witherspoon's attentions and Cam's consideration.

"That man deserved to be killed for causing her such trouble!" the chemist muttered in an aside to Cam, looking quite vindictive.

Cam felt it was rather hard on the murdered man to be blamed for his own death, but perhaps Mr. Witherspoon was hinting at Miss Penny's preliminary troubles.

To get the conversation away from the case, Cam mentioned conversationally that he had driven home with Miss Brown yesterday and had seen the wire netting for Mr. Witherspoon's vegetable patch.

"Wasn't it kind of her!" Mr. Witherspoon exclaimed. "Such a nice girl! And Dr. Robarts brought it round. But I'm not sure that I'll need it now. I think I've frightened the children away. I spoke to them—not harshly, you know, but firmly— and I wouldn't like them to think I didn't trust their promises not to walk on the bed."

"Which children did it?" asked Cam, unsympathetic to these problems of childish honour. "If it was the Barker children I should put in a fence and have it electrically charged into the bargain."

"Oh, I couldn't do *that!*" Mr. Witherspoon was shocked. "I never did find out which children. They all denied it. Perhaps the little things were afraid I might be cross with them."

"And very right, too," commented Miss Penny approvingly, while Cam tried to think of any child in the village so pusillanimous as to be afraid of Mr. Witherspoon's wrath.

After breakfast they went out and examined the unfortunate vegetable beds. The three walked gravely up and down the beds of transplanted seedlings which Mr. Witherspoon and Mr. Stone had together put out during the last few evenings. It had been a great labour for both of them, Mr. Witherspoon sighed, after a hard day's work. He hoped that their achievement was not to be undone by trespassers. It might prove a psychological defence to them if the Inspector could be seen by the neighbours examining the patch. Miss Penny observed that the bedroom windows of the house overlooked the vegetables.

"Well, while I'm here, Mr. Witherspoon," she promised fiercely, "I'll keep an eye on the beds for you!"

She clucked her tongue sympathetically over the devastated row of onions which had been trampled by the children. Mr. Witherspoon shot her what, in their young days, was known as a speaking look, and old Miss Penny really looked quite quaint, Cam thought, when she blushed prettily.

But he could not keep his mind off the case.

"By the way," he asked suddenly, "did I startle you yesterday, Mr. Witherspoon? When I spoke to you from Parry's window, I mean? It was rather sudden, I suppose. . . ."

Mr. Witherspoon blushed as prettily as Miss Penny.

"No, no, Mr. Cam. That was very silly of me. But really I was startled. You see, Mr. Parry himself once spoke to me like that. At least, I spoke to him. I happened to be passing down the alley, and I looked up, and there he was. So, naturally, I said how d'ye do. But he hadn't noticed me as I had just turned the corner from the Market—and he gave me *such* a look. He had a brick in his hand, and I really thought he would throw it at me! So when I saw you it all came back, and I suppose I was a little alarmed. Not that *you* would throw a brick at me, Mr. Cam!"

Miss Penny and he laughed merrily at the little joke, and Cam joined them heartily, with deep satisfaction at this confirmation of his own guesses. So Parry had noticed the brick. And no wonder he was startled to be found moving it if he used it as a hiding-place. Mr. Witherspoon had had a narrow escape.

He left this pastoral interlude about nine-thirty, passing Graham Stone on his way down Cat Alley.

"Hello, Mr. Stone," he called. "Are you returning to take over chaperone duties?"

The young man looked at him blankly, so the Inspector explained.

"Miss Penny is to stay with Mr. Witherspoon for the next few days, and they'll be needing a chaperone, I'm thinking—skittish young pair like that!"

Even the grim-faced Mr. Stone laughed rustily at that.

"I'll take care there's nothing improper, Inspector. So Miss Penny is back, is she? I'm glad she's all right."

"She's a bit nervy still," Cam warned. "I shouldn't mention the case to her if I were you."

"Aren't we all!" exclaimed Stone. "The atmosphere at the Ministry is so jumpy that Wassel House will lose its roof if you don't hurry up and solve the case."

"I'm doing what I can," said Cam uncommunicatively. "Well, good morning."

"Wait a minute." Stone stopped him hastily. "Have you any idea what's up at the House? We've suddenly been invaded by a host of grim-visaged MSR security officers: they arrived last night about tea-time. You know the sort of thing—checking up that we have all our files locked up at night, testing the locks, questioning the messengers. Are *you* responsible?"

Cam was interested. The Director-General certainly let no grass grow under his feet. But his face was manifestly innocent.

"No, Mr. Stone, I plead not guilty. But probably the murder has upset them."

Stone nodded doubtfully, and Cam suddenly thought that it would do no harm if his suspects knew he was now interested in more than the actual death of Parry. He leaned forward confidentially.

"By the way, Mr. Stone, you will remember the official order about Jose Maranda. Were you one of those who were asked by the gentleman for an interview?"

So far as Cam was aware, only one gentleman had been asked for an interview. But Stone was not to know that.

There was a definite trace of uneasiness in the young man's voice, though he replied unhesitatingly:

"No, I didn't know anyone had been asked. Do you mean he's mixed up in this, too?"

Cam nodded, and then shrugged disconsolately.

"Oh well, dead end again. Good morning, Mr. Stone."

Stone barely grunted a reply, but Cam did not feel it was so much bad manners as deep preoccupation. As they parted he looked at the young man over his shoulder, and there was a determined set to his profile which made Cam think that his question had not been as fruitless as the reply had indicated.

Cat Alley was busy that morning. Before he had gone a few steps he met Dr. MacDermot coming out of one of the Alley cottages, and the two friends walked along together.

MacDermot was anxious for more news of the case, and Cam, without much pressing, described to him his own acuteness in discovering Parry's hiding-place for spare cash. As they passed beneath the window he pointed out the system by which it worked. The Doctor was unappreciative; perhaps, Cam guessed, because he had not thought of it himself.

"What an open-air sort of hiding-place! Suppose it rained; the money would get soaked. And, although Cat Alley isn't much frequented, people do come down it, and might see him leaning out of his window. And what's to stop them nipping up to the 'Coach and Horn' bathroom and getting at the money from there? It's an easy reach. No Cam, I think you've proved your point nicely, but I don't really think it was very bright of Parry. And anyway I don't see that it helps the case."

Cam pointed out with dignity that the main thing was to build up a general picture of Parry, and that eventually all these unrelated pieces would fall into place. But the Doctor was obviously not convinced. On another point he was more constructive. Yes, he well remembered the death of Fred Penny.

That was an occasion when no one in the village shed any tears—except Miss Penny, of course, who had a mistaken sense of loyalty. Yes, he remembered, too, that the little bottle of pills had been almost empty, and he guessed the old man must have swallowed them.

Cam looked at his friend in amazement.

"But my God! Jack—why didn't you report it? Do you mean you just let it pass? Surely . . ."

The Inspector was speechless.

To his increasing astonishment, the Doctor burst into mocking laughter.

"Why, you old fool, do you think I gave Penny anything poisonous? Don't you know the fellow was threatening suicide every day? Not because he meant it, but just to frighten his poor daughter. He used to scream in the night, you know, just so as to get her up and fussing round him. Old devil! So I gave him some chalk pills—all impressive-looking, you know, and quite harmless—and when he took them he fell asleep without any trouble. I never told Miss Penny, because she wouldn't have thought it honest! No, if old Penny took those pills he probably *thought* he was committing suicide, and then died of fright because his daughter didn't come running when he shouted blue murder. Damn good death for a man like that!"

As they parted, Cam was laughing quietly to himself, but with a shade of melancholy. It was not MacDermot's fault—he could not know—but to think of the draper believing herself guilty of murder for so many years—and just because of some chalk pills.

★★★

At two o'clock the Inspector was back at his desk, chatting uneasily with Robarts, Ratcliffe and Stone. All three were obviously mystified by the meeting and somewhat peeved by being kept out of the secret. Even Robarts did not know why the DG had decided to summon them all by telegram that morning, and he looked weary-eyed and bad-tempered after a sleepless night. The Inspector himself was feeling cantankerous about the loss of his Sunday nap and the prospect of a difficult interview with the Director-General. At least, he thought, I shall be behind the desk this time. A man always feels more confident and masterful in his own office, with his own desk as a moral and physical support. But perhaps the Chief Constable would take the chair.

A rattling of doors outside and the hastening footsteps of Constable Wootton announced the arrival of the DG and the Chief Constable, and the three men stiffened unconsciously. The door was flung open, and the constable hardly had time to announce Sir Arnold when he slipped past him and into the office. The men jumped to their feet, and the Inspector nodded for Wootton to leave them. Cam looked enquiringly at Major Cottle, indicating the desk chair.

"No, no, Cam. I think you'd better run this. Do you agree, sir?"

Sir Arnold nodded curtly, and took a seat by the window. Cam was astonished at the change in his appearance. On Thursday he had looked worried, but today he was definitely haggard. Of course a leakage like this meant a lot to a man in his position. It might even, if bad organisation was proved, jeopardise his post. But worry had not softened his sharp tongue.

"I've missed a most important meeting because of this discovery, Inspector. I hope you can compensate for that by showing some progress in the case. With Major Cottle's permission I suggest you outline for us how the case as a whole stands at present."

Cam hesitated a moment. He wanted the rest of his audience, except the Chief Constable, who was in on the secret, to think that it was only the DG's pressure that forced him to be frank in front of them. He was anxious that they should not suspect that he had himself phoned Major Cottle and Sir Arnold this morning and asked that the three men should be invited to the meeting. It was a gamble, but in the interests of a quick solution he had reached the decision that by laying his cards on the table he might force the culprit to show his hand. In any case, it would be interesting to see the men's reactions. Perhaps none of them was guilty. One, he knew, was not. But Cam was a great believer in surprise tactics, and he hoped that his apparently artless description of the facts—or some of them—now at his disposal might provoke some interesting remarks from his victims.

"Well, sir," he said doubtfully, "it may be a bit awkward, because I shall have to mention names, and I don't want any hurt feelings. . . ."

The Director-General looked at him sternly.

"This is no time to bother about feelings, Inspector. I asked for these gentlemen to be present because the case has now become one directly affecting everyone in the department. Up to now, I confess, I had thought Parry's murder was the act of some villager. Now I am not sure. And I want to show my trust in three of the leading members of the staff here, by entrusting them with the facts of the case. Even if one of them is the guilty person"—here the DG cast a terrible look at the three men—"let him be assured that his race is almost run. But I refuse to believe that any of you gentlemen could be guilty of this terrible thing. So proceed, Cam, as if I were the only one present."

Cam was almost convinced himself that it was Sir Arnold who had decided to call in the three staff members. The latter were all looking suitably impressed, he noticed, though Ratcliffe had a faintly bewildered air, since the fact that Britex security was involved was still unknown to him and he was, apparently, unable to believe that the DG would refer to the murder of a messenger as "this terrible thing"—with real emotion in his voice.

With a rather mischievous look around him Cam began:

"It is too complicated a case to reduce to a few sentences, sir. There are, for instance, an unusual number of suspects. Let me begin by saying I have not yet made up my mind who is guilty, though I have made a few good guesses. I am going to tell you briefly the case against each of the suspects. You must forgive me if occasionally I sound as if I were speaking of the actual criminal, not just a suspect. It saves a lot of 'ifs' and 'buts'."

Sir Arnold grunted impatiently, while the other men looked at Cam nervously.

"My first suspect is Miss Penny—the village draper. She has always been considered in this village to be a most respectable woman, but at the same time we know that she has some bad blood in her through her father, a notorious drunkard and waster. At first Miss Penny appeared the unlikeliest of suspects in a case like this, despite the fact that she had a better opportunity than anyone else—an empty house, a key to the bedroom, a helpless victim and all night to hide her traces. Yet, in view of Miss Penny's reputation and character, I found it difficult to consider her a serious possibility. Even when she ran away from the village I thought it merely an indication of her hysterical excitability. But second thoughts have shown that perhaps this excitability was the root of the whole case. Miss Penny was terrified of Parry. He had for months threatened her with prison or worse on account of some pretended crime committed many years ago. I will not go into it, but let me assure you she was deceived by a fantastic story that only a very simple-minded person could believe. Miss Penny was very simple-minded, and I believe that under the strain of this daily terror her mind may gradually have given way. Last Wednesday evening Parry was brought home drunk by Mr. Ratcliffe. He was locked in his room, and the key was placed in Miss Penny's own hiding-place. It was the chance of a lifetime for Miss Penny to rid herself of the lodger. Her terror of the man was at this point strengthened by an almost pathological detestation of drunkenness, stemming from the days when her father burdened her life.

"Having access to the room, the details of the murder offer no difficulties, except, I would point out to you; that the murderer used several strokes to kill Parry—more the sign of a hysterical woman than a determined man. She had all night to concoct her story, before she phoned Dr. MacDermot with news of the murder. This story was simply that she had heard and seen nothing, owing to the sleeping-pill she had taken. But under the strain of questioning, her strength of will, which had been bolstered by hysteria, began to crack, and full realisation of her position drove her to madness. She tried to escape, but wildly, without purpose. Brought back, she concocted another story—a story which probably sounded convincing to her half-crazed mind, but, to any normal human being, like a penny-thriller. That is why I say, gentlemen, that Miss Penny might have committed this crime, but she could never be hanged, because if she did it she was, and is, mad."

There was a pause for a moment. Cam looked around the men. Ratcliffe was looking aghast. Cam's method of putting theories as though they were facts had obviously overcome him. Robarts was faintly surprised, Stone glum as ever, Major Cottle rather absent-minded, the Director-General thoughtful. The latter broke the silence.

"But what on earth had that to do with Britex? You seem to be rather off the track."

Robarts shifted uneasily, while Ratcliffe looked up with interest. It was his first intimation that the meeting had anything to do with Britex. Cam returned Sir Arnold's question with stony confidence.

"I'm sorry, sir, but until I get orders to the contrary, my job is to investigate the Parry murder. I have no *proof* yet that it was because of his espionage activities, if any, that he was murdered. It may have been. I shall show you how in a moment. But there were a number of people with motives for murdering Parry who certainly were not spies. The mystery of the South American articles may be a quite different case from the murder."

He looked for support to the Major.

"That's certainly right, Sir Arnold. We're local police, you know, and the first thing for us, of course, is to solve the murder."

"Then what on earth am I here for?" asked the DG irritably.

Major Cottle answered for Cam, and in a tone that the Inspector would have hesitated to use.

"Because if we find out who murdered Parry we may at least find out something about his private life which will help solve the more important problem of who his espionage contacts were. That is intelligent procedure, isn't it?"

Unexpectedly the Director-General smiled, and signalled for Cam to go on.

"My next case is against James Ramsden, the hedger—also no connection with Britex, sir. In his case the motive was simple jealousy. Mrs. Ramsden, after her unpleasant experience with Parry on Wednesday night, left him in a highly excited state, and when she met her husband at the junction of Bramble and High Streets she blurted out to him what had happened. If she had been in a calmer state she would never have been so stupid, because she knew what her husband's temper was like. Well, when he had heard his wife's story, Ramsden flew into a passion and rushed down the Market in time to see Ratcliffe and Parry crossing into Cat Alley, and the draper's shop. He confesses that he hid himself in the 'Coach and Horn' back yard. What he did not confess, but what we can prove, is that from that position, through the unshaded windows, he could have seen Ratcliffe, when he came down from Parry's room, hide the key in Miss Penny's box. So when Ratcliffe had gone and Miss Penny returned upstairs and Mr. Robarts had paid his brief visit, Ramsden climbed through the shop-window, which had had a broken lock some time, removed the key from the box and went up to Parry's room. When he had killed the messenger he returned the key to its hiding-place and left the shop. His idea was to thumb a ride from a passing car and get as far away from Little Biggling as possible in order to have a good alibi ready for the day of discovery. Unfortunately the Vicar saw him, and he has been forced to fall back on the feeble excuse that he simply got tired of waiting—and decided to go off for a walk instead."

"That sounds a good case," said the Director-General, approvingly.

Major Cottle shook his head doubtfully.

"In both cases," he said, "you ignore the fact about the Ministry notepaper or memoranda burnt in the fire. Can you fit them in?"

Cam shook his head.

"Not very well, unless Parry was awake enough, when Ratcliffe left him, to feel cold, and staggered across to the fire and threw some paper on. He might do that if he didn't feel well enough—or hadn't the sense to shovel coal on."

The Chief Constable agreed.

"Well, temperamentally he's the likeliest suspect. I can't believe Miss Penny is mad, Cam. Simple, perhaps, but incapable of violence."

Cam shrugged.

"My next suspect is Mr. Ratcliffe."

There was a gasp from Ratcliffe, echoed by Stone, at this sudden declaration. Robarts, Major Cottle and Sir Arnold remained impassive.

"You don't mind, Mr. Ratcliffe?" asked Cam tenderly.

"Oh no, no! Why should I mind?" the young man muttered.

"Mr. Ratcliffe was always a favourite suspect of mine," Cam continued, with a genial look at the other's gloomy face. "Because if Mr. Ratcliffe did it, there was no more question of how the murderer got in. We all know. It was too easy. All he did was carry the unconscious man upstairs, unlock the room with his victim's key and hit him with the walking-stick he carried on his walk over Wassel Peak, and which, I have observed, is an unusually tough one. Then Mr. Ratcliffe burnt some papers in that room which were of interest to him. He has two possible motives. One, which he has admitted, and which is purely personal, Sir Arnold, is known to you, and I will not discuss it except to say that it is a very adequate motive—if it is true. His second motive"—Cam paused tantalisingly—"is more serious. And perhaps. Sir Arnold, you would like to explain the situation as regards Britex."

The Director-General took over with quick authority. Briefly he recounted to the staff members the story which Cam had heard from Major Cottle the day before. While he talked, Cam examined his victims. Robarts, who had heard part of the story before, looked merely depressed. Stone and Ratcliffe listened with horror, though whether for personal or public reasons it was difficult to tell.

At the end of his strictly factual tale the DG abruptly signalled to the Inspector and sank back in his chair. Speaking quietly after the other's abrupt tones, Cam went on:

"I have discovered evidence that Mr. Jose Maranda, a South American agent of whose activities you are all aware, and who seems the likeliest intermediary for the leakage, was in touch with someone at Wassel House. A scrap of paper with his name and address on it was discovered hidden in Parry's room. That name and address was written, apparently, Mr. Ratcliffe, in your handwriting."

With an abrupt gesture Cam opened a desk drawer, brought out the paper and threw it on the desk in front of Ratcliffe. The young man looked at it dazedly under the gaze of the rest of the group. He shook his head slowly, as much in confusion as in negation.

"No, sir," he said, more to the DG than to Cam, "It looks like me, but I never wrote it—I've never seen it before."

There was silence in the little room, broken by Cam taking back the scrap of paper and putting it away.

"Quite likely," he said calmly. "As a matter of fact, that's forged. I just had the report from Stroud before we met."

This time the surprise included the Major and Sir Arnold. But the news did not seem to please or relieve Ratcliffe. He only looked more bewildered than ever.

"Can you tell who did the forging?" asked Sir Arnold quickly.

"No, sir. That's impossible. It's even possible to forge one's own handwriting by copying it upside down."

Ratcliffe swallowed a nervous laugh, and the DG looked at the unhappy man critically.

"But even Mr. Ratcliffe, Inspector, would surely have taken more pains to hide his tracks after the murder. Your case is almost too obvious. Surely he took some steps to direct your attention elsewhere—assuming, of course, that Mr. Ratcliffe *is* the murderer, either for the first or the second motive."

"That's the beauty of it," Cam explained enthusiastically. "Everything he did after the murder points *to* him. He shut and locked the window, for instance, when it would have been far simpler to leave it open and then leave us to suspect that someone had come in that way after he left. And again, he hid the key for Miss Penny, instead of suggesting that they simply leave it in the lock of Party's room—a suggestion she would undoubtedly have accepted. So naturally I couldn't think that anyone could be such a fool as to leave all the clues pointing his way, and I assumed he must be acting in all innocence. But isn't that, perhaps, what he intended me to think? Or perhaps we are overestimating his subtlety. Perhaps, having acted on the spur of the moment—for I do not think Mr. Ratcliffe had planned this crime—he simply acted without thought, stunned by the horror of his act."

"That's more like it," Ratcliffe commented bitterly. "Make me stupid, not malevolent. That's much more in character."

He subsided into deep gloom, only to be startled into a groan by Cam's next words.

"My next suspect is Dr. Robarts."

CHAPTER XIII

$\mathbf{C}$AM continued quietly, his eyes moving from listener to listener as he spoke.

"In the case against Dr. Robarts two points are outstanding. First, Dr. Robarts' chess set was, we know, used once, and might have been used many times before, as a hiding-place for highly secret information. Secondly, Dr. Robarts' intimacy with Parry is in striking contrast to the general suspicion which was felt about the messenger. Dr. Robarts had dismissed—rather high-handedly, perhaps—several charges by members of his staff that Parry was guilty of reading private correspondence. It is known that Dr. Robarts made a practice of lending Parry his chess set—this cache for secret information, remember—and that on one occasion at least he had the key to Parry's room, although he claims to have returned it several weeks ago. It is evidence of a close relationship between the two men, I think, that Parry should lend his key to Dr. Robarts, while against everyone else he kept his room severely locked. Perhaps this relationship had deeper roots than a mutual pleasure in chess. Dr. Robarts had excellent opportunities for obtaining information highly valuable to foreign commercial agents. He earns £1500 a year in this country as a civil Servant. For the same expenditure of time and thought in a commercial concern he might earn £10,000. Moreover, Britex, invented and perfected by him, brings him no direct benefits except prestige—not a very valuable reward if one is never able, so to speak, to 'cash in on it.' There was certainly temptation, therefore, to sell these secrets, which were in a sense his own property, as they were the product of his own mind. Parry would be a useful associate, as he went frequently up to London and could dispose of the material which Robarts provided . . ."

"One thing," the DG interrupted. "When Britex was invented I discussed with Dr. Robarts the question of some special reward—a title, promotion, advance in salary. He refused, saying he was quite adequately paid, wouldn't like further promotion and would detest a title. As long as Britex was not used as a private monopoly, he was quite satisfied."

"Very fine," said the Major approvingly. "But of course it may have been a bluff. And you couldn't offer him anything like a South American combine could. But why was the partnership dissolved, Cam?"

Cam shrugged his shoulders.

"We know Dr. Robarts and Parry had a disagreement during their chess game on Wednesday night. Dr. Robarts claims it was because he challenged Parry on the question of reading private correspondence. But perhaps it was because Parry was attempting to blackmail him with threats of turning King's Evidence or, less likely, refusing to co-operate further."

He looked at Robarts questioningly, but the latter simply nodded politely.

"But how did he get in?" asked Ratcliffe, joining in with zest. "And what about a weapon? I bet he hasn't anything as good as my walking-stick."

Cam smiled.

"Well, we have only his word for it that he returned Parry's key. If they were working as partners, it's more likely he kept it, isn't it? And as for the weapon—there is a bar loose in Dr. Robarts' bed. It is a brass bed, and the bar would make a very handy weapon to slip in one's pocket. You will remember that Dr. Robarts called at his lodgings before he went out for the evening."

"Oh, bravo!" Ratcliffe exclaimed. "But what will Mrs. Cottenham say when she hears you've been using her bed for illegal purposes, Robarts?"

The DG subdued the young man with a glance.

"The burnt papers in the fireplace, I suppose, would be any secret papers that Parry had in the room. But Robarts was only upstairs five minutes, wasn't he? That doesn't seem very long."

"It's long enough when you know exactly what you are going to do," said Cam, "And Dr. Robarts, unlike Ratcliffe, would have planned his crime."

"And am I," asked Robarts, rather grimly, "supposed to have forged Ratcliffe's writing and hidden it in my chess men to lead suspicion that way? Why?"

"I'm afraid if you did that, Dr. Robarts, it was just spite. You had certain reasons to be jealous of Mr. Ratcliffe, hadn't you?"

The two men avoided each other's look with some embarrassment.

"What utter rot!" exclaimed Ratcliffe. "You must have terrible nightmares, inspector—or do you read the women's magazines?"

In the awkward pause that followed, Cam again surveyed his victims. Cottle and the DG remained as expressionless as though Cam had been describing the case against some obscure villager. Robarts was looking more unhappy than alarmed. Stone and Ratcliffe, however, were looking both uneasy and embarrassed.

Cam went ruthlessly on:

"My next suspect is Mr. Stone."

Stone's expression of embarrassment turned to one of consternation. Even Robarts' calm was broken momentarily, and he looked sharply at Cam. A yelp of slightly hysterical laughter from Ratcliffe drew an angry look from the DG. The Inspector went on firmly:

"The clues pointing to Mr. Stone are that first he was one of the two men who had easy access to the secret information published in South America and, secondly, he was comparatively friendly with Parry. All the arguments I have suggested which might have led Dr. Robarts to sell the secret and to use Parry as a partner also apply to Mr. Stone."

He paused a moment, and Stone broke in protestingly:

"But I don't think I spoke to Parry more than twice in my life. Surely, sir . . ."

He turned to Sir Arnold, but a glance quelled him abruptly. Cam, watching Robarts, saw no change in the scientist's expression.

"Mr. Stone also had opportunity for the murder," the Inspector continued quietly. "During the first half-hour after he returned to his lodgings, Mr. Witherspoon, the only other occupant of the house, was in the bathroom. No doubt Mr. Stone is aware from bitter experience that Mr. Witherspoon likes a 'good soak'. This time it may have served him well, because during that half-hour he could get out of his window by way of the tool-shed roof beneath his window, cross the vegetable garden to the side gate into Cat Alley. (Mr. Witherspoon has complained of children trampling over his seed-beds, and told me this morning that it had now stopped—since the murder, you notice.) Once into Cat Alley, Mr. Stone could get to Parry's lodgings in a moment—a matter of twenty yards or so—and let himself in by the key which, if we accept the fact he was Parry's espionage collaborator, he probably had. You may not know that as Dr. Robarts was leaving Parry's lodgings he claims to have heard footsteps coming up the alley behind him. Perhaps that was Mr. Stone."

"I am afraid," interrupted Stone again, "that I was in no fit state to undertake all these activities. Dr. Robarts will confirm that I was drunk on Wednesday night, so will Acton. If I had tried to get out of the window, which in any case would be difficult because of my leg, I should probably have broken my neck."

"It is not difficult to feign intoxication," Cam said politely, but feeling rather a cad at having forgotten the crippled leg.

He laid down his pencil and sat back. He had not placed all his cards on the table, but enough to startle his audience. It was now up to Sir Arnold to make the next move.

When the Director-General spoke, after a pause of several minutes, it was to turn to the members of his staff and say:

"I think you gentlemen will understand why I am giving you all a week's leave. In a very short time we hope that the Inspector will be able to make his choice among such a rich supply of suspects. Personally, gentlemen, I do not and cannot believe that it is a member of my staff who committed this murder. But until we are all cleared of suspicion it would be most uncomfortable and unpleasant for us to frequent the office. The Inspector has been most frank in telling each of you exactly where you stand *vis-à-vis* the police. In the light of what you now know it should be easier for you to consider what information you still hold which would be of use to the Inspector in his investigations. You all realise the importance of maintaining the secrecy of our research. Hitherto we have even tried to conceal the fact that work is being done on the subject. We have failed in that. Soon all the textile world will know from South America. But the important details of production are still, we think, secret. These must be guarded. Obviously someone has been undermining the essential security of Wassel House. I must ask you to put aside personal friendship or admiration and to consider it your imperative duty to report anything suspicious or unusual in the actions of your associates which may have come to your attention. Dr. Robarts will excuse me, I am sure, inviting Mr. Ratcliffe and Mr. Stone to this meeting over his head, as it were, but in a case like this I thought it best to treat you all as 'equal in the sight of the law.'"

Robarts nodded solemnly as the Director-General paused a moment and looked round the ring of tense faces.

"That is the reason I requested your presence at this meeting, gentlemen. Personally I trust you all. I want you all on an equal footing. If this meeting and the Inspector's manner have alarmed you, remember that this is no time for schoolboy honour, and that the man who is responsible for taking the Britex secret, as well as the murderer of Parry, must be traced without waste of time. I ask you to leave now. When you have thought carefully about the case, and if you decide you can give further help, come back either to Mr. Cam tonight, or to me tomorrow at the office. And remember, all of you, the responsibility which we have, not only towards our department, but towards the whole country."

His voice faltered slightly as he stopped, and he turned his face away towards the window. Silently the three men got up and trooped out. Cam was reminded of the headmaster's study and the inspirational sermons of his childhood. But even he was impressed by the evident sincerity and emotion with which that usually impassive man, the Director-General, had spoken. He found it difficult to break the silence which fell on the room as they were left alone. For a minute or two they remained motionless, Sir Arnold still looking into the distance beyond the window, Major Cottle examining his finger-nails and Cam gazing fixedly at his blotter.

At last Sir Arnold Conway moved, and as his eyes came back to the room, Cam raised his to meet them.

"And which of your suspects do you really think did it?" asked the DG softly.

"Of those suspects?" asked Cam. "I don't know. Perhaps none of them." He looked at Major Cottle, who nodded slightly. "Something is still missing in this case. I haven't got all the pieces in the jigsaw—or, if I have, I haven't managed to fit them all together yet. Sometimes I think I'm playing with three or four puzzles all at the same time. Damn Parry and his curiosity and his everlasting tricks!" he ended, with quiet venom.

Sir Arnold did not seem surprised, but looked at him with a lurking humour Cam had never seen before. Again he asked a question.

"You imply you have other suspects. Who?"

Cam remained silent, but the Chief Constable spoke up for him.

"Yourself, sir," he said quietly.

In the silence that followed, the Director-General's expression gradually changed. To Cam's amazement, its hard efficiency and self-control melted into a rather wistful humour. There was certainly no surprise or shock manifested. On the contrary he seemed to find some entertainment in the situation.

"But why?" he asked rather plaintively.

Cam shifted uneasily. He felt as if he were the one under suspicion. If he were wrong, this was the most suicidal action of his career. If he were right, it was the most agonising duty. He looked desperately at Major Cottle, who again answered.

"At seven o'clock on the night of the murder, Sir Arnold, you left Wassel House to dine with friends in Stroud—Sir Walter Gilpin. You reached there at seven-thirty, and dismissed your driver, who has relatives in Stroud. You told him that he could stay the night and you would drive yourself back. At nine o'clock you left Sir Walter's on the excuse of feeling extremely tired and needing an early night. At ten-thirty you arrived back at Wassel House and were let in by the porter to the laboratories flat. Between nine and ten-thirty your time is unaccounted for. It is a half-hour drive to Stroud. You have an unaccounted-for hour, sir, during which to park your car, walk into Little Biggling and visit James Parry."

"But why?" repeated the DG. "Why should I do such a fantastic thing?"

He seemed genuinely surprised.

"You are a proud man," Major Cottle said earnestly and rather gently. "You have much to be proud of—including the fact that you rose from poverty, by your own strength of will and mind, to a position of great honour and brilliance. It is impertinent of me to mention this. Because it is not of that rise you are proud. You do not want to be pointed out as a freak who has by some fluke climbed the whole way up the ladder, from bottom to top. You want to be judged simply on your merits as an intellectual and cultured man. As a Civil

Servant you do not, fortunately, suffer from much publicity, and habit has made you hate it. Few people know anything about your early life. We know only a little more than most people. But I put it to you, sir, that you were born in Bolton, that your father, James Conway, died when you were still an infant, and that your mother died soon after when she gave birth to a son by her second husband. Her second husband's name was Parry, and James Parry was this son and your half-brother. But you never saw him, or even knew of him, as a child, because when your father died and your mother re-married, your father's family in Hull took you in and raised you. They were respectable small tradespeople, and managed to give you a good education, while James Parry and his other half-brother, Robert Parry, were running wild in the streets. Of the years between I know nothing, but a year ago James Parry was appointed to the Ministry to be your personal messenger—and at your personal request. I suggest that Parry came to you a year ago with the information that he knew of your relationship and was prepared to capitalise on it, and that he blackmailed you into appointing him. And, knowing Parry, no doubt that was not the end of the blackmail!" the Major concluded. "Ample reason for murder, Sir Arnold."

"The Inspector has been busy," said the DG courteously, turning to Cam. "Just out of curiosity, what gave you the idea?"

The Inspector grimly fiddled with his pencils and replied expressionlessly.

"I was rather puzzled by that unexplained hour on Wednesday night when I got the report on your movements which my man collected as part of the routine of the case. But my first real hint was when I noticed this morning in Parry's personal file that you had yourself requested his appointment. Yet, if you remember, when I saw you last Thursday you seemed to have difficulty in even remembering his name. That struck me as rather odd. And that reminded me of another thing—Robert Parry told me yesterday that his half-brother's mother had been married to a Conway, and that James Parry sometimes used that name before he joined the Ministry. At the time it struck me as an amusing coincidence. But Parry had also said, apparently, that he had a friend at the Ministry who was 'just like a brother' and over whom he had some influence. When I first heard this phrase I thought it was used figuratively—and that is certainly how Parry meant it to be understood. But as soon as I began to suspect that there was a relationship between you two I also guessed there might be a deeper—or, rather, a more direct—meaning to the phrase: that you were in truth his brother. A couple of telephone calls to Bolton and Hull this morning proved my suspicions—or at least made them appear extremely probable. So I spoke to Major Cottle."

Sir Arnold smiled.

"I won't insult your intelligence by denying the main structure of your thesis, Mr. Cam. Perhaps you gentlemen would like, in confidence, my own version."

Cam nodded, rather embarrassed.

"Well, then, your family genealogy is remarkably correct. My mother was one of those weak little waitress types who do very little good and not much harm in the world. Her first husband was my father, a skilled mechanic of considerable strength of character who might have made her into something. Unfortunately he died when I was six months old, and three months later she married again, a building labourer of bad reputation and low intelligence. She died giving birth to her first child by this man. Fortunately for myself, my grandparents had already removed me from her care—I don't think she cared much—and henceforth I was raised by them in Hull. They were ill-educated, rough people themselves, but they took a pride in my accomplishments and, without understanding but with great faith, helped me in the struggle to rise out of their own poverty and ignorance to a richer life. I loved and respected them."

The Director-General shut his eyes for a moment. But when he opened them his face hardened.

"The rest of my early life I loathed. The drudgery, the meanness, the sordid, crowded kitchen life! How I despised all those slatternly women and their jeers at any poor girl who tried to improve herself with a little extra care for her person and her clothes. They said she was putting on airs if she looked too clean! And the men were no better. For all their squabbles and petty jealousies, they were united in attacking and despising any man who dared to be different by seeking for knowledge rather than drink, and read philosophy rather than the racing news. There were exceptions, of course, and some of those men I still know; but the rest of the crew I threw out of my boat long ago! No, Inspector, I admit I despise the masses. I despise most individuals, when it comes to that! And as far as possible I associate with very few of them. Fortunately, in my position that is not difficult. No one knows much about me except that I am supposed to be brilliant. They are right. I am. And that, I consider, is all that it is necessary for anyone except my closest friends to know. I seek no sympathy, no understanding—only respect. As long as I do my duty and exercise my talents for my country, why should I submit to examination of my private life by strangers?"

The DG paused in the heat of the question. Receiving no answer he went on more quietly:

"What was my disgust, therefore, when last year a man called James Parry found his way to my office at the Ministry and announced that he was my long-lost half-brother. It was my first intimation that I had a half-brother, but he promptly produced birth certificates to prove it. My first instinct was to say how d'ye do and have him shown out. Even if he was my half-brother, I felt no responsibility towards him—and James Parry never looked other than he was—a scoundrel. Unfortunately he started to talk, and unfortunately I listened. He said that he knew it was awkward for a man like myself to have such a brother, and that he was ready to efface himself for my benefit. Nor did he want any money from me. That, he said, was unbrotherly! But he did want a job, and he would like to be a messenger. Could I fix it up? Mixed up in this argument was the shadow of a threat that unless I did something for him the papers might find out that my brother was walking the streets and that I had refused to help him. I knew what bad publicity can do, from the fate of many of my Ministers. That was bad publicity. At that time I was in need of a personal messenger. It would look odd if I started making appointments to the ordinary messenger staff. But it was not unusual to appoint one's personal attendant. So everything conspired to make it seem easy and natural to appoint Parry and make an end of the problem. Of course it was not the end. You have guessed it. It was the beginning of a whole series of petty blackmails, little degrading familiarities, a mean and despicable understanding with a man who had all the vices and none of the virtues of his class."

Unable to restrain himself, Sir Arnold got up and paced restlessly up and down the room. Cam watched him with undisguised curiosity, but just as he was about to ask a question, the Director-General answered it.

"When I came down this week to Wassel House I made an appointment with Parry. I wanted to bribe him, to persuade him, to take a position I had arranged for him in Scotland— where I would not forever be reminded of his presence by little humble services and familiar winks when he knew no one was watching. I never expected to be rid of him entirely until death did us part. I knew that, once having fixed his grappling-irons into me, he would never let go, and that by letter or in person I would always be plagued. But it would be something not to see him every day. I had found him a post as caretaker in a Glasgow block of flats. I wanted to make him go, so I told him on Wednesday afternoon to meet me by the stream below Wassel House about nine-thirty. That was why

I left Sir Walter's early. I parked the car down a lane when I returned and went down to the stream. I waited there until a quarter-past ten, and Parry did not turn up. There was nothing I could do except collect the car and return to Wassel House for bed." Sir Arnold paused a moment and smiled wryly. "I will not trifle with you, Major Cottle, by asserting that I did not kill Parry—that, curiously enough, I had never thought of that solution, that, even if I had, I have too much respect for the police to provoke them thus. If you did not believe me it would be insulting, and if you did, without further evidence, it would be absurd."

Major Cottle and Cam took deep breaths. The former spoke up.

"Well, that's very interesting, sir," he said, in a hearty voice as though he had been listening to the latest football results. "It puts quite a new complexion on the case, doesn't it? Perhaps I ought to question you now, but if you don't mind I'll think about it a bit more and then let you know."

"In other words," said the DG wryly, "I may go now. Well, gentlemen, I don't respect you less for your suspicions, but I hope sincerely for my sake now, as well as the country's, that you don't take long in selecting the right murderer. I would be within my rights, you know, to ask my Minister to request the Home Secretary to take over from here." He hesitated. "But, frankly, I would prefer not. I like the way you work. It would be better in your hands. And though I shall have to tell my Minister some day"—he grinned wryly—"I should prefer to put off the evil hour until I am proved innocent. Of course you may think differently. . . . Good afternoon, gentlemen. You can get hold of me at my London office for the next twenty-four hours."

He got up abruptly and without further formality left the room.

Left alone with such suddenness, the two men looked at each other uncertainly.

"Well," the Major said finally. "Your guess was certainly right, Cam. I'm glad you had the courage to phone me about it."

"But it can't have been him," exclaimed Cam desperately. "Surely, sir, he couldn't be mixed up in the Britex affair. I knew there was something odd about his relations with Parry. But that was a perfectly reasonable story he told us."

The Major shook his head.

"You wouldn't accept the bare word of any other suspect so easily, Cam. Perhaps the DG has his monetary troubles, too. And it would be a safe gamble that no one would suspect him." He paused a moment.

"No, you're right. It's fantastic. High Government officials just don't do that sort of thing. But you can't ignore him, anyway."

There was a depressed silence for several minutes while the two men gloomily considered the impossibility of the situation.

"Will you speak to the Minister, sir?" asked Cam. "Or the Home Secretary?"

The Major sighed.

"I suppose I should, but I don't think I shall. After all, if Sir Arnold's story is true he hasn't done anything wrong at all. And it's a serious thing to start throwing suspicion at Civil Servants—can ruin their career, even if they're not true. I'll keep it dark, say, until tomorrow evening. If you're still no nearer a solution I'll go up to Town and see the Home Secretary. It means bringing in the Yard," he added gloomily, and got up. "I don't feel intelligent enough at the moment to discuss the rest of the meeting, Cam. Come round to Wootton-under-Edge tomorrow morning and we'll talk about it."

He stalked out, and Cam got up to pace the room, restlessly shaking his head from side to side like a great bear. It was a fantastic situation that he—a mere Inspector—should have charge of the destiny of one of the most respected men in the country. Listening to Sir Arnold's story he had forgotten for a moment who he was—what he was—and had judged it purely on its merits. And certainly the story was not without flaws. Had the DG really been so innocent as never to ponder how he could finally and for ever rid himself of the incubus? What were the words that slipped out—grappled together "until death do us part"? Even a Civil Servant, surely, has his weak moments, his passionate impulses. And perhaps there was more to the story than the DG had told. Perhaps Parry, on the strength of an increased income from spying—or from blackmailing Ratcliffe—was threatening to throw over the whole agreement and to tell his story to the Press, just for the fun of it. Or perhaps he was asking for more money than the DG—never a wealthy man—could provide.

He stopped by the window and gazed moodily at a gaggle of police geese marching purposefully across the lawn.

All his satisfaction in the case had evaporated. For, after all, where was he? He had a whole legion of suspects and not one certainty—clues by the gross and not one bit of proof. That damn key, he thought bitterly. If only there were a key.

And that forged address of Jose Maranda. Why should someone want to implicate Ratcliffe? Or had his own suggestion that Ratcliffe forged his own writing hit the mark? He might do it if he wanted the police to think that Robarts was the criminal and was, out of jealousy, trying to lead suspicion to him. Every fool knows that forgery is the most difficult of all arts and that the police are on to every turn of it. So it was not likely that Robarts would use such a clumsy method or was it? He wouldn't know much about police methods.

The sounds of the police-station drifted in to him through the door and the open window—Wootton whistling some jazz tune, the scratching of a pen in the office, an occasional high-pitched remark from some woman complaining about police efficiency. And quite right, too, thought Cam bitterly.

When you come down to it, we can't do much without a little cooperation from the criminal!

The medley of footsteps down the corridor took form and concentrated into the irregular thump of a lame man approaching the door. Cam swung abruptly from the window, and as Stone opened the door he was standing behind the desk looking at some papers. He smiled genially as the young man entered.

"Well, Mr. Stone. I'm certainly glad to see you," he roared, the picture of self-confidence. "You've interrupted some rather gloomy thoughts."

Stone grunted without enthusiasm and took a chair, rubbing his leg nervously, as if it were aching.

"And what can I do for you?" asked Cam cheerfully, his depression quite forgotten. "Or, rather, what can you do for me?"

Stone looked at him unpleasantly.

"Well, I'm glad you're feeling happy, anyway. I suppose to a professional policeman there's always a certain pleasure in hounding some poor devil to death."

Cam laughed.

"Well, it has a fascination. But I suppose you think me sadistic."

Stone obviously did.

"I would have spoken to the DG, but he's gone off already, and I want to get this off my chest," he said jerkily. "What he said about the responsibility we had, and not letting personal feelings stand in our way, rather moved me. It may sound odd to you, but we learnt something in prison about the value of loyalty. And after what I've been through I'll be damned if I'll let some traitor—whoever he be—ruin all the work we've done here. It's been bad enough being stuck in this hole, without losing the fruits of our labour."

He paused for a moment, and when he spoke again his face was puckered rather childishly. "But the trouble is that I still can't believe it. He—he's such a decent fellow! And the old poison must have worked its way out by now!"

"Who?" asked Cam patiently.

"Robarts."

The name shot out like a blow, and, having delivered it, Stone seemed to sink into himself again. Cam, his eyes sparkling with excitement, tapped impatiently with a pencil to bring him back to the matter.

"Oh yes.Well, you remember that night at Dr. MacDermot's. I said I knew Chatsworth, the spy. I did.Very well.Well enough to despise him heartily. We were at Bonn together before the last war, and he was thoroughly taken in by the rather flashy set of young Nazis who almost owned the place. They didn't get me that way—perhaps because I was studying too hard—and eventually I quarrelled with Chatsworth, and when I left Bonn we weren't on very good terms. Nine months after the war started I met him on Bond Street, and with typical undiscriminating friendliness he asked me to lunch. I asked him what he was doing, and he told me with great *éclat* that he was joining the MSR. Robarts, he told me, had suggested him to Establishments, and he was pretty certain to get the post. At that time nothing but the fighting services seemed much to me, but I was politely congratulatory, and asked him what he thought of Robarts—who had left Bonn before I went up, but about whose brilliance I had heard a lot. Chatsworth went off into paeans of praise, and it was obvious they were great friends. It surprised me in a way, because I should have thought Robarts was too intelligent a man to bear well with Chatsworth's meretricious talents. But stranger friendships have been made. Just as lunch was over I asked Chatsworth jokingly about his Nazi friends. His face shut up tight at once. He said the usual thing about having been fooled, but I had the uneasy feeling that was only for my benefit. Something told me that Chatsworth was still a Nazi at heart.

"The next few months I was too busy fighting in France to bother my head about it. Then I was captured, and had even less time. I didn't have much news from home, but one of the letters which got through to me was from Chatsworth. It was an odd letter—full of hopes that I was enjoying life in Germany, and obviously insinuating that now was the time to turn Nazi. That only made me feel bitter. Two years in German prisons hadn't made me feel any more friendly to their philosophy. What worried me, however, was that Chatsworth said that, although he and Robarts were not in the same department, they were very friendly and 'working in close collaboration'. That was a phrase that lingered in the memory.

"A year later I heard of Chatsworth's arrest and execution." Stone stopped abruptly, and looked searchingly at the Inspector. "Mr. Cam, the reason I came into this organisation was in order to prove that Robarts should have stood beside Chatsworth to be shot; that they were working together, and should have died together."

Cam was gripping the edge of his desk.

"And can you prove it? I ought to tell you that all my information is to the contrary."

Stone laughed bitterly.

"You mean Robarts provided the information which condemned Chatsworth. Yes, I know that. It makes it worse, somehow, doesn't it? Throwing the baby to the wolves. No, Inspector, I haven't got my proof. But I've got something else which may help you. That's the background, because it explains why I did what I did this afternoon.

"I left here feeling pretty depressed by the situation and impressed by the DG's harangue. I don't care two hoots about the murder—Parry was an incumbrance on the face of the earth. But I care like hell about Britex. That's been my particular baby since Robarts took on administrative work, and though he did the preliminary work on it, I have had the main responsibility. And it's good. Well, we were pretty silent as we left here. Robarts said that he was going down to the labs to collect some papers to read on his enforced holiday, and he offered me a lift back to my digs. I sat beside him in the front seat. Just as I was getting in I caught him flashing a curious glance towards the back of the seat—towards the angle where the back meets the seat cushion. It was absolutely nothing—but it reminded me of something. I suddenly remembered that on the night when Parry, Robarts and I drove back from Wassel House, Parry sat beside Robarts on the front seat. And I remembered, too, that just as I was climbing out of the back seat at the 'Coach and Horn' I saw Robarts slipping his hand down behind the seat cushion as if he were feeling for something. It hadn't meant a thing to me then. It was one of those aimless gestures you see people make, without ever giving them a second thought. But Robarts' glance today reminded me. And I wanted desperately to know what he had behind the cushion. There was no reason why there should be anything, but I suppose your lengthy exposition had me all keyed up and curious. As Robarts was slipping round the car to get in I pressed my hand down the space behind the cushion and I found—something which may be of interest to you."

Stone paused a moment to savour, with childlike pleasure, his climax. Cam raised his eyes from the floor and waited while the young man fished in his pocket and produced, carefully and delicately—a key.

"Ah!" said Cam, in a long sigh of delight. "So there she is. At last!"

He got out his handkerchief and took the key from Stone with it. He laid it on his blotter and looked at it. He picked it up again and looked at it by the window. He removed a speck of dust from it and inspected that with concentrated attention. Then he turned to Stone and said with the deepest appreciation:

"Just what we want, sir. The essential clue. That was a really clever bit of work, and I shall mention you in my report, you can be sure. I know it must have been quite a tussle to come here, but you did right, sir."

Stone laughed wryly, but not without pleasure in his own success.

"Being mentioned in your report, Inspector, need not always be an honour, I suppose. But thanks, anyway. And what are you going to do now?"

"Nothing hasty," said Cam carefully—"nothing rash which will drive him away. I have just about enough evidence to make an arrest, but there are one or two pieces which still need collecting for my blessed puzzle. I think he's safe until we've got them." He admired the key again as it lay upon his handkerchief.

"Does Dr. Robarts know you came here, Mr. Stone?"

"I should hope not! No, I let him drive me home, and waited there a minute or two, and then scampered back. He's safe up at the labs, for an hour, I should think."

"Hm," said Cam. "I'd like to have the coast clear for a bit longer, if possible. I wonder if you would mind acting as decoy, sir? I don't think it's really dangerous—just a case of keeping him busy until I've got everything taped."

"My God!" said Stone. "Do you think I'm frightened? No, of course I'll do it. I've just got time to catch the Ministry bus up, and I'll keep him there, say, two hours."

Cam agreed heartily.

"Yes, that would be grand. And then, perhaps, if you could think of an excuse for bringing him back here. Tell him that the DG wants to see him, for instance."

Stone nodded casually, and got up with the help of his stick.

"Right, Inspector. I shall see you in two hours, then. Oddly enough, I still feel like a swine."

He left the room abruptly, and Cam, musing over the key, heard his heavy limp passing down the corridor and into the outer office. For a few minutes more he sat there, eyes gleaming with suppressed excitement, but body slouching back in the chair. Ten minutes passed without him moving. Then with a grunt he sprang up, seized the key in its handkerchief, and strode out of the room.

CHAPTER XIV

MR. WITHERSPOON was enjoying the peace of his garden on a Sunday afternoon. To his mind Sunday was the most precious of days, and the hour of tea-time the most precious hour in that day. He liked it in all weathers—when it was raining and he had hot crumpets and home-made jam in his little parlour before the fire; on bright, cold autumn days when the sun gleamed frostily through the window and made the firelight seem pale by comparison; in midwinter, when the wind howled outside in the early twilight and he could contrast the comfort of his own home with the misery of the weather. But best of all he liked tea-time on warm, sunny days in spring and summer, when he could set his tea-table on the patch of lawn half-way down the garden and, erect upon a dining-room chair, could proudly survey the fruits of his labour gradually taking form. That was paradise indeed.

But today was even better, he thought mischievously to himself. For Eve had come to Paradise, and he was no longer alone in his admiration of the beauties of that tiny, high-walled plot which formed his landed property. Miss Penny, sitting very erect on the other side of the table, her hat with the cherries secured with a decorative hat-pin and her thin face beaming pleasurable interest and delight, made a perfect tea companion. She did not want to talk much. Just occasionally she said with a sigh of rapture: "I've never seen such pruning, Mr. Witherspoon," or "This jam is so much better than shop jam, Mr. Witherspoon". Otherwise they sat silent ("Just like an old married couple," Miss Penny thought coyly), exchanging occasional happy smiles.

It was a good thing, Mr. Witherspoon was musing, that Mr. Stone had been called away that afternoon. He was a fine fellow, certainly, but perhaps a bit gloomy for a little tea-party like this. And, then, one would have to make conversation with him. For a moment the chemist's heart had sunk when, just as he was carrying out the tea-table, Mr. Stone appeared in a breathless hurry in the garden. But by the time Mr. Witherspoon came out again with the cake the young man had disappeared, and although Mr. Witherspoon had set another cup, he thought it safe to presume that he and Miss Penny could count on privacy.

"More tea, Miss Penny?" he asked rather shakily, "and you must have some more seed cake."

"Oh, I couldn't," she protested. "Well, if you insist, Mr. Witherspoon. Yes, I suppose I do need to keep my strength up. The inquest tomorrow will be such a strain. Never before—well, yes, perhaps just a spot of jam with it. Really, Mr. Witherspoon, I am quite ashamed of myself—you are such a good cook and I am such a bad one!"

"But you have other qualities, Miss Penny," said the chemist, leaning closer and gripping the edge of the tea-table. "Miss Penny."

But at that moment, when Miss Penny was preparing herself for an interesting remark—and desperately telling herself not to be silly—a sound of marching feet broke the Sabbath peace and the propitious moment. And hard upon that military sound the side door of the garden leading into Cat Alley swung open and Cam appeared, grim-visaged, and buttressed by the unprecedently large force, for Little Biggling, of three police constables.

Mr. Witherspoon sprang to his feet in consternation. For a second he wondered wildly what a property-owner should do to defend his privacy in such a situation. But the next moment his course of action was clear, because Miss Penny fainted with a preliminary scream, and for the next ten minutes he had not time for anything but running for glasses of water and desperately begging Miss Penny, please, to come back to life because he loved her so.

Even in the midst of this breath-taking occupation, however, he could hardly remain completely unconscious of the extraordinary and inexplicable actions of the police. For, without so much as by your leave—though Cam did vaguely flourish in Mr. Witherspoon's face, during one of the latter's dashes to the kitchen, an important-looking document—three constables had started walking up and down Mr. Witherspoon's own vegetable seed-beds, carefully examining the seedlings with an intensity which would have done credit to judges at a flower show. And up and down the path beside them Cam stalked, grimly surveying the little plants as though they were being paraded at a police line-up. Even in the excitement of proclaiming and resuscitating his love, Mr. Witherspoon was conscious that this Sunday afternoon had lost its tranquil quality.

By the time Miss Penny had begun to revive, however, and was murmuring "Oh Claude", in tones which a few minutes ago would have sent him into a swoon of delight, the situation had deteriorated. Poor Mr. Witherspoon clutched his hair wildly in the strain of dividing his attention between his reviving beloved and his threatened seed-beds. For, with a bellow of excitement and command, Cam had suddenly pointed at some unoffending cabbage plants, and all his three constables were down on their knees examining the soil like so many terriers.

"Oh, look!" cried Miss Penny, with a wail. "They're ruining our seed-beds, Claude! Do something, dear!"

Blessing heaven, which had provided him with such a jewel of a woman—a woman who could put first things first—Mr. Witherspoon arose from his knees at a bound and rushed to the scene of the disaster. He seized Cam by the arm, but for a moment, in the extremities of his emotion, he could hardly speak.

"There, there," said Cam rather absently, his eyes glued on the kneeling constables. "Don't worry, Mr. Witherspoon. I'll replace——. Whoa there, you fools! Not so rough! Here, get away; let me do it."

With tears in his eyes Mr. Witherspoon saw the vast bulk of Inspector Cam descending upon his helpless plants, and saw three weeks supply of vegetables disappear as he knelt beside a cabbage which his constables had already started to excavate. Delicately and with the utmost care, the Inspector proceeded to make a hole, bringing out the earth in handfuls and depositing it neatly in a pile. The constables leaned over him eagerly, like schoolboys at an exhibition. All Mr. Witherspoon could see was a broad phalanx of police backs. From the midst of this suddenly emerged a stentorian "Ha!" and then there was further silence while the constables held their breath. Mr. Witherspoon held his, too.

Then the phalanx fell aside, and out of it emerged Cam, bearing in his hands, preciously wrapped in a handkerchief, a small tin box. The excitement in the atmosphere helped even Mr. Witherspoon to overlook the firm steps which Cam took across his precious onions.

"Why!" he exclaimed in surprise. "That's my old tea-caddy! Now how did that get there? Those children, I suppose."

Cam was busy. He had produced a phial, and into it was scraping a little earth off the tin box. He scribbled on the label, "Earth specimen from tin box found in Witherspoon's garden" and the date. Then he took from another pocket a second phial, apparently containing nothing.

"Peak," he said, "get off to Stroud and have these analysed. You know what we want. Have the answer phoned to my office as soon as it is available. Off with you."

Peak jumped to it, and in a split second Mr. Witherspoon dazedly heard the exhaust of his motor-bicycle diminishing in the distance. Cam turned to another constable.

"Colley, you stay here and guard that hole. Erect a little shelter over it in case it rains. And don't let anyone near it on your life! Mr. Witherspoon, you don't mind, do you?" Cam suddenly remembered the chemist. "No, of course you don't. I know I can rely on you. This is a matter of life and death, you know. Perhaps you could provide Colley with some tarpaulin to cover the hole."

Miserably, Mr. Witherspoon, feeling no longer the captain of his soul, went off to collect materials to make a shelter for he knew not what. Cam, meanwhile, went into the house, hardly conscious that this was a private home, and proceeded to phone Stroud to warn them of Peak's impending arrival and to ask that a photographer be sent at once to Mr. Witherspoon's, the chemist's. That done, he went upstairs with Sergeant Rowley, and Mr. Witherspoon could hear them tramping about in the upstairs back bedrooms and murmuring distantly to each other.

He was going to the kitchen for some string needed by Constable Colley when Cam called to him down the stairs.

"Mr. Witherspoon, have you got a key to the bedrooms, please? I'm afraid we shall have to lock them."

So shattered was his sense of property now that Mr. Witherspoon gave not a second thought to the request, and instantly surrendered the key to his own bedroom, which fitted all the upstairs rooms. The policeman came downstairs again. Cam for the first time seemed conscious that there had been something abrupt in his behaviour. He smiled genially at the chemist.

"This rather breaks up your Sunday, I'm afraid, Mr. Witherspoon. But it's an emergency. You'll understand soon enough. Didn't I see Miss Penny out there? I wanted to speak to her."

Mr. Witherspoon realised with horror that in the bewildering activity of constructing a shelter over a hole in his cabbage bed he had forgotten Miss Penny. He leaped ahead of the Inspector out of the back door into the garden. Ah, there she was, walking across the lawn from the back gate, pale but otherwise composed. She smiled wanly at him and said:

"But what is it, Claude? I've never felt so bewildered in my life."

"It's just some enquiries in connection with the case," interrupted Cam, coming to the rescue of Mr. Witherspoon, who was obviously even more bewildered than she was. "Don't worry. It will soon be over. But I was wanting to see you."

Miss Penny turned pale at these fatal words, and put out a hand to Mr. Witherspoon for support, which he seized with a look at Cam of concentrated ferocity.

The Inspector laughed.

"Don't worry, Miss Penny. As a matter of fact I might tell you right now that those pills you were interested in were completely harmless. They couldn't hurt a baby. You have, I'm afraid, been suffering unnecessarily for a long time."

He ignored her stammered expressions of delight and gratitude and dashed on.

"That's all right. Only next time come and ask Mr. Witherspoon; he would have known. But now for business. I want you to describe again the noises that you heard when Parry's friend was visiting him."

She wrinkled her forehead.

"Oh, very vague noises mostly, Mr. Cam. Just thumps, you know. But there's a substantial wall between the two rooms."

"Can you say what they were like?"

"We-ll—like a stick on the floor, perhaps. Only heavier."

"Someone—limping, perhaps?"

"Yes, perhaps. They *might* have been steps, anyway—only very uneven."

Cam grunted without enthusiasm. She was not very sure of herself. A good barrister would break down her evidence without much trouble. Still, perhaps he had enough.

"Before I forget," Miss Penny was saying blandly to Mr. Witherspoon, "Mr. Stone will be back for supper."

The two men looked at her blankly.

"He couldn't wait," she explained. "But he said yes, he would be in for supper. Mr. *Stone,*" she ended with slight exasperation at their slowness.

"When," roared Cam, with such venom that Miss Penny started back.

"Why—he didn't say. I suppose the usual—"

"When was he here? I mean, have you been speaking to him?"

Cam was literally dancing with emotion.

"Why—just now, of course. I don't . . ."

"He's been here?"

"Yes, he just came to the back door to collect something. I was telling him about you being all over the place, and he was quite shocked. Anyway, he said he wouldn't bother us now, and would be back for supper. . . ."

But Cam waited for no more. With a bellow for Rowley to follow him he was rushing out into the alley and up to the Market and into his little car. "Which way? Which way?" he was murmuring desperately. "My God, if something happens! Blast that woman! Which way—ah!"

He saw Charity Brown strolling down the hill in the direction of Wassel House, deep in conversation with Bill Ratcliffe. They disappeared, but as Rowley jumped into the car, Cam, with a noisy flourish on his horn, was after the pair.

As the car turned the corner out of the Market he again hailed them, and they stopped, both with expressions of rather apprehensive curiosity.

"Have you seen Stone?" he shouted as he drew up beside them.

"No." It was Ratcliffe who answered, rather sullenly. "What do you want him for?"

Cam ignored the question, and scowled angrily up and down the Sunday peace of the Market.

"Have you seen anyone?" he exclaimed.

Charity had never seen him in such a temper.

"I saw Robby—at least, his car. But why?"

The Inspector's face underwent a rapid sequence of expressions, ending in one of alarmed understanding.

"Which way?" he rapped.

Charity glanced at Ratcliffe, who nodded ominously. Her mouth had a stubborn line as she answered.

"If you're after Robby you can find your own spies. I don't know."

"That's right," Ratcliffe joined in. "You're on the wrong track, Cam, and we're not going to help you along it."

Cam shot him an angry look, but he addressed himself to Charity.

"You damned little fool," he said unofficially but intensely. "If you want to keep Robby alive you'd better jump into this car and tell me which is his car when we catch it!"

Charity still hesitated, though clearly impressed by his fury, and with an impatient gesture Cam threw open the car door and seized her by the wrist to yank her into the seat beside him.

"I say . . . Look here!" Ratcliffe cried protestingly, and grabbed the Inspector's arm.

Cam winced at the young man's powerful grip and muttered an order to the Sergeant in the back seat. In a moment Rowley, the light of battle in his eye, was out on the pavement, and with an experienced twist of Ratcliffe's free arm had laid him groaning on the ground.

"Take him to the police-station and lock him up," ordered Cam. "Meet me at Wassel House—use a motor bike!"

He turned again on Charity, who, without a word, got in beside him.

"If you hurt Robby," she said quietly, "I'll never forgive you. But you are Uncle's friend."

She pointed silently down the road towards Wassel House, and Cam set off. They drove at a rate Cam had never in his life attempted before. But he knew already there was not the slightest chance of catching Robarts' roadster—which the scientist once said took ten minutes to get from the village to the House. All he could hope for was a puncture or a breakdown. They turned in at Wassel House drive, still without seeing the car. But the guard there said yes, it had come in about ten minutes ago. Who was in it? He really hadn't had time to see. The gate had been open and the car just whizzed through. But he recognised Dr. Robarts' car, so he hadn't bothered.

Cam drove grimly on, and Charity, who had caught all his tenseness, leaned forward, staring through the windscreen as though she still hoped to see a car which had passed ten minutes before. They drew up at the House with a squeal of brakes, and in an instant the pair were out of the car and up the steps. Martins, the porter, lounging in the hall, jumped to his feet at their precipitous entry.

"What *is* this?" he exclaimed. "Has everyone gone mad today?"

"Is Mr. Stone here?" Cam rapped.

"No, sir. He just went out again about five minutes ago."

"He was here twice?"

"Why, yes. He came up about three and stayed an hour. Then he borrowed Dr. Robarts' car to go somewhere, rushed back again about twenty minutes ago and then off again. And here you come, running like wild people. And who's this now? I really don't know why people don't take their Sundays more quietly!"

The old man looked reprovingly at Sergeant Rowley, who had just appeared, hot and breathless, having rapidly disposed of his prisoner and driven to the House at a speed in defiance of all traffic rules. The Sergeant was tripping on the tips of his boots as though he could hardly bear to stay in one place so long.

"Stone, sir?" he gasped. "Is he here?"

Cam looked at him absently. All his excitement of the last hour seemed to have vanished suddenly in calm thoughtfulness.

As if fascinated by the fire, he stared again at the sparks flying up the chimney, and when he spoke it was rather impatiently, as though his thoughts had been disturbed.

"No. He's left. All right, Rowley. You go after him. He's probably struck across country to Wipton station. Here, take my gun; you may need it. And bring him back here."

He looked around the hall as Rowley joyfully departed.

"Now, where's Dr. Robarts, Martins?" he asked.

Again he seemed all urgency, and Charity felt rather bewildered by these rapid changes of mood.

"Down in the labs, sir," Martins replied.

"Then take us down there. I've got to see him."

The old man did not move. He shook his head stubbornly.

"Oh no, sir. I couldn't do that. You 'aven't a pass, 'ave you? Only special passes allowed in there."

Cam suppressed his impatience and said calmly:

"Then phone down to him and ask him to come up here a moment."

Still shaking his head, old Martins went across to the switchboard which was built into a little room off the hall and rang the number. There was silence in the great hall except for the sound of Cam's boots pacing up and down. They could hear the buzz of the telephone from the little room. It went on and on. Martins poked his head round the door, his earphones awry and a puzzled expression.

"No answer yet. That's odd."

"Could he have left without you seeing him?" Cam asked.

"Why, I suppose if he *wanted* to—by a window. But why should he? And Mr. Stone told me Dr. Robarts was very busy and didn't want to be disturbed. He just told me that a few minutes ago."

The old man shook his head, and disappeared to continue his ringings.

A few more precious seconds passed. Cam begged again to be allowed to go down into the laboratories, but Martins was adamant. Police warrant or not, he wasn't going to allow anyone down into the laboratories without special permission. Those were his orders. And it was no good looking as if he were going to be violent, because Martins was the only one who knew where the key was, and wild horses wouldn't tear it out of him.

Cam mentally tore his hair, but, collecting himself with a great effort, he turned again to the old man.

"Then phone the Director-General. Get your London office and find him, wherever he is. If he gives me permission I suppose you won't over-rule him?"

Martins was deeply shocked. To ring the Director-General, on a Sunday afternoon, at the behest of a mere Inspector of Police—it was unthinkable.

Ten minutes passed in giving him some idea of the urgency of the situation, but eventually Cam had him back at the switchboard putting his call through to London by the direct line. To Cam's heartfelt relief, Sir Arnold had just got to his office after the two-hour drive, and within a minute or two he was speaking to him.

"Cam here, sir. Yes, I'm at Wassel House. I can't very well tell you what the position is, but it's essential I get down into the laboratories. I think Robarts is down there. Would you please give the porter authorisation to let me in? Yes. Thank you. I'll put him on. And one thing more, sir. I think I can give you your answer tonight—as soon as you can get down. Tonight? Well, if you can make it. Right. Thank you, sir. . . . Here's the porter."

He shoved the receiver into Martins' hands and stood restlessly while the porter murmured,

"Yes, sir. Yes, sir. I will at once, sir."

The old man looked at Cam with some awe as he reverently replaced the receiver. A man who could ring the Director-General on Sunday and almost *tell* him to come down to Little Biggling must be someone. In response to Cam's impatience he retrieved the key from its hiding-place—a hook behind the switchboard—and led the way down stairs. The way to the laboratories was through a wine-and-beer cellar where the forlorn and empty racks stretched from floor to ceiling, and where the pleasant smell of home-brewed beer had penetrated the very bricks of the walls with its comforting odour. At the end of the cellar was an iron door. Martins unlocked it, and Cam stepped inside—leaving the other two, like Bluebeard's frailer wives, curious but frightened, on the other side.

He was in a long, low corridor, with doors on both sides of it. Cam remembered hearing that Lab 2 was where Dr. Robarts usually worked, so he went quickly down to the door with that number stamped on it. It was unlocked, and he entered. There was every sign of immense activity—papers strewn all over the desk and floor, an inkwell upset in the middle of the desk spreading its slow, dark stain across the papers, the desk chair overturned. But there was no sign of Robarts. Cam went farther into the room and looked at the desk. There was no pencil or fountain pen lying there to indicate he had just stepped out for a moment. As he turned again, the door had swung to behind him, and hanging upon the hook was an old mackintosh and a hat—Robarts' mackintosh and hat—mute witnesses of their owner's presence somewhere in the laboratories.

For fifteen minutes Cam ransacked the underground workrooms—looking in every room, every cupboard. He noticed that there was a strange absence of the scientific equipment which one expected in a place of this kind. But he soon realised that at night the laboratories were practically stripped of their equipment, which was locked away, probably in the large corner safes—sunk into the wall, or, rather, into the earth. Coming back into Robarts' room, Cam looked at the safe there. It was even larger than most of the others, and its green-painted door had an impressive solidity.

With a gasp he dropped down upon his knees in front of

it. Something had caught his eye. Lying at the foot of the door was a piece of shoe lace, raggedly torn off from the main piece—a brown shoe lace for brown shoes. Robarts had been the only man in a brown coat and shoes at the meeting.

Cam got to his feet feeling ten years older. Dead or alive, Robarts was in that safe. And there was no one who knew the formula within a hundred miles—except Stone.

Charity was waiting for him at the door.

"Is he there?" she asked, in a voice so tight that he was afraid it would break in a moment. She saw in his face that something terrible had happened and turned her own away to hear it.

"He is there, I think," Cam said gently. "But I can't get at him. He is in the safe. We must find Stone."

Charity swayed convulsively and then, seizing Cam's arm, said pleadingly:

"I shan't be any help in finding Stone. Please let me go in there and sit near him. Please, Mr. Cam. It sounds silly, but perhaps I can help him by just being near. Please!"

Cam looked at Martins, whose expression of horrified bewilderment had softened into one of sympathetic misery. He shrugged, and Cam looked at the girl again.

"All right, Charity. Only you mustn't get frightened. You must hold fast, and remember that tears never helped anyone. When we get him out he'll want to see you smiling."

Neither of them mentioned the possibility that he might not come out at all. Cam showed Charity the room, and then dashed out himself and up the stairs. He instructed Martins to stay where he was and, if Mr. Stone should come back, to say that no one had been since he left. But on no account was he to let Stone down in the laboratories again.

Out in the sunlight again Cam took the path down by the river, where Ministry staff had their lunch in summer-time. He did not run, but he walked steadily and purposefully at a great rate along the river-bank, over the footbridge and up the hill meadow on the other side. This brought him out on the Wipton Road, and he wondered momentarily which direction to go. But away from danger was the instinctive route, so he turned towards Wipton. Five minutes brisk walking, his face grim and determined, still brought him no sign of either Sergeant Rowley or Mr. Stone. Striding along, he hardly noticed a car which passed him, going towards Little Biggling, until it drew up and a voice hailed him.

"Inspector! Sir!"

It was Sergeant Rowley, very flushed and triumphant, and sitting beside him, contemptuous and indifferent, was Stone. They were in the back seat of a little Ford car, driven by a rather dazed travelling salesman.

"I commandeered it," said Rowley proudly. "I didn't like walking with this fellow."

"Good work," said Cam briefly, climbing in beside the driver. "Now drive like blazes for Wassel House. It's first on the left and first on the left again."

The commercial gentleman in face protesting, but in action obedient, started off. Cam turned to see his prisoner, and for a moment a gleam of humour relieved the anxiety in his eyes.

"Well, Mr. Stone. We arranged to meet again in two hours, didn't we? I like punctuality."

Stone flushed, although he tried to sneer.

"Make the most of this, Cam. It won't be long before you're being ticked off in court for making an arrest on insufficient evidence. Why aren't you after Robarts, you fool?"

"Your story was not quite convincing. Not that I wasn't delighted to hear it. And it provided me with some most interesting evidence."

"The key?" asked Stone quickly. "You know where I found that."

"Yes, I do now," said Cam. "No, it wasn't the key itself that I was grateful for, though that was a pleasant surprise. It was the common or garden dirt on it. Just a few grains, Mr. Stone, but worth your weight in gold. They are at present on their way to Stroud, whence I expect to hear that they are proof unimpeachable that the key was buried in Mr. Witherspoon's back garden—together with a tin box containing further important details of Britex."

"You sound like a sixpenny spy story," said Stone rudely. "Anyway, I shall wait for my lawyer now."

There was silence for a moment. The car was now turning into Wassel House drive, where the guard looked rather bewildered to see Mr. Stone, the Inspector and Sergeant Rowley appearing all together and in an entirely different car from any that they had used so far.

"Why are we going to the House?" asked Stone abruptly.

"You have some work to do there," Cam replied.

Stone laughed unpleasantly, and Cam shot him a threatening look.

"Dr. Robarts," he said calmly, "has somehow or other got himself locked in the laboratories' safe. I do not care how. We shall ignore that part of the case. No doubt it was his own carelessness. But you, fortunately, know the combination, and you can let him out."

"I don't think I can remember it," said Stone sweetly.

Cam turned white.

"Listen, you fool. God knows you've got enough charges to face. Don't add to it by another murder, man! It can't help you, letting Robarts die. It may very possibly hang you."

"I'm afraid," said Stone, with steely excitement in his eyes, "that in the agitation of the last few hours the combination has escaped me. Even if it hadn't, I would feel unable to help you. I *know* that Robarts is the murderer in this outfit. I know you don't think so. In the cause of justice I should be right to let him die. And let God curse his soul!"

The man's eyes were glittering with fury as he spoke, and there was metallic hardness in his voice. Cam realised sinkingly that argument would be useless. He was beginning to understand the mentality of this man who had committed one murder already, simply in order to encompass the destruction of his enemy.

He drove up to Wassel House with the wretched certainty that, so near the end of his game, he had lost the most precious of his pieces.

He could hear the telephone ringing as they trooped up the steps, and old Martins was answering it.

"Hello. Wassel House. Oh, yes, yes. Thank you. I'll tell him when he gets back, sir."

"Wait a moment!" shouted Cam, taking the last few steps at a bound. "Is that for me?"

"It's the Ministry," Martins explained. "Just phoning to say the Director-General is on his way."

"Has he left? Give that to me!" Cam seized the receiver and barked staccato questions down the line. The Director-General would just be getting into his car, his secretary supposed. "Then stop him! Get him if it kills you! I'll hold on."

For wracking minutes Cam waited, eyes shut as if he were praying. It was all his fault, he was thinking bitterly. Not a thought had he given to Robarts' safety, when, in order to get Stone out of the way for a few hours, he had sent him off on a fool's errand to guard Robarts. He should have detained Stone at the police-station on some pretext while he had made certain of those last essential facts. Glancing over at the prisoner, standing comfortable and self-confident with his back to the fire, his fury reached boiling point.

"What the hell," he roared down the receiver, "is happening there?"

"That's Cam, I suppose," said a calm voice in reply.

"What's all the fuss about?"

"Robarts is locked in the safe, sir," Cam rapped out.

"I don't know whether dead or alive. I've got to have the combination if we are to get him out alive. What? Oh, Stone. Yes, he's here, but he won't talk.

I want it now, sir." He could sense the DG's hesitation at sending these details by phone. "The lock will have to be changed anyway, sir. Right. Thank you. I'm ready to take it down, sir."

In five minutes Cam had the combination scribbled on the backs of several envelopes. With an abrupt final "Thank you, sir," he put the receiver down and headed for the stairs.

"You come, Wootton. Yes, bring him, too."

Down in the laboratory Charity was sitting on the floor pressed close to the safe door, her face grey with strain and despair. She looked up dully as they came in. Cam, without a word, pushed her roughly aside and kneeling down himself laid his envelopes on the floor.

"Now, quiet!" he said fiercely, looking around him.

As concentrated as if he were doing a scientific experiment, he twisted and stopped, first one way and then another, the large dial which controlled the safe mechanism. It was a complicated combination. Four times, with a curse and a twist of his wrist which sent the dial spinning, he over-passed his mark or turned in the wrong direction and had to start again the whole series of movements.

The fifth time, working slowly and moving the dial by centimetres, he completed the combination. One last pressure was rewarded by a click.

The group swayed forward and the door swung open. Lying on the floor of the safe was the body of Robarts. And Stone burst out laughing.

EPILOGUE

SIR ARNOLD CONWAY came down to Robarts' wedding. It was an unprecedented honour, but, as the DG said to Cam at the reception held in Wassel House, he felt he owed the scientist something for his earlier suspicions. The bridal couple looked customarily radiant, though Robarts was still a bit pale after his unpleasant experience six weeks before. It had been a short engagement, they were busy explaining to curious relatives on both sides, but they liked short engagements, and they had known each other a long time. The best man was giving another version on his side of the room—after Charity had proposed to Robarts on the floor of the safe, and had forced him to accept on his hospital bed, she decided to enforce her claim while he was still too weak to put up a fight! But Ratcliffe, as Charity cheerfully explained to the guests, was simply raging with jealousy and, personally, she was quite convinced that it was he who pushed Robby in the safe and that the only mistake Mr. Cam had made was in letting Bill out of gaol.

Mr. and Mrs. Witherspoon were also receiving the congratulations of the guests, as they had been married quietly the day before. Mrs. Witherspoon was looking as happy and excited as any young bride, and was busy explaining to her friends that she had no intention of closing the draper's shop, but that she would live at the chemist's. And Mr. Witherspoon was going to do the cooking and she was going to make new slip-covers. So wasn't it a good arrangement? And the inquest hadn't been nearly as bad as she expected, what with that nasty Mr. Stone being arrested and she herself hardly questioned at all. But to think of such a young man being so wicked! And the police-station had given Mr. Witherspoon as a wedding present a whole day of "Hard labour," they called it, in the garden, and were going to build them a summer-house for two. So everything had worked out very nicely, hadn't it?

Cam and the Doctor were also there, of course, arguing in the corner whether the Doctor's idea about a second key wasn't the most important feature of the whole case. The arrest of Stone had caused considerable excitement in the village, but already interest was subsiding. After all, it had proved to be entirely a Ministry affair, and what else but murder and blackmail could you expect of these wild Londoners? The espionage aspect of the case had not been fully brought out in the trial. Cam had secured conviction simply on the ample evidence of Parry's murder. The other and more curious aspects of the case were passed over.

The Director-General was unusually gracious at the reception. He chatted with Miss White, laughed at a joke by Ratcliffe, spoke kindly to old Martins, remembered and said "How d'ye do" to the Doctor. He kissed the bride gingerly on her cheek and declared that he was sorry her marriage would deprive the Ministry of her valuable services. Finally, before he was leaving, he beckoned Cam and drew him aside into the garden, where, among flocks of meandering and inattentive guests, they could talk quietly. They walked down to the river in silence.

"Well, Cam," the DG eventually said, "it's all gone very well, I must say. You've handled it neatly. No one seems to have a very clear idea of *why* Stone killed Parry, though they are all convinced he did."

The two men smiled.

"Of course Parry was a fool," Cam mused. "Too many irons in the fire—and all crooked. If he'd stuck to blackmailing one person—you, sir, or Ratcliffe, for instance—or had kept to his profession of espionage, he might be alive today. Stone only took advantage of his weakness."

"Curious idea," Sir Arnold said thoughtfully. "To murder to cause another murder. Obviously Stone didn't give a damn whether Parry lived or died, but he was a convenient instrument for securing the legal murder of Robarts. It was also clever, one must admit, to select the one man in the establishment who was often seen together with Robarts— over those chess games. And, of course, Stone himself only spoke to Parry about once, and except for that one meeting, which Mrs. Witherspoon overheard, never met him alone."

"That's it," Cam interrupted enthusiastically, oblivious for the moment of the great man's condescension in discussing the case. "And that's where the brick in the window was vital. Once Stone and Parry had agreed to co-operate— Stone to get the Britex secrets and Parry to take them to Jose Maranda—they never met again, or spoke again, as far as I can find out. But that was when Stone took up drinking. Because he had to have an excuse to get into the 'Coach and Horn' and leave his notes under the brick. That's the way he paid Parry, too."

"I wonder why Parry let him keep the room key, then," Sir Arnold questioned.

"In case of an emergency, I suppose. Stone could think up some excuse. He had to—because that was really what he was interested, in—to get into the room at some convenient time, murder Parry and start the trail which was to lead us to Robarts."

"And he used his heavy walking-stick to murder him. It was a piece of luck Parry being drunk, of course. Not that he couldn't have managed it anyway. But the cleverest idea was leaving the address of the South American agent in the chess piece. He knew that this would appear to us an excellent information exchange point for Robarts and Parry. But we would never believe that Robarts was such a fool as to leave evidence in there. Hence the forging of Ratcliffe's writing rather than Robarts', because everyone knew that Robarts was jealous of Ratcliffe—or at least so I hear now, though there doesn't seem to have been any reason for it."

"I must admit," Cam said ruefully, "that his story about Robarts and Chatsworth almost got me. It sounded very plausible. Just two things didn't ring true. How did he know that Robarts was the man responsible for the spy's conviction? No one else did. Everybody thought it was Parry. And what did he mean about getting two letters from Chatsworth while he was in prison? I had heard him, only two nights before, saying he hadn't received a line all the time. And, in any case, though Chatsworth was a fool, he wasn't *such* a fool, surely, as to say in a letter, which must have been censored, that he and Robarts were 'working in collaboration.' So I decided, on the basis of the second point, that he was lying, and on the first that he had had access to details of the case not generally available."

"I don't see that that helped you," said Sir Arnold reasonably. "Until Stone confessed that those five years in 'prison' he had actually spent in the comfort of the German secret service. I'm glad," he added, "that the man was found guilty but insane. There was nothing mad about the way he planned the crime, but only a madman could have spent such time and thought on the sole purpose of avenging, as cruelly as possible, the death of a friend. He and Chatsworth must have been very close. But any sane man would have known that what Robarts did in reporting Chatsworth's activities was only what a Government servant had to do."

Cam picked a rose and put it in his buttonhole. He remembered rather sadly Stone, in his office, stroking the petal of a daffodil.

"He was mad all right," he said gloomily. "Many a sane man has wanted revenge, but only a lunatic expects an eye for an eye to quite the extent Stone did. He didn't just want Robarts to die. He wanted him executed like Chatsworth and convicted of espionage like Chatsworth."

"It was a bit too thickly laid on," the DG commented. "When you started repeating to me that rubbish about Robarts being a confederate of Chatsworth's during the war, I knew something was wrong. Did he really think MI5 were such fools? Of course they'd thoroughly investigated the Doctor. I knew Stone was guilty then."

"*I* knew he was guilty," said Cam, with bland satisfaction, "even before he entered the room that Sunday afternoon. I didn't see *why* he had murdered Parry, but I knew he was the man."

"So you have said before," sighed Sir Arnold. "Frequently. But although the mysteries of your trade are wonderful to a layman, Inspector, you must admit that you wouldn't have convicted Stone on the grounds that the sound of his limping coming up the corridor reminded you of the thumps which Miss Penny—I mean Mrs. Witherspoon—had associated with Parry's friend."

"No," Cam admitted. "And what's more, it didn't help my case when Stone's lawyer made him limp up and down the court for us to listen to his steps, making all the jury feel like cads and reducing Miss Penny to hysteria. But they couldn't get round the key."

"Careless of him to leave dirt on the crowning piece of evidence with which he was going to convict Robarts! But I suppose he was hurried in those last few hours."

"That was it. But it was clear as daylight that the damp brown speck of dirt on that key hadn't come from behind the cushion of a car. Grey, dry dust is what you get there. And so, of course, I remembered Mr. Witherspoon's garden and his new seedlings, and the fact that the one place in a garden where you can hide things without fear of a gardener disturbing the soil is under seedlings—and Mr. Stone had helped Mr. Witherspoon plant his seedlings. Oh, it was easy from there on."

They turned back to the house.

"I hear Dr. Robarts is leaving here," Cam said tentatively.

"Yes," replied the DG. "He's been appointed head of the chemistry school of a northern university."

"Is that a good thing?"

"Excellent. The Britex work is over now. A year from now our factories will be ready and the drive begins. But the scientific work is done. Robarts is going on to do something else. He's delighted, I believe."

They reached the house, and the Director-General announced that he must go.

With a last good wish to the couple he went down the familiar steps to his car. Mr. and Mrs. Witherspoon were wandering through the rose-beds selecting varieties for their own garden.

Ratcliffe was having a delightfully intimate talk with Miss White. After a long lecture and a warning about his future conduct, the DG had arranged that he could get an advance on salary to pay his debts, so, although a long period of penury loomed ahead, at least he could rely on his career being uninterrupted. He beamed self-confidence and, in the enthusiasm of whisky punch and pretty girls, he waved with cheerful camaraderie to Sir Arnold.

Somewhat to his own surprise, the Director-General waved back. "Well," he thought, as he got into his car, "it doesn't hurt to relax occasionally. Tomorrow we can get back to work."

THE END